The Curse of Septimus Bridge

A Novel

Scott R. Larson

www.ScottLarsonBooks.com

Cover illustration
by
Tamlyn Zawalich

To

Teresa and Maggie
my loves for all centuries

Dan Curtis, Art Wallace, Gordon Russell, Sam Hall,
Ron Sproat, and all the other creative minds
behind the TV series Dark Shadows,
who fired my youthful imagination
and inspired this book

All the souls who have been taken
in the waters of Western Washington
and the families who mourn them

Many thanks to

Dayle Moss
for three decades of cherished friendship, for extraordinary generosity,
for lavishing so much precious time on my silly books
and making them better than they deserve to be

Claes Johansen
for feedback, guidance and for giving me the benefit
of his vast writing experience and regaling me
with some rather intriguing anecdotes

Michael Morrow
for getting all my arcane references, for coming up with just the right detail
in exactly the right place, including, unsettlingly,
the precise physical effects of a hanging

Marcella Peralta Simon
and M. Diane Moss
for sharing thoughts, impressions, reactions,
and observations that were helpful
in refining my story

Contents

1 The Blue-haired Girl *1*

2 Transcendence *11*

3 Riesgado Island *23*

4 The Children *32*

5 Bridge House *41*

6 Sleepless *50*

7 Grandfather *59*

8 Eliot *69*

9 The White-haired Girl *77*

10 Septimus *90*

11 Justine *101*

12 Cnoc Meadha *113*

13 Ceremony *123*

14 The Diabolusbane *132*

15 Sapphire *144*

16 Orpheus *155*

17 Izanami *165*

18 Koschei *174*

19 Cultists *183*

20 Journey *193*

21 Hell's Guardian *208*

22 The Netherworld *218*

23 Reckoning *229*

24 Ballard *240*

25 Chiharu *250*

1
The Blue-haired Girl

FROM THE moment she saw her, Lola Blumquist was drawn to the blue-haired girl.

There was something about her. The way she moved. The way she held her head. The way she laughed. And of course, the blue hair.

The band had not shown up yet so, in the meantime, a Blondie song was playing. The tune was catchy. Lola sang along under her breath. She liked being at the tavern. Sure, some people might think it was sad she was still hanging around the U District two years after she graduated from college, but she didn't care. She liked the music. She liked the atmosphere. She even liked the smell of beer mixed with the stubborn odor of smoke still lingering so long after smoking was outlawed. Besides, she was only visiting the U District. It wasn't as though she still actually lived there.

Lola tried to stop looking in the blue-haired girl's direction. She did not want to be weird or creepy. Finally, though, she just gave up and stared more or less continuously while sipping her beer. In the end she picked up her glass, slid off her stool, and made her way through the crowd. She had decided she needed to introduce herself.

The blue-haired girl was sharing a laugh with a friend. The two were dressed in clothes that Lola guessed might have been purchased at Value Village, but she had to concede the dresses totally suited them. They each wore a small backpack. Lola imagined that they were on a brief layover during a grand world tour. She wished that she could join them on their tour. Lola's plan was to get close enough to hear what they were talking about and insert herself into the conversation.

"You're absolutely mad, Maria!" exclaimed the friend in a rather shrill voice that carried over the hum of the crowd. "I mean, absolutely lunatic, like."

The friend had short-cropped black hair with streaks of blonde. Her hair was cool, but not as cool as Maria's blue hair. The friend was laughing so hard that she did not notice she had spilled some of her beer.

"Pure bonkers, so you are!"

"I'm telling no lies, Sinéad. It's all true. I swear. Every last word."

This was going to be easy, thought Lola.

"Hey, you two aren't from around here, are you? Where are you from anyway?"

The two women were so involved in their conversation that they did not even notice Lola. They continued as if she were not there.

"Swear all you like, ya chancer," said Sinéad. "I copped onto you a long time ago, so I did. Ever since we got on the plane. I know better than to believe anything that comes out of your gob."

"Excuse me," interjected Lola, not used to being ignored. She spoke more assertively this time. "I was wondering where you are from?"

The pair turned in Lola's direction, looking mildly surprised to find her there.

"Is it us yer talking to?" asked Maria, looking around.

Normally, Lola found people—even ones she did not know—were delighted to have her strike up a conversation with them. She flashed her best smile, determined to charm them.

"Sorry. I didn't mean to interrupt. It's just that I heard your accents and wondered where you were from."

She could tell from the expression on Maria's face that she had heard this before and was not particularly impressed. At least, though, Lola now had the blue-haired girl's attention.

"Myself, I'm from Cork," said Maria. "This one's from Dublin."

"Really? From Ireland? Your accents are so cool."

"Yeah, we hear that a lot," said Maria. "Oh, I *love* your accent!" she continued, doing her best exaggerated impression of the way an

American would talk. "Sure, 'tis a strange thing, indeed," she concluded in an exaggerated stage Irish accent.

"'Tis a strange thing, indeed," repeated Lola, giggling and mimicking Maria the best she could. "God, I wish I could talk like that. So your name's Maria, huh?"

"'Tis indeed."

"'Tis indeed," Lola mimicked her again. "Maria! It's so funny that that's your name."

"Is it? And what's so funny about it?"

"Listen. It's the song they're playing right now. Haven't you been listening? This song is about a girl named Maria."

"Ah, so it is. Well, now there's a right coincidence for you. I haven't heard this song in yonks. What is this, Oldies Night?"

"Every night is Oldies Night when Kurt over there gets to choose the music. It must be fun to have the same name as a cool song. I wish there was a cool song with my name."

"Can't say I've really thought about it. Why, what's your name?"

"Lola."

Maria looked at Sinéad and then back at Lola again.

"You're joking me, right?"

"Joking you? No, why?"

"I mean, you're taking the piss."

"No."

"Hello? The Kinks?"

"The Kinks? Oh, yeah, right. But that song doesn't really count."

"And why not?"

"Well, I mean, it's not really fair. You get a song that goes on and on about how totally cool Maria is, and I get the song about a transvestite."

"Transvestites can be cool."

"You do understand that you're totally missing my point, don't you? I've just always hated the song. I hate the fact that she turns out to be a man. By the way, I totally love your hair. I always wanted to have blue hair, but I never thought I could pull it off. How did you decide to dye it?"

"What do you mean dye it? This is my natural color, don't you know?"

"Now you're the one 'joking *me,*' right?"

"Maybe I am, maybe I am't."

"Come on. How did you convince yourself to do it?"

"Truth be told, I was not unlike yourself. I always wanted to have blue hair, but the principal at my school was not exactly keen on the idea. Once I did it, she drove my mam cracked with all the parent-teacher meetings. In the end, though, she was a good mam and stood in my corner. And after having gone through all that, I have never dared change it back. It became a matter of principle, you see. Hey, see what I did there? A matter of principal."

"What are you doing in Seattle?"

"We went to San Francisco on our J–1 visas," said Sinéad, trying to get back into the conversation. "It was this one's mad idea to come all the way to Seattle, just for the weekend. This was after finding out I had an uncle living here."

"What's a J–1 visa?"

"It's rite of passage for us Irish youth. Your government kindly gives us visas so we can go work for the summer in your lovely country. Bright, young people like ourselves come to kill ourselves with a bit of hard labor, and there's not drinking or messing, so it's not like it's a holiday at all," said Maria with a wink.

"How cool," said Lola. "I wish we had something like that here so I could go abroad. So what are the two of you planning to do during your big weekend in Seattle?"

Maria and Sinéad looked at each other and burst out laughing.

"You don't want to know," laughed Sinéad. "Sure you don't. Then you'll know this one is mad for sure and for certain."

"Go on. Tell me."

"Your one had a dream," said Sinéad, pointing at Maria with her thumb. "She's been hopping to go to the Pacific Northwest ever since she saw the bloody mountain in her sleep."

"Really? In a dream?"

"Yeh," said Maria. "I'm always having a load of weird dreams, but the image of that mountain just somehow stuck with me. I can't get it out of my feckin' head. Finally, I found a photograph of it—the exact same mountain—in a travel book about Washington. That's how I was able to put a name on it."

"What mountain is it? Mount Rainier?"

"Yeh, you'd think it would be the obvious one, wouldn't you? But no, it wasn't. It was the one called Mount Baker."

"So you had a dream about Mount Baker?"

"Yeh, mad, isn't it? And me never being in the States before or anything. I never even saw a picture of it before. So how did I know to dream about it?"

"Are you sure you didn't see it sometime in a book or on television?"

"I'm sure and certain."

"It's nothing unusual," said Sinéad. "Like she says, she's always having bizarre dreams. The mountain isn't even the oddest of the lot."

"Really?" Lola asked.

"Yeh, I'm always going mental in my sleep," said Maria. "I think it must be because I'm reincarnated."

"Reincarnated?"

"Yeh. I must have been. It's the only thing that makes any sense. I'm always dreaming the strangest things. Things like they're happening to someone else. In a whole different time like. A whole different place. Places I've never been in me life, like on an island where I can see that Mount Baker as clear as anything. I have that dream all the time."

"Wow, that's wild. So you think you lived here in Washington in another life?"

"I know I have. I've always known it. Like I don't even question it anymore."

"Do you know which island?"

Before Maria could answer, Lola was distracted by someone she saw coming toward them.

"Oh great," she said, "Here comes Joe Cool."

Tall and with moderate-length dirty-blond hair, the young man did indeed look cool to Maria. His colorful shirt and blue jeans made him look as though he had just walked off the beach. In her eyes, his tanned skin glowed like gold.

"Hi, Lola," he said shyly.

"Did you lose your sunglasses, Kyle?" she smirked.

"No, why?" he asked with a confused look.

"Because they're on top of your head. You can probably put them away since you're indoors. And it's nighttime anyway."

He put his hand on top of his head and was surprised to find she was right.

"I guess I forgot they were there," he said, embarrassed. He quickly changed the subject. "So, who are your friends?"

Maria and Sinéad shared a look between them as they eyed Kyle appreciatively. Maria was taken with his eager, puppy-dog grin. Sinéad could not take her eyes off his perfectly straight, white teeth. His only flaw, as far as they could see, was a large black mole on an otherwise perfect cheek.

"They're from Ireland. They're just here for the weekend," said Lola protectively.

"You came from Ireland for the weekend?"

"Yeh, we flew in on our private jet, don't you know?" said Maria, giggling as she sipped her beer.

"Really? You have a private jet?"

"No, they don't," said Lola, annoyed at the way he had barged into their conversation. "You have to know them a while to get their sense of humor."

"So how do you two know Lola?" he asked.

"We don't, to be honest," said Maria. "We're only after meeting her for the first time."

"Hey, your accent is really cool."

Lola rolled her eyes.

"Yes, that's how Irish people talk, Kyle," said Lola impatiently. "Say, maybe you could make yourself useful and get us a round of drinks?"

"Sure, no problem. You ladies want a Guinness?"

"I'll have a Budweiser myself," said Maria. "The Guinness never tastes right here, and they never pour it proper anyway, sure they don't."

"I'll have the same," said Sinéad.

"I'm drinking Ballard Bitter," said Lola.

Once Kyle had left to fetch the beers, Sinéad leaned over and asked, "Is that yer fella, Lola? My, but he's a fine thing, if you don't mind me saying."

"He *wishes* he was 'my fella,'" said Lola. "He's just a friend who has an annoying habit of following me around everywhere."

She lowered her voice and put her finger to her temple.

"He may be good-looking, but there's not a lot going on up here if you know what I mean. His parents are geniuses, but he doesn't seem to have inherited any of it. His mother is a vice-president at a big software company, but he's just working at a sales job at a sports store."

"I don't even mind if he's not the full shilling," said Sinéad, watching him order the beers. "All's I know is he's fierce lovely to look at. He's the real American surfer dude, so he is."

"I suppose. I mean, if you like that sort of thing. You definitely got the surfer dude thing right anyway. He moved here from California, and all he talks about is how much he misses the beaches down there. It gets old after a while. On the positive side, though, his parents have a boat. He takes me sailing sometimes."

"Deadly," said Maria. "A boat? Really? I'd love to go sailing on a boat here."

"Maybe if you play your cards right, he'll take us all out," said Lola slyly. "He'll do just about anything for me."

"Perhaps he could bring you to your island, Maria," laughed Sinéad.

"You know," said Maria, "that's an absolutely brilliant idea you have there, Sinéad. Do you think he would really bring us, Lola?"

"Maria, I was only joking," said Sinéad. "You do remember we have tickets for the train tomorrow, don't you?"

"But I'm so close, Sinéad. I'm actually here. I'm actually in the very place. I can't be this close and not see the island. And maybe see *him*."

"Him? Who are you talking about?" Lola wanted to know.

"The man in the dream."

"What man in what dream?"

"It's tricky to explain. Everyone thinks I'm daft. You see, there is a man in my dreams. A fine, tall fella with wild black hair and a weathered face like a fisherman. He is always in my dream. He lives in a house on an island. The one that looks across the water to some land with trees on the other side,. Beyond that there is a huge mountain covered with snow."

"Well, I can't say your dream lacks detail," said Lola.

"What dream?" said Kyle, handing the women their beers.

"Maria has very detailed dreams about an island with a view of Mount Baker."

"Yeah? Which island?"

"I haven't a clue, but the island in my dream has a massive house. Very old. Like centuries old. Have you ever seen it?"

Kyle thought for a moment.

"You know, I have seen a house like that on Riesgado Island. It's a small island, but you can see a big old house from the water. And it does look right out toward Whidbey Island and the Cascades. I've never docked there. I always figured it was private. Come to think of it, I don't remember ever seeing a pier or a dock."

"Do you hear that, Sinéad? He's seen my island. It's a real place. We have to go. It's like I'm fated to go there. We have to go."

"You're mad, I keep telling you. Remember the train?"

"This is important, Sinéad. This would be worth missing the train. I have to see that island. Please say you'll come with me."

"Not on your life. You know what will happen if we do not keep to our schedule and are not back in time. You need to cop on, Maria. You do know the difference between dreams and reality, don't you? The island he is talking about is not going to be the one in your dreams. It makes absolutely no sense."

Maria paid no attention to her. She turned to Kyle.

"Are you serious about bringing me to 'race gato' island or whatever you called it? You're not just messing with me, are you? Will you really bring me?"

Kyle shrugged.

"Sure. I'll take you. No problem."

He looked at Lola.

"You'll come too, right, Lola?"

She smiled serenely. She could not believe her luck that she would get to spend more time with the blue-haired girl.

"I wouldn't miss it for all the coffee beans at Vivace."

"I can't believe you're doing this to me," said Sinéad unhappily. "What will I tell Trevor? You're putting me in an awful position, so you are. You know, I'm the one he'll give out to. He'll eat the face off me."

"It'll be grand," said Maria. "I won't even be missed. Besides, I know you'll do a brilliant job covering for me. I cannot pass this up. I simply can't."

Sinéad looked at her watch.

"I think I might as well head out. I have some packing to do for the journey tomorrow."

"Ah, Sinéad. It's early yet. Don't be like that. I know I've offended you by changing the plan, but there's no reason not to stay and have a few more jars."

Sinéad had made up her mind.

"Enjoy your adventure. I'll see you on Wednesday or whenever. It's all right. Really."

Maria turned to Kyle.

"So where will I meet you tomorrow? What time?"

"We should get an early start," said Kyle. "I'll have to check the weather forecast. How about we meet at the marina at around eight?"

"Where's the marina?"

"It might be easier to stay at my place tonight," said Lola. "I know where the marina is. The two of us can go there together from my place."

"You sure it's no bother? I don't mean to impose on you."

"Not at all. I'm always having friends stay over. It's no big deal. Do we need to go get your things?"

"No," said Maria, turning to show off her backpack. "This is everything. I travel light, so I do."

"So that's it then," said Sinéad, looking a bit sad. "I'll say goodbye now."

Maria gave her a hug.

"Thanks a million, Sinéad. You're a star. Tell your Uncle Brian thanks for letting me stay last night."

"I hope you'll be all right," said Sinéad, looking uneasy.

"Don't give it another thought. It'll be grand. In a day or two I'll be telling you all about it. I'll text you when I'm on the train back."

After Sinéad left, Kyle bought another round.

"To Riesgado Island!" toasted Lola.

"To Riesgado Island!" said Kyle.

"*Sláinte!*" said Maria, now beginning to wonder if Sinéad might actually have been right about her being crazy.

2
Transcendence

LOLA HAD BEGUN cataloguing in her mind all the ways that she and Maria were different. For one thing, Lola was an early riser.

As she did most mornings, Lola had gotten out of bed early and made coffee. With a warm mug in her hand, she sat in her robe and watched Maria as she slept. She noted each time the Irish girl's chest rose and fell softly. Random strands of blue hair lay across her forehead. She was intrigued by the way the lids of her eyes, dark with eyeshadow, fluttered. Perhaps Maria was dreaming. She might even be dreaming about that island that fascinated her so much. Lola wondered if it was a deliberate choice or an oversight that Maria's blue lipstick was a slightly different shade than that of her hair.

Lola could simply not take her eyes off her. It frightened her that Maria fascinated her so. She had never experienced anything quite like this before.

Suddenly the Irish girl's eyes were open.

"Janey Mack. What's the time?"

"About seven-fifteen. I was just about to wake you. We should be heading to the marina soon."

Maria looked at her warily.

"Were you, like, just sitting there watching me?"

"I made coffee. Do you drink coffee?"

"I'd murder for a cup of Barry's tea, but I'll take the coffee so."

"I can make tea for you if you want. It's no problem. I have some herbal teas."

"No, if it's not Barry's—or maybe Lyons in a pinch—then there's no point. The coffee will be grand. I've heard coffee is a big thing in Seattle."

"You definitely got that right. Here's a cup. Do you take anything in it?"

"Anything? I take everything. Milk, sugar… I'll have everything that's going."

After a quick breakfast of cereal and toast, Maria gathered up her backpack, and Lola threw a few things into her day pack. Maria followed Lola out of the house and down the street. She looked back at the modest, two-story, wood-frame house where she had slept. Wedged between two similar houses, it sat on a small lot that left barely any room for a garden in front.

As they walked, Maria asked, "So where is this marina we are going to?"

"Shilshole Bay. It's about a mile and a half. Hope you don't mind walking. There isn't a bus that goes there from here. Should only take half an hour."

"And what is this place called where are we now?"

"Ballard. It's where I've lived my whole life."

"Seems like a nice place."

"There used to be an old joke about Seattle. They said, the old people live in Magnolia, and their parents live in Ballard."

"Do *your* parents live in Ballard?"

"They did. In fact, they lived in the very same house where you spent the night. They're gone now."

"I'm sorry."

Lola shrugged.

"It's just the way things worked out."

They walked to the end of a long street where they had an expansive view of Puget Sound and Bainbridge Island in the distance. Lola led her down a path that wound down the hill. At the bottom was a bike trail paralleling a set of railroad tracks. They walked along the trail, which soon turned and then followed a wide road. Soon they were at the marina where Kyle was waiting.

"I've been listening to the weather forecast," he said. "There's a storm blowing in off the Pacific, but it won't reach here until late tonight. We should be okay as long as we're back before dark."

"I cannot believe you have your own boat," said Maria, admiring the vessel's long, gleaming, white hull and its tall mast. "This is going to be savage. It all feels so posh."

"The boat is actually my dad's. He doesn't mind me taking it out, although I usually don't go out as far as Admiralty Inlet by myself."

"But you're not by yourself," said Lola. "Maria and I are with you."

"I mean without him or someone else who has sailing experience."

"Aw sure, it'll be grand. Look how fine the day is. Jeepers, I cannot believe I'm really going to see that place from my dreams," said Maria, setting down her backpack next to Lola's.

"I hope it looks how you think it's going to look," said Kyle. "I don't know how you can dream about a place you've never been to before."

"Very metaphysical your boat's name," said Maria, noting the word *Transcendence* painted on the hull in a flowery script.

"That was my mom's contribution," said Kyle, climbing on board. "Buying the boat was Dad's idea, but Mom insisted on naming it. It had something to do with a self-actualization course she was taking at the time."

As the women joined him on the deck, Kyle said, "Here. Put on these life vests. That's one of the rules. In fact, it's the most important rule."

Maria looked disgusted.

"Just so you know, I'm not really big on rules. Are you really going to make me wear this yoke?"

"Yeah, I am," said Kyle. "It's no joke. The sea doesn't forgive mistakes, and this boat isn't leaving the harbor until we're all wearing life vests."

"You should have more confidence in your sailing skills," said Maria contrarily. "If you know what you're doing, these things shouldn't be necessary at all. You're not planning to land me in the water, are you, bhoy?"

"Just put it on," he said impatiently.

Maria slipped it over her shoulders, but in a pique of stubbornness, she made a point of not buckling the straps. She braced for another lecture, but Kyle, who had already begun preparing for the boat's departure, had not noticed.

"Just so you know, it doesn't really flatter me."

"It's about safety, not about looks. Besides, the two of you look great." After a pause, he added self-consciously, "I really like the way you're wearing your hair now, Lola."

His face blushing, he went back to checking the lines and the tiller. Maria could not believe how broad his shoulders were. Easily over six feet, his frame was well filled-out. A definite improvement over the skinny lads back home. And his tan. Even though Seattle seemed to have as much rain as Ireland, Kyle's skin positively glowed from being bronzed by the sun. The best thing she liked about him, though, was the line of his jaw. It was the slightest bit over-large, which she found very attractive, and she found the mole incredibly sexy.

"He's lovely, so he is," said Maria when she was sure he would not hear her. "Do you seriously have no interest in him? It's so obvious he's mad about you."

"Definitely not my type. I mean, he's handy to have around if you need something heavy lifted or want to go sailing, but he's definitely not my choice for an interesting conversation."

Kyle started the engine and began maneuvering the sloop into position.

"Conversation? Who needs conversation? I'd be happy enough to sit there looking at him all day. If he's not your type, then what on earth is?"

Lola smiled slyly.

"I'll tell you after I've gotten to know you better," she said with a wink.

"I don't know how much better you'll get to know me. I'm going back to San Francisco tomorrow, remember."

"Maybe you should stay longer," said Lola, a bit wistfully.

Maria continued to watch Kyle intently.

"He's doing all the work. Should we not be doing something to help?"

"He likes doing it all himself. Besides, he has his own way of doing things. It's easier just to leave him to it."

"I'm surprised you're not insisting on getting in there and sharing the work."

"Why?"

"You strike me as the DIY type. You know, a woman of action. You are obviously very fit and, I'm guessing, quite athletic. I'm sure you could be doing all this boat work as well or better than him."

"Well, I was on the gymnastics team for all four years I was at U-Dub. That's the University of Washington. Martial arts is kind of an obsession of mine. I not only took a Tsun Jo class all through high school, but afterwards I got my own private instructor. I decided a long time ago I was going to walk wherever I wanted at night without being paranoid."

"Fair play to you. I was never very athletic myself, but I definitely like looking at lads who are."

Lola watched Kyle and tried to see him through Maria's eyes. As he went about his various chores, the outlines of his muscles were visible even through his sweatshirt and jeans. The breeze rippled through his hair. The glint of morning sun reflected against his dark glasses—the ones he insisted on wearing in good weather and bad. As good as he looked, though, Lola still saw only a guy who had nothing very interesting to say.

The dock lines having been untied and put out of the way, Kyle backed the boat out of its berth and guided it toward the marina exit. Maria felt a thrill in her stomach when she first felt the vessel bounce on the water. The cold slap of wind on her face and the smell of salt excited her. It brought back childhood memories of her uncle Fintan's boat at Kinsale. Lola could not take her eyes off the smile on Maria's face.

The marina and its acres of boats shrank behind them. Their own boat, which had looked so large by the dock, now felt small as it glided up and down over the shifting waters of Puget Sound. Maria turned and watched the city's profile on the receding horizon. Seattle was a collection of hills. The Space Needle looked small from this distance. Beyond the city was a range of snow-capped mountains. Much bigger than any mountains in Munster.

"Coming about!" warned Kyle, as the boom swung from one side of the boat to the other. "We're heading into the wind, so I have to tack."

Maria carefully made her way toward him. She was not yet entirely steady with the boat's motions in the water.

"Is there anything I can do to help?" she shouted over the wind.

"Not really. I'll let you know if there is."

"I'm feeling a bit useless. You're great to be bringing us out."

"I really like sailing a lot. It's definitely more fun if there's somebody to go with. I always like it when Lola comes with me. I don't know if she really enjoys it that much. I always have to talk her into coming. Except today. She was definitely happy to come today. I think because you were coming."

"Who wouldn't enjoy this? This part of the world is so beautiful. It's great to get out for the bit of *craic*."

Kyle looked at her a bit suspiciously.

"You didn't bring drugs on board, did you?"

"No. Why?"

"You mentioned crack."

Maria laughed.

"No, I didn't mean crack like heroin. *Craic* is Irish. It's means having a bit of fun, a laugh."

"Why, don't you just say 'fun'?"

"*Craic* is different than simply 'fun.' It's difficult to explain. Maybe you just have to be Irish."

"Ireland must be really different than America. I can see why Lola finds you so interesting. I can tell she likes you a lot."

Kyle bit his lip. His tone turned confessional.

"*I* really like *Lola* a lot."

"Yes, I can tell that."

"I don't think she feels the same about me, though. I think she finds me kind of boring. I never know what to say to her."

"I can't imagine a fine fella like yourself having any problem with the ladies, Kyle. Maybe it's only a matter of finding the right woman."

"I don't know about that. Lola is the only one I'm really interested in. There's just something about her."

As coyly as she could manage, Maria said, "Do you think you might ever fancy an Irish girl?"

He laughed.

"That's cute. 'Fancy.' I like the way you talk. I don't know, maybe I could 'fancy' an Irish girl, but it doesn't seem too likely. I mean, I've never even been to Ireland."

Maria was beginning to see Lola's point about Kyle being a bit dim.

"You don't have to go to Ireland to find Irish girls. We're everywhere. You might even find one here in Seattle."

She put the tips of her two fingers on her shoulders, to draw his attention to herself. Kyle blushed.

"But won't you be going home soon?"

"Well, who knows? I mean, if I had a reason to stay, I might not go back at all."

"But what about your visa? Won't it run out? I thought you were just here to work for a few weeks."

"I think you're missing my point, Kyle, but no matter. I just want you to know I think you're really sound. You know?"

"Not really."

"I'm just saying, you're a really good guy. That's all."

This had become too much work, so Maria gave up. She glanced back at Lola, who smirked as she watched them from the other end of the boat. Kyle turned and looked intently toward the mountains across the water in front of them.

"There are mountains everywhere," said Maria. She pointed at the range behind them. "Which ones are those?"

"Those are the Cascades." He then pointed at the range on the opposite side of the water. "Those are the Olympics. On the other side of those is the Pacific Ocean." He continued to stare at the horizon. "I don't like the look of those clouds."

"Sure, a bit of rain isn't going to be any bother, is it? If there's anything I'm accustomed to, it's rain."

"Yeah, me too. At least since I've been living here. It's just there's a forecast for a big storm coming in off the ocean. It wasn't supposed to get here until late tonight, but I'm starting to worry that it's getting here early. I'm wondering if we should go back."

"Ah, it will take ages for those clouds to get here. Besides, we can't turn around now when I'm so close to seeing the place in my dreams."

"You might be right, but I'd rather be safe than sorry."

"How much longer until we get to the island?"

"Well, we're about halfway there, I suppose."

"Well, there. That'll be no time at all. And then you'll have us back in port in a flash. Long before those clouds get here."

"I don't know…"

She put her hand on his shoulder. Even through the sweatshirt, his arm was every bit as solid as she expected.

"Come on there, Kyle. Surely, you're not afraid of a wee bit of weather. Don't disappoint me now."

She could see the indecision in his face. She found his furrowed brow adorable.

"Okay," he said, "We'll keep going for now, but if the wind picks up at all, I'm turning around. Trust me, you really don't want to be out here in a storm."

Maria carefully made her way back toward Lola, trying not to fall as the boat churned through the water. She ducked when Kyle again shouted, "Coming about!"

"You're absolutely mad," she said to Lola. "He so obviously has the glad eye for you. What a waste of a fine lad."

"No thanks. Besides, I think you're the one who likes him."

"I won't lie. If he would only give me the time of day, I'd overstay my visa, no problem. But it is definitely not me he's interested in, sure it's not."

"That just proves what a moron he is. Someone would have to be an idiot to pass up a chance with you."

18

"Ah, you're too kind, boosting a poor girl's bruised ego like that."

"There it is!" shouted Kyle, pointing at the horizon. "That's Riesgado Island."

It was just a bump in the distance, but as they drew closer, the shape became clearer. Maria could barely contain her excitement. The nearer they got, the more the island's distinctive outline matched what she had seen in her dreams. It rose high out of the sea but was mostly flat, except for a tall peak on one end that made its silhouette look like a giant sea creature. She could scarcely believe it was real.

"So, does it look like your dream?" Kyle called to her over the wind.

"If you only knew. My dream has well and truly become reality."

She glanced east back toward the mainland. On the horizon Mount Baker stood majestically with a crown of snow. It was all exactly as she had seen it.

Kyle, meanwhile, looked west.

"This is bad!" he cried. "The weather front wasn't supposed to come in until after dark."

Beyond the Olympics the blue sky had been covered by a dark, murky gray. The boat shook as gusts of wind whipped at its sails. The three of them watched apprehensively as the giant gray wall of rain swallowed the mountains.

Kyle looked anxiously in one direction, then another.

"We have to head for the island!" he shouted. "We'll never make it back to the marina before the rain hits!"

He worked frantically, adjusting the sails so that the strengthening wind would propel the boat toward Riesgado.

"Tell me what to do!" Lola shouted at him. "How can I help?"

He did not seem to hear, as he worked even faster. Anxiously, he watched the swells surrounding the boat.

"Grab hold of something!" he shouted at the two women. "Hold on tight! This could get rough!"

Maria felt her stomach rise to her throat. It was the same queasy feeling as being on the rollercoaster at Tramore. She clasped one hand on a gunwale cleat while grabbing the seat beneath her with the other. Lola did the same. They watched in disbelief as the gray wall raced toward them and blacked out the sky. The boat was thrust by the swirling water. Then unexpectedly, there was an eerie calm. A chill went through them, as the temperature dropped precipitously. It felt as though the air was being sucked in the direction of the looming gray wall.

In no time at all, the rain battered them. Within seconds they were drenched to the skin. The force of the deluge was so great, it was like being struck by a physical object. The boat now seemed positively tiny. With no warning, it rose high in the air and then fell. It landed at an angle, and Maria felt as though it would turn over. She looked at Kyle, hoping for a reassuring look, something to indicate that panic was not warranted, but he looked every bit as terrified as she was. Her ears filled with the wind's violent roar.

Once more, the boat was pushed high into the air. To her dismay, Maria could not keep her hands from slipping on the wet surfaces. She choked as the water battering her face found its way into her mouth. She tried to wedge herself under the seat, but there was no room. Again, she had the sickening feeling of the boat falling through the air. She felt the thud of the vessel ramming against the water's surface.

Kyle had lost control of the boom. Careful to avoid being struck as it swung one way and then another, he crawled closer to the two women.

"Hold on the best you can!" he shouted at the top of his lungs.

His words were all but lost in the gale. Lola wondered how the weather could have changed so fast and dramatically.

The boat rolled starboard as a massive wall of water rose up on the port side. They felt as if they were about to fall from the boat and into the air, but then the sloop slid down the water's nearly vertical surface and righted itself. It rested there calmly for a precious few seconds, as the three stared in awe at the mountains of water around them.

Another mass of water rose above them. They found themselves again sliding into a deep valley surrounded by swells. Then the boat was propelled upward, struggling against gravity as it neared the top. To their horror, the vessel stood on its stern, the bow reaching high into the air. Maria prayed that it would slide back down the same way it had risen. Instead, the boat fell backward, casting its terrified occupants into the empty space between it and the water.

Maria fell through the air. She feared the boat would land on top of her, but its trajectory took it in a different direction. Her last view of it was dominated by the name *Transcendence* smashing into the churning sea. Maria hit the water with a smack and felt its coldness grip her body. She sank beneath the surface. Desperate to get a breath, she felt as though it was an eternity before she got back to the surface. Shivering with fear and cold, she looked in every direction, trying to spot Kyle and Lola. She sucked air in huge gulps between splashes of sea water. She wondered how long she could last, struggling on the surface of the angry water. She did her best to get control of her panic.

Then, to her horror, she sank again beneath the water. She felt her arms slip through her life vest. She watched it rise to the surface without her. She stared in disbelief and then remembered how she had foolishly unclasped the buckles. She reached upward desperately for the vest, but the swirling water carried it out of sight. The cold was horrible, and every movement was a struggle. She worked her arms and legs as frantically as she could, hoping to reach the surface.

She managed to get her mouth above the water and take a breath. She refused to think about the likelihood of death. Suddenly, something grabbed her and held onto her. She turned and saw Kyle, his body wrapped around hers. For an instant she was hopeful, but it was no good. The two of them were sinking beneath the water. He held on to her ever more tightly. It felt as though he was deliberately pulling her down, as if he wanted her to drown.

She struggled against him frantically, trying to get away, but the more she struggled, the more he writhed and twisted and kept a grip on her. She could not understand why he was trying to drown her. She continued struggling, but her strength was nearly gone. At the very point when she thought she would black out from holding her breath, she rose suddenly to the surface. Kyle had let go.

She saw him struggling in the water. He was being carried away from her. She wondered why she was not sinking and then realized that she was wearing a life vest. Somehow, Kyle had managed to remove his own life vest and, without losing it in the roiling water, had put it on her and had even buckled all the clasps. She watched him float farther away. He struggled to keep his head above the water. She watched him gulp for air each time he struggled back to the surface.

Finally, she saw him sink and disappear completely. Hoping against hope, she continued watching, but in her heart she knew he was not coming back up. By this time the bitter cold of the sea had completely numbed her body. She could neither feel nor move her arms and legs. Attempting to swim was out of the question. She closed her eyes—just for a second, just to rest them for a moment—and then did not open them again.

3
Riesgado Island

MARIA WAS SURPRISED by her complete lack of panic. She did not struggle for air. In fact, she was quite comfortable. It was as though she had become a sea creature that had always lived underwater. She took in her surroundings with childlike curiosity and took note of the different kinds of fish that swam past her. It was hypnotic.

Then she spotted Kyle. He looked as though he too was quite relaxed. He had shed most of his clothes, and she admired his muscular body, as he floated in front of her. He was surprisingly smooth and hairless, like a Greek statue. Only now did she question if this was really happening or whether it was some sort of dream. But she did not care. She was happy just to stare at him. Kyle propelled himself with his brawny arms and drew near. His face was full of sorrow. His eyes locked with hers, and she was lost in the blueness of his irises. The expression on his face broke her heart. Mesmerized by the way his hair floated in every possible direction at once, she reached out and lightly stroked his cheek. He closed his eyes, as she pulled herself closer and put her lips against his. The shock of their coldness startled her. His skin had lost its golden glow and was now turning a dark shade of blue. She kissed him again, but his lips did not react. Then she tried once more, and she pried his mouth open as she put all her feelings into the kiss. Her mouth filled with water, and she gagged. She could not catch her breath—and panicked.

Maria was no longer underwater. Sharp stones pressed against her back. She gasped for air but found none. She was frozen. The pain from the cold was so intense she feared her heart would stop. Something blocked her mouth and nose, and she tried to push it away but found she could not. Finally, she felt the air she desperately craved in her lungs. She struggled to focus her eyes and saw Lola's face drawing away from hers. Water dripped from her lips. It had been Lola's mouth over hers and Lola's fingers pinching her nose. Maria coughed and spit up water. She was relieved to find she could draw a breath, even though her throat ached as she did it. She drew one grateful breath after another, not taking for granted the air around her.

"Stay with me, Maria," Lola said with concern in her voice. "Please, please, stay with me."

Maria had no idea where she was. She tried to speak but could not.

"Don't try to talk. Just nod if you know where Kyle is."

At the mention of his name, Maria became anxious. She wanted to cry but was too exhausted.

"Kyle... Kyle..." she gasped.

"Don't try to talk. I'm sure he's okay. I mean, he's such a jock, he's probably swimming back to Seattle for help. He'll be all right."

"No... You don't..."

She could not get the words out, and her frustration at not being able to communicate desperately upset her. Lola rubbed her arms and shoulders. This did not make Maria any warmer. Lola was every bit as cold as her, but at least her efforts to warm Maria were comforting.

"Take it easy. There will be plenty of time for talking. We're probably going to be here for a while. I have to say, I miss your blue hair."

"What?"

"Your hair. The color must have all washed out of it. I can understand now why you colored it."

"What?"

"I've never seen anybody your age with completely white hair before. I mean, without coloring it. Is it some kind of condition or something?"

Maria was confused by Lola's words, but at least she found it easier to talk now.

"No, my natural color is brown. It has always been brown."

"Really? Strange. Anyway, that's the least of our worries right now. We need to find a way to dry ourselves off and get warm. Then we need to figure out how to get off this island. I don't suppose you managed to hold on to your cell phone."

"My mobile? Let me check. No, everything's gone out of my pockets. I've lost everything."

"Too bad, but it probably doesn't matter. We probably weren't going to get a signal here anyway."

They were on a narrow, stony beach bordered on two sides by large rocks. In front of them was the wild, churning sea. The wind roared in their ears and chilled their bones. Behind them were thick woods. The rain had stopped, but a heavy dampness lingered in the air and swirling black clouds filled the sky.

Lola said, "When you feel up to it, I suggest we explore as far as we can in either direction. With any luck we'll find Kyle. I hope he was washed up like we were."

"Lola, Kyle's gone."

"I know. That's why we should look for him."

"No, you're picking me up wrong. He's gone. I mean, really gone. I think he's drowned."

"Don't think like that. We made it, and I'm sure he did too."

"Do you not hear me? He's gone, and it's my fault."

Lola put an arm around Maria and gave her a hug.

"It's nobody's fault. Kyle checked the weather forecasts. There was no way anyone could have known the storm would blow in so fast. It's just something that happened."

"I saw him sink in the water. He had no life jacket."

"What do you mean? Of course, he had a life jacket."

Maria was close to tears.

"He took off his life jacket. He gave it to me."

"What are you talking about?"

"I never fastened it. I was acting the maggot. It came off as soon as I landed in the water. He saw me struggling and somehow he managed to take his one off and put it on me. He sacrificed himself for me. I was so stupid. I cannot believe how pure stupid I was. And now he's gone."

Despite being alarmed by Maria's story, Lola kept up a brave front.

"Get a grip there, Maria. He could still be okay. After all, he's a really good swimmer."

Maria took heart from her words.

"You're right, of course. The two of us survived, didn't we? You'll think I'm crazy, but I believe in guardian angels. I have to hope that Kyle's guardian angel is looking after him."

"Do you feel up to walking now?" Lola asked. "We should start to look around. Maybe there is a cabin or something. I know there's a big, old house overlooking the water somewhere, but I think it's been abandoned for ages. We were pretty stupid to set off without being better prepared. Who knows how long it will take before anybody realizes we're missing?"

Maria struggled to stand. It was an effort at first simply to keep her balance, but they walked carefully, doing their best not to stumble on the stones beneath their feet. The clouds parted to reveal a patch of blue sky, and the unexpected sunlight warmed their faces. The weather cleared just enough so they could look across the water toward Whidbey Island and beyond. Maria gasped to see the mountain suddenly revealed.

"There it is!" she cried. "Just like the dream. It's exactly like the dream."

"Well, that's something," said Lola. "At least you got to see your mountain."

As quickly as it had appeared, the mountain vanished again behind a stream of clouds. The sunlight was gone, and the temperature felt as though it had dropped ten degrees.

"It wasn't worth it," Maria said glumly. "It's the worst mistake I ever made. I thought it would be a bit of fun, but I made a right bollocks of it, so I did. I'd give anything to know that Kyle is all right. That's all that matters now. How could I have been so stupid?"

"Stop beating yourself up, Irish girl. Things could still turn out all right. I bet in a few days you and Kyle and I will all be back at the tavern, having a big laugh about this. You'll see."

"Do you think the house is far from here?"

"I have no idea, but I don't think this island is very big."

"I'd feel better if we had shelter. Do you think there's a chance someone could be living here? Or here on their holidays?"

"I don't think that's too likely. I've lived in Seattle all my life, and I can barely remember anybody even talking about this island, let alone hearing about anybody living on it. But who knows? There's only one way to find out."

They continued toward the woods, thinking perhaps they would find a trail. Suddenly, a cracking noise could be heard over the sound of the wind.

"What was that?"

"I don't know. Probably a branch blown down by the wind."

"Please don't think I'm going mad or anything but…"

"But what?"

"I think someone's watching us."

"Do you see someone?"

"No, it's more of a feeling."

"Well, if there is someone, that's good news, right? They would have a way to get off the island or at least a way of communicating with the rest of the world. Let's keep going."

"It's just that…"

"What?"

"I have a strange feeling. As if I can remember something from the dream. Something I haven't remembered before. It's giving me the willies. Seriously."

"What do you want to do then?"

"I don't know, but I know we can't stay here. It only makes perfect sense to seek out anyone else who might be on this island, but something puts me off it. I can't explain. Do I sound completely mad?"

"No, of course not. You've been through a shock. We both have. But you're right. We can't stay here. Let's keep going."

They took a few more steps. Then Maria stopped and stared ahead into the woods.

"Did you see something that time?"

"No."

"What was that sound?"

"I'm sure it's just branches," Lola said. "It's the wind."

"There's definitely something moving over there, isn't there?"

"Just branches in the wind."

"No, on the ground. There in the shadow."

"Okay, you're starting to kind of creep me out, blue-haired girl, I mean, white-haired girl. Look, if you absolutely don't want to go into the trees, stay here. I'll go and see if there's anything or anybody there. Then you can follow me."

"I'm really sorry to be such a bother, Lola. I'm not normally like this. I don't know what it is that makes me so apprehensive."

"Don't give it another thought. Just stay here."

Lola continued toward the woods. The stones hurt her feet, and she wished she had worn more sensible shoes. But at least she still *had* her shoes, although like the rest of her clothes they were soaking wet, which gave her feet an unpleasant wet, squishy feeling. It became easier to walk after she reached the trees and there was solid earth beneath her feet. The trees swayed around her. It was not hard to imagine they were angry creatures, and she could understand why they would make Maria uneasy. The wind made a strange whistling sound, as it blew through the branches. Normally she was not the type to get scared without good reason, but Maria's nervousness had affected her. She peered into the shadows to reassure herself there was no danger.

Out of the corner of her eye, she thought she saw something dart between the trees. She turned her head quickly but saw nothing except the motion of the branches. The more she studied her surroundings, the more the idea preyed on her that there was something behind her. She quickly turned and saw there was nothing.

She found an overgrown path and followed it. Then she heard the cracking sound again, this time much louder. When she looked around again, she definitely saw something running between the trees.

"Hello? Is there somebody there?"

She heard nothing but the sound of the wind.

"We could really use some help here. Is there somebody there?"

The branches swayed indifferently.

She walked on, brambles scraping against her bare ankles. With each step, the foliage enveloped her more and more in darkness. She looked back toward the beach. There was a patch of gray light where she had entered the woods. She could no longer see Maria. She resolved not to be so cautious and picked up her pace. The path took her uphill. She was anxious to move even faster, but given the shoes she wore and the unevenness of the ground, she knew she needed to be careful not to turn an ankle.

As she stepped over a small tree that had fallen across the trail, she was sure she saw something ahead of her—something that moved. She blinked twice to make sure it was not a trick of the eye. No, there was definitely something moving on the trail. Not particularly large, but large enough to be a person. So she rushed up the hill to get a better look. She was sure she was gaining on it, whatever it was, but then she lost track of it when she glanced downward for a moment to check her footing. Nevertheless she continued as fast as she could. Even after she had stumbled and banged her knee on a stone, she kept going. Finally, she paused to lean against the trunk of a particularly large fir tree and catch her breath.

As she stood there, she heard a sound from behind the tree. With no hesitation, she circled around to the other side and came face-to-face with a small figure with an unruly mop of black hair. He looked up at her with huge eyes.

It was a boy.

Lola froze in surprise. She had only a few seconds to take in his appearance before, after a quick shake of his head, he sprinted up the hill. He looked to be about twelve or thirteen years old and wore a black coat made of heavy woven material—not vinyl or polyester, as she would have expected. His pants were of similar material, and his shoes were large and heavy. He was definitely not dressed like any of the kids in her neighborhood.

As soon as she had recovered from her surprise, she set out after him. He clambered up the hill like a frightened rabbit, and she knew she would not be able to catch him.

"Stop!" she called after him. "Sorry if I scared you. I'm scared too. Please stop. I won't hurt you. I promise."

He paid no attention and, if anything, fled with even greater speed until he disappeared down the other side of a rise in the hillside. She followed as rapidly as she could, but when she got to the top, there was no sign of him. The trail went down into a gully and then rose up another slope. He hardly had enough time to make it up the next hillside, and there were plenty of places among the trees and bushes where he could hide.

She tried one last time to coax him back.

"Please come back! My friend and I need help. If you won't come back and talk to me, will you please go ask your parents to come help us? Please!"

She stood quietly, hoping to hear something—if not an answer then perhaps the sound of him running—but all she could hear was the restless movement of the tree branches and the faint sound of a stream at the bottom of the gully. She had gone farther into the woods and spent more time than she had intended, and she knew she needed to get back to Maria.

Carefully, she made her way back down the hill and toward the beach. At least she would have good news to share. There were people on the island! It was unlikely the boy was there entirely on his own. Other people had to be on the island with him, and they would surely have a boat. Lola felt a huge relief. She could not wait to tell Maria. Now, if only Kyle would turn up. She was counting on it and hoped Kyle's parents had good insurance on the boat and would be understanding about what had happened.

Lola reached the edge of the woods and stepped onto the stony beach. It was good to see the sky again, even if it was still full of oppressive, dark gray clouds that swirled in the gusts. She walked toward the water, looking curiously from one side to the other. She looked behind her and studied the woods. She walked the entire length of the beach. She climbed on one of the large rocks for a better look around.

Finally, she called, "Maria?"

But there was no sign of the Irish girl.

4
The Children

LOLA CALLED AGAIN.

"Maria! Where are you?"

Instead of an answer, there was only the sound of waves lapping furiously at the stones.

Lola fought back a sudden sense of panic and did her best to think logically. Had Maria tried to follow Lola into the woods? Not likely. If she had, they surely would have met each other. What possible reason would she have had for leaving the beach anyway? Did something frighten her? Given the shape she was in, she would hardly have gone rock climbing, which would have been the only way to leave the beach without going through the woods.

Lola paced up and down along the edge of the woods. She could see no other place Maria could have gone. The whole thing made no sense, and it made her angry. Why did this have to happen just at the moment when she had begun to feel optimistic about their situation? Lola decided the only thing she could do now was go back to the trail in the woods and follow it. She just hoped that she would find Maria somewhere along the way.

She took one last look out toward the sea. The dark gray water still roiled, topped by foaming whitecaps. She scanned the seascape, refusing to consider the possibility that the water could have somehow taken Maria or that it had taken Kyle. It gave her some peace of mind that there was no sign of anyone out there. Nor was there any sign of *Transcendence*. She saw only the sea and sky in turmoil. She feared that daylight would soon be drawing short, and she needed to get moving if she was to find anybody before dark. Resolutely, she walked back into the woods.

While she was worried about Maria, Lola was at least not bothered to be alone. She had hiked alone many times in the Cascades and always enjoyed her own company. On this particular walk, her only real concern was her shoes. She could not forgive herself for not choosing a better pair of shoes that morning. Her feet were now very sore, and she knew it would only get worse.

Climbing the hill, she found herself looking continually to one side and then the other. It was only prudent to watch for animals, and she also thought she might see the boy or somebody else. Beyond that, though, something had her on edge. She could not forget Maria talking about her nagging feeling of being watched. Lola herself could not shake the feeling of something or someone lurking just out of sight.

Her way of dealing with the apprehension was to walk faster. She descended into the gully where the boy had disappeared and then climbed the other side. When she got to the top of the ridge, she paused for a look around. There was something hypnotic in the way the tree branches never ceased to sway in the breeze. The wind played tricks on her ears. With just a little imagination, the whistling through the firs could nearly be voices. The sound was like whispers—quiet, taunting whispers, just a bit too distant to make out clearly.

As she was about to resume her walk, she heard a sound that was clearly a voice. It was like a child's laugh. Lola played it back a few times in her mind and then gave her head a shake. No, it had to have been her imagination. She walked perhaps another fifty yards and then stopped. She had heard it again. It was more distinct this time. She looked around.

"Is somebody there?"

For several minutes she waited and listened.

"It's okay. I won't hurt you. Come out and talk to me. I won't bite."

Still nothing but the wind.

"Maria, is that you out there? Talk to me. Please."

She had once again convinced herself she was imagining things when she heard a giggle and something scrambling in the bushes just ahead of her. She rushed forward and then saw her. A little girl in a long, frilly, white but very dirty dress. She had long, curly, brown hair and looked about nine years old. She ran up the trail ahead of Lola.

"Come back! Don't be afraid! It's all right."

Because the girl was not as fast as the boy had been, Lola was able to catch up to her. She grabbed the girl by her arm. She was surprised at how strong and solid it was for such a small person.

"Ow! You're hurting me! Let go!" she whined in a loud, high-pitched voice.

"I'll let go if you promise not to run away. Okay?"

"Let go! Let go!"

From the way she spoke, Lola wondered if she was not from Washington. Maybe the East Coast?

"Promise you won't run away, and then I'll let you go."

The girl stopped struggling, and Lola released her grip on her sleeve. As soon as she did, the girl bolted, and Lola rushed to catch up to her and grab her arm again.

"I'm not going to let go this time until you stop and talk to me. I promise I won't hurt you. I need you to help me. Won't you please help?"

Again the girl stopped her struggle, and again Lola let go of her sleeve. This time she did not try to run away. She wiped her hands on her dress and stared defiantly.

"My name is Lola. What's yours?"

The glaring child stayed silent.

"Please tell me your name. Listen, I almost died today and I'm actually very scared. Please help me."

The girl's face softened a bit. She looked down at the ground and shuffled her feet. Lola was struck by her black, high-button leather shoes.

"Was that your brother I saw before?"

She said nothing and kept her head bowed.

"If you don't tell me your name, I'll have to make up a name for you. Let's see. I think I'll call you, um, Gertrude."

The girl looked up crossly.

"My name is not Gertrude!"

"Then what is it?"

Silence.

"Okay, Gertrude it is. How are you doing, Gertrude?"

"I told you! I am not Gertrude!"

"Until you tell me your real name, you're Gertrude as far as I'm concerned. Gertrude. Gertrude. Gertrude."

"Stop calling me Gertrude! I'm Celia!"

"Celia! Now we're making progress. It's very nice to meet you, Celia. I'm Lola."

"You already told me."

"You're right. I did. Okay, Celia, are your parents here with you on the island?"

"No."

"No? You mean, you and your brother are here all by yourselves?"

"That is not what I said."

"Yes, you're right. That isn't what you said. Can you tell me who else is here on the island?"

Celia shrugged.

"There must be grownups with you. If it's not your parents, who is here with you?"

She shrugged again.

"Are you here on a visit? Or do you live here?"

"We live here, silly."

"You do?"

"Of course," she replied, as if it was the most ridiculous question she had ever heard.

"Can you take me to your house?"

Celia went silent again.

"Don't you want to take me to your house?"

"I shall be in trouble."

"Why? Are you not supposed to be in the woods by yourself?"

"No."

"I'm sure, when you explain how you found me and helped me, your parents—or whoever is in charge of you—will forget about punishing you. I'll tell them not to."

"She will be angry."

"Who? Your mother?"

"She is not my mother. She minds us. And she keeps the house."

"Who is she?"

"She is our minder. I told you."

Lola took the little girl's hand and led her up the trail. She was surprised how cold Celia's hand was.

"You should wear gloves. You are going to freeze your fingers off."

"I do not like gloves. Maybe *you* should wear gloves."

"I would love to be wearing gloves. I would love to be in dry clothes."

"Where are you taking me?"

"We are going to see your minder. While we are walking, I think I will make up a name for her. I think I will call her... Brunhilda."

"Her name is not Brunhilda."

"Well, until I hear a different name, Brunhilda is her name as far as I'm concerned. Brunhilda. Brunhilda. Brunhilda."

"If you call her that, she will give you a whipping."

"Who will?"

"Judith."

"Judith is it? Well, I bet Judith will be very nice to us when she finds out you saved someone from a shipwreck. I bet she wasn't expecting to meet me today."

"You say silly things."

"And you aren't silly enough. How old did you say you were, Celia?"

"I did not say."

"Well, say it now. How old are you?"

"I... I do not know exactly."

"You don't know how old you are?"

"Not exactly."

"Come on now. How many candles were there on your cake the last time you had a birthday party."

"I do not remember my last birthday party."

"How can you not remember your last birthday?"

"You ask too many questions."

"And you don't have enough answers. Tell me, Celia, have you seen another woman today? She would be about my age, and she is very beautiful, and she has fabulous blue, I mean, white hair. Have you seen her?"

Celia laughed.

"Which is it? Blue or white. Who has blue hair anyway? You are very silly."

"Maybe you don't see people with blue hair on Riesgado Island, but sometimes you see them in Seattle."

Celia looked perplexed.

"So, have you seen her? Have you seen my friend with the white hair?"

"She must be very old if she has white hair."

"No, I told you, she's my age. Young people have white hair sometimes. Her hair turned white just today."

"Grandfather has white hair."

"Is your grandfather here on the island?"

Celia nodded silently.

"You still haven't answered my question. Have you seen my friend with the white hair?"

Celia shook her head.

"You ask too many questions, and you talk too much."

"Sometimes asking questions is the only way to learn things. Do you want to ask *me* any questions?"

"Yes. Will you *ever* stop talking?"

While talking, they had climbed to the top of a hill and were now descending. Soon after, they reached the end of the woods. When they emerged into the gray daylight, Lola saw that the trail had brought them through the interior of the island and then to a different point on the sea. As they continued across a grassy expanse, she saw a tall, sharp promontory. At the top was a large, old stone house. It was like a fortress, standing defiantly against the lashing gales blowing in from the sea. It had narrow, high turrets, making it look somewhat like a castle. Clearly, it had been battered by storms for many years, maybe even centuries. It looked more like a ruin than an inhabited residence. The house looked as though it were leaning—and perhaps even in danger of falling into the sea.

Lola gaped at the impressive—and rather frightening—edifice. She wondered who had built it and what its history was. Was this actually what Maria had seen in her dream? If so, no wonder she had become consumed with finding out more about it.

Her musings were interrupted by a loud, piercing scream. She stopped and spun around to see the black-haired boy following them at a gallop out of the woods with a grotesque look on his face. He came to a dead stop just short of running into them.

"Peter!" yelled Celia. "You are not one bit funny."

"Ha! I scared you. Admit it. I scared the life out of you."

"Not as scared as you will be when I tell Judith."

"You will not tell Judith. You know I am not the one who will be in trouble. It will be you for bringing *her* here. You are the one who will get a smack this time."

The children's bickering unsettled Lola.

"Judith doesn't actually smack you, does she?"

The two of them said nothing.

"Peter, is it? Hello, Peter. My name is Lola."

"Lola?" he laughed dismissively. "That is a strumpet's name."

She had never been called a strumpet before and did not quite know what to make of it. It also struck her that Peter spoke differently from Celia, as though he might be English.

"Where do you guys come from anyway? Where did you live before you were on this island?"

The two went silent.

Something about Peter impressed her. Normally, she did not care for boys, but there was something about this one that fascinated her. Being an only child, Lola had never been particularly comfortable around children in general, although she was now finding she was better at talking to them than she had thought she was.

"Come on, you two," she said. "I need to talk to a grownup."

The path circled away from the house and toward the water. It then led them toward the house along a high bluff with a sheer drop to the swirling gray water below. Bracing herself against the wind, which seemed intent on blowing her over, Lola stopped to take in the view. From this vantage, she could see that there were many large rocks at the base of the promontory. Waves crashed against them with surprising fury. It was as though the sea were actively trying to hasten the old house's inevitable plunge into the water.

She found the salty smell of the sea both reassuringly familiar and yet also otherworldly. The wind's slap against her face reinvigorated her.

Looking again toward the old house, she asked the children skeptically, "Is that really where you live?"

"Yes, silly," said Celia. "Do you think we live in the woods?"

The sky darkened. It would soon be night. Given that she had been wandering around for hours now in soaked clothing, Lola was not surprised to be shivering. She needed to get somewhere she could dry herself and remove her wet clothes. Accompanied by the children, she made her way along the edge of the bluff and to the house's front door. It was large and made of oak with a big, rusty iron knocker in the center. She thought about using the knocker but decided against it.

"Go tell Judith I'm here, will you? I'm guessing she will be pretty surprised to see me."

"She might not, you know," said Peter. "Judith always knows everything."

"She does," agreed Celia. "Maybe your friends told her you were coming."

"My friends?" said Lola in surprise. "Do you know something about my friends?"

Celia shrugged.

"Wait a minute. Why did you say 'friends'? I only told you about one friend. Do you know anything about the man who was on the boat with us?"

Celia shrugged again.

"Celia, you stay here with me. Peter, go inside and get Judith for me. Please."

"Very well," he said. "I only hope for your sake that she is not contrary today. You do not want to see her when she is contrary."

Peter opened the iron latch, pushed the door open, and disappeared inside. As she waited, Lola assured herself that surely Judith could not be as fearsome as the children were suggesting. The wait seemed an eternity.

"He will tell her to come see me, won't he?" she asked Celia.

She shrugged.

"So tell me. Why did you say 'friends'?"

"I do not want to talk anymore. I get in trouble when I talk too much."

"Not with me you won't. I will be your best friend in the world if you answer all my questions—honestly."

"I used to have friends," said Celia sadly. "They are all gone now. You cannot fool me. You will be gone soon too."

Lola was about to respond when she was startled by the door's sudden movement. It opened wider, and there stood a tall, thin woman in a full-length black dress. Lola's eye was drawn to an unusual pendant hanging on a chain around her neck. Her face was long, severe, and lined with deep wrinkles. Her light auburn hair was laced with strands of white and tied tight behind her head.

She looked Lola up and down, taking in every detail. Her voice was deep, almost like a man's.

"You are right, Celia. This one is not for staying. She will be wanting to go back to her own."

5
Bridge House

"ARE YOU JUDITH?"

The woman in front of Lola nodded without altering the severe look on her face.

"I can't tell you how happy I am to finally find an adult," Lola said. "My friends and I were on a boat, and it sank in the storm. I am cold and tired and wet, and I think I'm going to catch pneumonia. Can I come in?"

"Grandfather does not like strange people in the house."

Lola was dumbstruck for several seconds by this response. Then she said, "I understand, but this really is an emergency. One of my friends may have drowned. The other has disappeared. People may be dead."

Other than involuntarily raising one eyebrow, Judith's demeanor remained unchanged.

"I see," she said.

"Please help me. Just let me come in and dry off. That's all I ask. Oh, and use your phone. If you let me use your phone, I promise to pay for any calls that I make."

Lola did not understand the woman's hesitation. She had always heard that people on the islands were quick to look out for each other or anyone else who got into trouble in the water.

Judith finally stepped back and reluctantly motioned her to enter. Relieved, Lola entered the large hallway. Her first impression was that the house, seen from the inside, did not look any more fit for habitation than it did from the outside. The wide staircase was certainly impressive, but it also looked as if it could collapse under someone's feet. In the gloom, she could not see much beyond the hallway except for a large doorway to the left.

Judith led her through the doorway to a sitting room. There was a large fireplace with two burning logs, and Lola rushed to kneel in front of it and warm her hands.

"I need to get out of these wet things," she said.

"I shall bring you some blankets," said Judith in a resigned voice.

"Thank you, Judith. I really do appreciate this."

The older woman tightened her face and said, "Welcome to Bridge House, Miss."

It seemed to Lola that never had a welcome felt so unwelcoming.

"Bridge House, huh?" she said. "So where is the bridge then? No chance it would lead to the mainland, I suppose."

Though she was joking, Lola would have given anything for a bridge to any place where people were not so strange.

"There is no bridge, Miss. Bridge is a family name. I shall be back with the blankets shortly."

Lola warmed her hands eagerly in front of the fire. The flames were the only source of light in the room. She saw no electrical fixtures—only an unlit candle on the mantle and an oil lamp on a small ornate table.

She heard the children whispering in the hallway. She strained to make out what they were saying over the crackling of the fire.

"You tell her."

"No, you tell her."

"No, I am in enough trouble as it is. She will not smack you. She likes you. You are her favorite. Always have been."

"If you do not tell her, then Audrey will just have to tell her herself."

"You know Audrey will not tell her. Audrey gets away with everything."

"I know. We should tell Grandfather. He would understand better than Judith. He would know what to do. He would put everything right—just like he used to do."

"Grandfather cannot even get up off his bed. No, we have to tell Judith and just take whatever comes."

Lola crept to the door and stepped into the hallway.

"What are you talking about?" she asked. "Can I help?"

The two startled faces vanished down the hallway. As apprehensive as she was, Lola was about to follow when she heard Judith's imperious voice from somewhere near the top of the staircase.

"I have the blankets. You should really stay close to the fire if you are worried about contracting consumption."

"Yes, thank you, I know."

Judith emerged from the darkness on the stairs and followed Lola back to the sitting room. She handed her the blankets. Lola eagerly slipped out of her clothes and wrapped one of the blankets tightly around her.

"Thank you so much, Judith. I'm almost afraid to ask, but I don't suppose you have a telephone?"

The older woman shook her head.

"How do you communicate with the mainland?" Lola asked.

"There has been no need, Miss."

"But what about food and supplies? I mean, you must leave the island to go shopping—or else someone must bring you supplies."

"We manage, Miss."

Lola was finding Judith no more satisfactory to talk to than the children.

"Can I ask? Where are the children's parents?"

"There is only their grandfather."

"But what about their parents? Where are they?"

"Do you need anything else, Miss?"

"And what about you? Are you a relative of theirs? Or do you work here?"

"I mind the children."

"What about school? They must need to see a doctor once in a while. How can they live here in such isolation?"

"If you will pardon me, Miss, I have things to attend to."

"But how am I going to get off the island? There has to be a way for me to get a message out."

"Perhaps when Grandfather is feeling better, he might sort something out. Things have been… difficult—since Grandfather has not been well."

"Would it be possible for me to talk to the grandfather?"

"No, Miss. I fear not. Certainly not until he is better."

Judith turned to leave when she and Lola spotted a little girl standing like a statue in the doorway. Lola had not seen her before. She appeared to be a year or two younger than Celia. She had blonde curls that framed a distinctively unhappy face.

"Audrey," said Judith sternly. "Why are you hanging about there?"

"I have something to show you."

"Can it not wait? I have been pestered enough for one day."

"She is not well."

"Who is not well?"

"My friend."

"What friend?"

"My new friend. I have a friend."

The girl pointed at Lola.

"I found a friend, just like Celia found a friend."

A cautious smile came over Lola's face.

"A friend?" she asked. "Like me? Is your friend a woman like me?"

Audrey nodded.

"Where is she? I have to see her," Lola said.

Audrey looked at Judith. After a show of exasperation, Judith nodded her assent.

"Come," said Audrey. "Follow me."

With surprising speed, the little girl scampered through the hallway and out the front door.

"Hey, wait for me!" Lola called after her.

Reluctantly, Lola put her jeans and top back on. She then went after Audrey. It was now completely dark outside with no sign of the moon or stars. Her ears were filled with the sound of wind and crashing waves. She spotted the child running along the bluff and rushed after her. She caught up with her at a gazebo perched on the

44

cliff, where it no doubt had a lovely view on a fine day. The structure was beaten by the elements, and Lola thought it a miracle it was even standing—given the storms it must have endured.

Inside the gazebo, two benches had been pushed together. Someone lay on top of them. Lola held her breath as she drew near.

"Thank God," she said aloud with huge relief.

Then she dropped to her knees and took her friend's hands.

"Maria, wake up. It's me. It's Lola. Wake up, Irish girl."

Maria opened her eyes.

"Janey Mack," she said.

"Are you okay?"

"I'll be honest with you. I've been better."

"Can you walk? I'll take you to the house. It's a big, cold, drafty place, but at least there's a fire in the fireplace. We need to get you out of those wet clothes."

Maria made a wobbly attempt to stand. Once she got her balance, Lola guided her slowly out of the gazebo and down the path toward the house. Little Audrey followed silently behind.

"Where were you?" Lola said. "Why didn't you wait for me at the beach?"

"It was so strange," Maria said. "After you went into the woods, a little girl appeared out of nowhere. I reckoned it meant there were other people around. She wouldn't say anything, but she seemed to want me to follow her. She brought me to the rocks at the edge of the strand and showed me the entrance to a cave hidden among the large stones. I would never have spotted it but for her. Despite being a bit claustrophobic, I followed her inside and we came out on a different part of the island. There was a path. I knew I should have gone back and waited for you, but the little *womaneen* wouldn't stop. I knew if I didn't stay with her, I would lose her—and I didn't want to miss a chance of finding people who might help us. I got as far as the place where you found me and had a weakness. That's all I remember. Thanks be to God you found me."

"Are you sure you're okay?" Lola asked.

"I'll be grand. I just need to catch up with myself. Tell me..."

"Yes?"

"Did Kyle ever turn up? Please say yes."

Lola shook her head.

"I'm afraid not," she said, "but I haven't given up hope. Anyway, we're not alone anymore. The good news is that this big old house here has people in it. The bad news is that they are mostly children. I've only met one adult, and she's the strangest woman I've ever met. I really don't know what to make of this place. None of it seems quite right."

"Like a dream, you mean? See, wasn't I telling you? Didn't I dream this place?"

"So is this actually what your dream was like? Is this really the place you saw? Were all these strange people there?"

Maria gaped at the house. Even in the dark she was able to recognize it.

"I don't remember anyone in the dream except for the man. The fine, tall man. But, yes, this is definitely the house I saw. It was on the edge of a cliff—just like this. The waves were crashing on the rocks below too—just the same as this. It is absolutely the strangest sensation being here and seeing it in the real world. I can scarcely believe it. Does this mean that I am not mad—or that I am?"

"If you're crazy, Maria, then we both are. I haven't seen your fine, tall man, but I wouldn't mind if I did. He might be more help than the ones I've met so far."

They were startled by a crow, which had been perched on a nearby rock, suddenly spreading its wings and taking flight amid a commotion of noisy fluttering. Battling the brisk winds, it flew upward and alighted on the highest point of the house's roof where it let out a grating, taunting caw.

"Awful things, crows," said Maria. "When I was small and my granny gave out to us for not eating, she would say, 'You'll follow the crow for it!' Well, here I am now following the crow, but where on earth am I following it to?"

Lola led her into the house and into the sitting room. She was happy to see another log had been added to the fire. They both slipped out of their wet clothes, wrapped themselves in the wool blankets, and installed themselves in front of the flames.

There was a divan in the room, but it was so old and musty they did not go near it. They preferred sitting on the floor.

"I don't know what I would have done if I hadn't found you," said Lola. "I was going bonkers."

"Yeh, I was going a bit mental there myself."

"I'm going to have to start calling you Blondie."

"Eh?"

"Well, I can't call you my blue-haired girl anymore. You've gone platinum blonde on me. Kind of like Debbie Harry. You know, the one who sings your song."

"I'm absolutely knackered. I don't think I'll be awake for much longer."

"Me either. Thank God for the fire, but there's still a chill in this room. I think we're going to have to huddle together for warmth."

"Sounds good to me, so it does. I honestly feel as though I will never be warm again."

Lola snuggled close to the Irish woman and put an arm around her shoulder. Maria yawned.

"Lola," she said, "we will be able to get off this island, won't we? I mean, this place seems so strange—like we're not even in the same world anymore."

"Sure, of course. It's not like we're prisoners or anything. At this time tomorrow we'll be back at my place in Ballard."

"How many people have you actually met?"

"Well," Lola replied. "let's see, not counting you, I have seen three children plus Judith, who seems to be their nanny or something. She's not exactly the friendliest person I ever met."

"And no sign of the man? The man I saw in my dream?"

"No. They all talk about a grandfather, but it sounds like he is pretty old and not very well. The way they talk about him, though, I get the feeling he might be the most normal person here. Judith doesn't sound like she's going to let me anywhere near him, but we definitely have to talk to him. I bet *he* will make sense of this place for us. Everything will look better tomorrow. Things never seem as weird in the daylight."

"Lola…"

"Yes, Blondie?"

"I just had this strange thought."

"Yeah?"

"I know it will sound completely daft."

"Just tell me."

"It's just that... what if we're dead?"

"What are you talking about?"

"How can you explain this place? It's as though time has forgotten about it. As if we are the only people to ever come here—except for the people who are already here."

"You mean, why is this place so isolated?" asked Lola. "Kyle explained that to me one time when we were out sailing. It has something to do with the currents and the fact that there is no good place to dock a boat. And I think there may have been legal complications with the ownership. I don't know. I'm sure there's a logical explanation for it."

"Lola," Maria said solemnly, "what if this is the afterlife?"

"What?"

"I mean, what if we actually drowned when the boat sank? What if we're dead and we just don't realize it? What if the people here are ghosts? And we are too?"

"You've definitely been watching too many episodes of *The Twilight Zone,* Blondie. Of course, we're alive. Feel this and tell me I'm not alive."

Lola ran the back of her hand along Maria's cheek. Lola was happy to feel warmth returning to her face.

"And what about the kids? I held Celia's hand. You can't do that with a ghost, can you? My hand would pass right through. God, I can't believe we're even talking like this. And what about Kyle? If this is the afterlife, where is he? Shouldn't he be here too?"

"That's the thing. Maybe we have it backwards. Maybe Kyle's not here because he survived. We thought he drowned, but maybe he's the only one who is all right—and it's us who drowned."

Lola hugged her tightly.

"I can feel my heart beating, and I can feel yours too," she said. "Whatever's going on, we're definitely not dead. We'll figure this out, and we'll get off this island. Everything will be fine. You'll see."

"I'm so glad you're here, Lola. I was so scared when we got separated. I was afraid we wouldn't find one another again."

Lola rested her head comfortably against Maria's.

"You needn't have worried, Blondie. There was no way I was going to lose you. I'm so glad I met you. I can't tell you how glad."

"You're very good, so you are."

"As long as we're stuck here, why don't you teach me some Gaelic?"

"Like what?"

"I don't know. Let's see. For example, what word would I use for someone I loved?"

"That would be *grá*."

Lola pressed closer and said, "*Grá mo shaol.*"

"Hey, you're taking the piss, aren't you? And me thinking you knew no Irish."

"What do you mean?"

"You know full well. You're using words I didn't teach you."

"I am?"

"Yes, you are."

"That's impossible. How would I know Gaelic? I think one of us must be telepathic. Anyway, I'm really enjoying this."

"Yeh, in spite of everything, this is lovely," said Maria, her voice fading with exhaustion. "Reminds me of times at home when I was a child. Nights snuggling in the bed with one or other of my sisters."

"Sisters, huh?"

"If only…"

"If only what?"

"If only we knew that Kyle was okay. He's all I can think about."

6
Sleepless

LOLA'S HEAD WAS tortured with dreams.

More than once during the night, she relived the capsizing and sinking of *Transcendence*. She experienced again the trauma of being thrown into the sea and struggling to keep her head above the churning waves. She again felt the terror of the icy water and not knowing where Maria and Kyle were. She struggled for breath and flailed her arms. Her heart pounded with panic.

She woke with a start and sat up. She needed a moment to catch her breath. The room was dark and cold. A few orange embers glowed in the fireplace, and a smoky wood smell hung in the damp air. She gasped upon noticing a figure a few feet away.

"Who are you? What are you doing there?"

It did not move, and she wondered if she might be imagining it. It then stepped closer.

"Peter! What are you doing there?"

"I did not mean to scare you."

"Well, you did!"

She glanced at Maria, who slept undisturbed.

"It's the middle of the night, Peter. You should be in bed."

"I cannot sleep."

"Well, you should be in bed anyway. You shouldn't be prowling around in the middle of the night scaring people."

"I can never sleep."

"I'm not surprised. This house is absolutely freezing. Now you've woken me up, and I'm not going to be able to sleep either."

Lola got up and found the candle she had spotted earlier. She removed it from its base and held it in the fireplace so that the wick would touch the embers. After a few moments it began to burn. She put the candle back in its base and looked around. She was happy to see additional logs had been left near the fireplace. She put two of them on top of the embers.

"Let's see if those will burn. Then at least the room will warm up a bit again. Tell me, Peter, why were you standing there looking at us?"

He shrugged.

"You and your sisters are not very good at answering questions."

"They are not my sisters."

Lola sat in front of the fire and beckoned the boy to join her.

"Sit down, Peter. Let's have a little talk."

Reluctantly, he sat.

"So, if Celia and Audrey are not your sisters, tell me, who are they then? How come all of you are living here on this island together?"

"Because."

"Because why?"

"That is just how it is. This is where we live."

"But you must have lived somewhere else before?"

"I do not remember."

"What about your parents?"

"What about them?"

"Did they live here too? Where are they now?"

"I do not remember that either."

"No, of course, you don't. What about your grandfather? What can you tell me about him?"

Peter shrugged again.

"He is just Grandfather. He has always been here. This is Grandfather's house."

"What's his name?"

"Grandfather."

"Grandfather what? I had two grandfathers. Grandfather Blumquist and Grandfather Hansen. What is your grandfather's name?"

"Grandfather Bridge."

"Okay, now we're getting somewhere. Do you know Grandfather Bridge's first name?"

"His first name is Grandfather. Grandfather Bridge."

Maria stirred under her blanket. "Who are you talking to? It's not morning, is it?"

"I have no idea what time it is," said Lola, "but it's still dark. I'm having a little chat with Peter."

Maria sat up and yawned. She gazed at the boy and an expression of profound sadness came over her face.

"Is something wrong, Maria?" Lola asked.

"It… it's uncanny."

"What is?"

"He looks exactly like my cousin."

"Okay, but you seem upset."

"You don't understand. My cousin Fionn, he was just about this boy's age when he died. He was killed in a road accident a few years ago. Our family were totally devastated. He was such a beautiful lad. It broke my aunt and uncle's hearts. They've never got over it, and they never will. None of us will. Seeing this lad brings it all back."

"But this isn't actually him, right?" said Lola, not believing she was even asking that question. Though she did not want to admit it, Maria's talk about being in an afterlife had been preying on her mind. "I mean, it's just a coincidence, right?"

"Yes," she replied sadly. "It is only a coincidence. I'm sorry. So your name is Peter?"

"Yes, Miss."

"Hey, wait a minute," said Lola. "How come she gets called Miss? You never call me Miss. You called me a strumpet."

Peter shrugged.

"You're a fine young lad," said Maria. "C'mere, tell me who are your people?"

"My people, Miss?"

"You know. Where do you come from? Who are your parents?"

"I already told the other one. I have always lived here. I do not remember anywhere else or anyone else."

"I'm sorry. You must be so very lonely."

"I am not lonely. There is Celia and Audrey and Judith. And Grandfather."

"And who is your grandfather?"

"You ask too many questions. Just like her. I am leaving."

Lola followed him as far as the hallway. "Go to bed, Peter. Get some sleep."

"I told you. I cannot sleep."

As she was about to go back to the sitting room, Lola noticed Celia joining him in the hallway.

"Celia shouldn't be up at this hour either," Lola called after him. "Make sure she goes to bed too."

"Celia cannot sleep either."

"How weird is that?" said Lola, as she rejoined Maria by the fire. She could see her friend was still upset. "You don't really think Peter is your cousin Fionn, do you?"

"I know he isn't. It's just that seeing him brought back so many sad memories. I'll be all right."

"Well, one thing is definitely for sure. I don't think we are going to get any answers or any help until we talk to Grandfather. As soon as it's light, we're going to find out where he is and insist on talking to him."

"Is it just me or has this night been going on for a very long time now?"

"It just seems long because we're awake. We should try going back to sleep."

The two women lay down again under the blankets.

"Lola, what if...?"

"What?"

"It's silly."

"Tell me."

"What if the sun isn't ever going to come up? What if it is going to stay nighttime forever?"

"You're kidding, right? Why would the sun not come up?"

"It's just that, well, nothing else seems to be normal here."

Lola snuggled close to her.

53

"That's crazy talk, Blondie. You'll see. Trust me. Just close your eyes. The next thing you know, it will be morning and then things won't seem so weird at all. At least not as weird as what you're talking about."

"Thanks, Lola. I don't know what I'd do without you."

"Don't worry. I'm not going anywhere."

The next thing Lola knew, she was blinking her eyes at the morning sunlight streaming through the window. The room was cold again. The fire had died completely. Though she hated to admit it, even to herself, she was extraordinarily relieved to see the daylight.

Maria stirred. She stretched and clearly also appreciated the sunlight.

"Guess I was quite silly last night."

"Hey, we've been through a lot. Yesterday was a terrible day. I think we're both still in shock."

"Have you been awake long?"

"I just woke up."

"So, you haven't seen anyone yet?"

"No."

Lola did not know what to make of the look on Maria's face. "What is it?"

"I just wonder if they are still here."

"What? Judith and the kids?"

"Yeh."

"Why wouldn't they still be here? Where would they go?"

"I just thought, you know, that maybe they couldn't exist in the daytime."

"You mean like vampires?"

"Well, yes, or ghosts."

"But we saw them in the daylight yesterday."

"You're right. I'm being silly. I wonder if there's tea."

"Or coffee. Somehow I'm not too hopeful. This place doesn't seem too well equipped. We should find Judith. I'm sure the old crone is lurking about here somewhere. The first problem, though, is what to wear—unless you feel like wearing damp clothes."

"Um, were those dresses there last night?"

Lola followed Maria's gaze to the couch. Two long white dresses were draped over it. Intrigued, Lola stood and, unembarrassed at being undressed, walked over and slipped on one of the dresses. She turned in the direction of a tall, narrow, stand-alone mirror in a corner of the room and saw herself wearing the old-fashioned frock in the centuries-old room.

"My goodness," she laughed. "How very Gothic novel!"

More shy than her friend, Maria kept her blanket around her as she crept to the couch. Lola was impressed that Maria was somehow able to put her dress on while staying underneath the blanket. She was even more impressed by how beautiful she looked in the dress.

"My God, Blondie, that dress really suits you. Are you sure you're not just visiting from a different century?"

Maria laughed.

"Well, this is fun. A bit of fancy dress. Are there any shoes?"

"Don't see any, but they'll probably turn up mysteriously too."

They felt a sudden cold draft and turned to see Judith standing in the doorway. She entered the room and collected the jeans and tops that had been left on a chair by the fireplace.

"I shall hang these outdoors. They will dry more quickly that way. If it does not rain again."

Lola glanced out the window. There were only a few clouds in the sky. The storm had passed, although she could see from the trees' movement that there was still a strong breeze.

"Any chance of a cup of coffee, Judith?"

"I shall show you the kitchen. You are welcome to whatever you can find."

They followed her down the hallway and into the kitchen, where there was a very welcome warmth from a wood-burning stove. Maria was particularly pleased to see steam coming from the large metal kettle.

"I suppose a latte is out of the question," Lola said ironically.

Maria got two earthenware cups from the shelf and put them on the wooden table. Among the glass jars on the shelf, one contained tea leaves and another had ground coffee.

"No tea bags," observed the Irish woman.

"And no coffee machine," said the American woman.

"No bother," said Maria, as she put her hands on a stoneware teapot. "This is how my granny used to make the tea."

"My grandma had a Mr. Coffee. I guess I'll just try to make coffee-press coffee-but without the coffee press."

Maria was quite happy with her cup of tea, although she missed having milk. Lola was less happy, as she did not like feeling the grounds in her mouth as she tried to drink her coffee.

"Does it seem strange to you, Lola, that there is tea and coffee but so little food around?"

"Now that you mention it, yeah. A bowl of cereal or a slice of toast would be nice. At least there is bread, and it seems to be freshly baked. And there are apples. At least we won't starve."

"It is as though the tea and the coffee and the rest are meant only for us. What do Judith and the children eat?"

"You're not going to say it's because they're ghosts or vampires, are you?"

"You have to admit, it is all so very strange."

"You're right. It is. We have to talk to Judith."

Even as she said her name, the minder appeared at the door.

"I am sorry if we do not have everything you would like. We are unaccustomed to visitors."

"We can see that. Look, it wasn't our idea to come visiting you. All we want is to leave as soon as possible. How can we do that?"

"I am afraid that may be difficult."

"Is there a boat?"

Judith shook her head.

"And definitely no telephone?"

Again, Judith shook her head.

"Telegraph? Internet? I don't know. Carrier pigeon? You must have some way of communicating."

"Grandfather has always cherished his privacy."

"This is crazy, Judith. What are we supposed to do? Start swimming and hope for the best?"

"Can we hoist an emergency flag of some sort," asked Maria, "that a passing boat might see?"

"There is no flagpole."

"Or light a bonfire somewhere to attract attention?"

"I cannot stop you from doing whatever it is you think you need to do, Miss."

"Judith, I think we need to talk to Grandfather."

Her face tightened.

"That is out of the question. He is not well."

"Is he conscious? Can he talk?"

She did not reply.

"We promise not to upset him or tire him, but we need to talk to him. Somebody has to explain to us what is going on, and it sounds more and more like he is the only one."

"I am sorry."

"Not as sorry as I am, lady."

Judith left the kitchen, but the women immediately heard her engaged in conversation with two of the children.

"What? Where? Show me."

"Come on, Maria," said Lola, giving up on her gritty cup of black coffee. "Let's find out what's going on."

They went outside where they saw Celia and Audrey leading Judith in the direction of the woods. At the edge of the woods stood a boy. At first they thought it was Peter, but then they saw that his hair was a much lighter shade than Peter's.

Judith walked back toward the house with the three children. The new boy looked like he was a couple of years older than Peter. He had a dazed look on his face.

"Hello. My name is Maria. What's yours?"

The boy said nothing.

"He is Caleb," said Celia.

As the others went into the house, Maria turned to Lola with a look of astonishment.

"Lola! Did you see what I saw?"

"What are you talking about?"

"Does Caleb not remind you of someone?"

"I don't know. He's just another kid to me. Why, who does he remind you of?"

"Lola, I may be going mad, but I think that lad is the absolute spit of Kyle!"

7
Grandfather

"WHAT DO YOU mean 'the spit'? You mean he *looks* like Kyle?"

"Doesn't he?"

Now that Maria had pointed it out, Lola could see that Caleb did indeed look very much like Kyle, although quite a bit younger.

"What are you saying, Maria? Do you think he actually is Kyle? That's impossible. It's just a coincidence that they look alike. You know, the way Peter reminded you of your cousin."

"This is different."

"How?"

"I could tell Peter was a different person from Fionn, that it was just a resemblance. This is more than a resemblance."

"What do you mean, more than a resemblance?"

"It is difficult to explain. He simply seems to *be* Kyle. Did you see the mole on his cheek?"

"Now that you point it out, I have to say it is a strange coincidence all right, but a lot of people have moles. I think this is just you *wishing* it were Kyle. That boy is way too young to be him."

"I know you're right from a logical point of view. It's just that there are things going on in this place that do not seem very logical to me. You'll probably think it is silly, but I trust my own intuition about certain things, even when it doesn't make sense to anyone else."

"Okay, I'll tell you what. Let's talk to him. Once you see him more closely and talk to him, you'll realize he's a completely different person."

"Fair enough."

They went back to the house, where they arrived in time to see Judith leading Caleb up the staircase. When Maria looked at her stern visage, her courage suddenly drained away.

"Maybe this is a bad idea," she whispered to Lola nervously.

Lola paid her no heed. "Judith! We need a word with Caleb."

"He is busy."

The old woman stiffened visibly as Lola continued ascending the stairs.

"This is important, Judith. Caleb, how long exactly have you been in this place?"

"He is one of us. He has always been here."

"I want to hear *him* answer. Caleb, how long have you been on this island?"

He appeared confused.

"Judith told you. I have always been here."

The longer Lola gazed at him, the more she could understand Maria's thinking. Given his age, he was shorter and skinnier than Kyle and did not have his physique, yet the resemblance was uncanny.

"How old are you, Caleb?"

"Why do you need to know that?"

"Because I do. How old are you?"

He appeared confused. He looked to Judith, as if for help.

"We do not worry about ages here," said the old woman with a tone of finality.

She turned to continue up the stairs, but Lola refused to give up.

"Kyle, do you remember what you told me the last time we went sailing together? Do you remember what you said to me?"

He looked baffled.

"I don't know you."

His voice definitely sounded like Kyle's, although maybe half an octave higher.

"Yes, you do. Think hard. Try to remember."

He shrugged.

"I don't know what you want me to say. Why are you asking me questions I can't answer?"

Now it was Lola's turn to shrug.

"I don't know. Maybe I'm starting to go crazy."

Maria, who at first had stayed at the bottom of the stairs, now climbed past Lola and stood directly in front of him. She pointed her finger at Lola.

"Kyle, look at her again. You were in love with her. I know you were."

"Uh, Maria, this is getting a little weird," muttered Lola under her breath. "I mean, he's only about fifteen years old."

"Do you not remembered saving my life? If not for you, I would be dead. You sacrificed yourself for me. How could you forget that? I'll never be able in all my life to get over it."

Caleb was more confused than ever.

"That is quite enough," said Judith sternly. "Leave us now."

"Judith," said Lola, "we have to talk to Grandfather, and we have to talk to him right now."

"That is quite impossible."

"Why is it impossible? Is he unconscious or something? Is he deaf and dumb? Or is he not actually here? Does Grandfather even exist? You have to give us some answers that make sense."

"He has not been well for some time. The past few days in particular have sapped him completely. Have you not done enough to him already?"

"What are you talking about? What have we done to him? We haven't even seen him."

"I do not have to answer your questions."

"Listen," said Lola, losing her temper, "I know you didn't invite us onto your little island, and I'm sorry for the intrusion. But don't tell me you don't have to answer my questions. I didn't have breakfast this morning, the coffee situation is unacceptable, and all I can think about is getting home. I'm in a bad mood, and the longer I go on without an adequate amount of caffeine, the worse it's going to get. I need you to answer my questions right now."

Judith turned and led Caleb up the stairs where they disappeared into the gloom.

"That does it," Lola said. "We have to talk to the old man. As far as I can see, it's our only hope of getting any answers and getting home."

"How do we do that?" asked Maria. "She's guarding him like a hawk."

"I think I could definitely take the old bat in a fight."

Maria looked at her impatiently.

"Okay, you're right, we're not going to force our way past her. We just need to find a time when she's not around. We need to distract her. One of us needs to find a way to get her out of the house, so the other one can go upstairs and talk to him."

"Why does your idea sound scary to me?"

"I don't know, Maria," said Lola sarcastically. "Maybe because you think we are in mortal danger from a crabby old woman, a bunch of kids, and an old man lying in a bed?"

"Okay, what do you want me to do?"

"Think of something that would make Judith leave the house. Get the children to help you. Tell them it's some sort of game."

"But then you will be searching the house alone."

"Yeah, I guess I will."

"I have a bad feeling about this."

"Is this your intuition again? What kind of feeling do you have about being stuck on this island for the rest of our lives? And come to think of it, that won't be all that long since there doesn't seem to be very much actual food in the house—never mind the coffee situation."

"All right. I'll go look for Audrey. She will be the easiest one to convince we are playing a game." Maria gave her a hug. "Please be careful, Lola."

"Don't worry about me, Blondie. I can look after myself."

Lola waited in the sitting room where she could see the woods through the window. She watched the clouds float across the deep blue sky. The storm had made the air fresh and clear, but in the far distance, she could see darker clouds gathering. It was only a matter of time until the next storm blew in.

Eventually she saw movement between the house and the woods. Maria was talking to Audrey enthusiastically as she led the little girl away from the house. Audrey jumped up and down with excitement. So far so good, thought Lola. Maria stayed by the woods as Audrey ran back toward the house. Soon she was running back to Maria, now joined by the other two children. Maria had a conversation with all of them. It appeared to be going well.

Maria, Peter, and Celia walked down the path into the woods, while Audrey ran back to the house by herself. Lola held her breath, waiting to see what would happen next. She heard Audrey scamper up the stairs. She could barely make out the sounds of her and Judith conversing. The old woman sounded testy. After a few minutes she heard them come down the stairs. Through the window she watched, as Audrey led Judith and Caleb across the grass. Halfway to the woods, Judith stopped and spoke impatiently to the little girl and then looked back toward the house. Lola stepped back quickly in case she was looking at the window. After some discussion, the group continued until it disappeared into the trees.

"It's now or never, Lola," she whispered to herself, heading for the stairs.

She knew she had no time to waste, but she did not rush. She was careful to look where she stepped, as she did not trust the state of the stairs or the floorboards. She had no logical reason to be apprehensive, yet she was nervous. Despite thinking Maria's fears were irrational, she was affected by them. She did her best to shake them off.

At the top of the stairs was a long, dark hallway with several doors on either side.

"I guess I'll have to try all of them," she said under her breath.

The doors had handles rather than knobs. She turned the handle on the first door, opening it to reveal a dusty, bare room. She closed that door and tried the next one. It was similar except for an old steamer trunk in the middle of the floor. Lola wondered if she was going to find Grandfather—or anyone else—upstairs. She also wondered where the children and Judith slept.

Moving quickly, she tried the remaining doors. Every room was either completely empty or contained only a minimal amount of furniture. None of them had a bed. She had all but concluded that Grandfather did not exist when she noticed a door at the very end of the hallway. She tried the handle, and it opened out to reveal a set of narrow, steep stairs leading upward. Wondering how much more time she had before Judith returned, she took a breath and started up the steps.

The closeness of the walls on either side made her feel claustrophobic. She reached a landing where the stairs continued upward in a different direction. By now the light from the hallway below was lost to her. She did not like climbing in the dark. The stairs appeared to stop at a ceiling, but when she felt around with her hand, she realized that there was a hatch door that opened upward. She pushed against it, nearly hoping it would not budge. A dead end would mean she could give up and go back downstairs. Instead, it creaked open.

She pushed hard against the door until it swung on its hinges and slammed on the floor. She raised her head above the floor level and tried to make out whatever she could in the dimness. What little light there was came through a small, dirty skylight at the far end. Everything was deathly quiet once the sound of the slamming door faded from her ears. She listened in vain for the sound of breathing or anything else that would indicate someone was in the room.

Carefully, she climbed the rest of the way and stood on the floor. She thought she could make out a bed in the gloom, but she needed more light. The slant of the roof confirmed this was the attic. She saw a second skylight near her, but it allowed in no light as the glass was covered with black paint. She saw a rusty latch on it and realized it could be opened like a window. She could only open it an inch or so, but it was enough to let in a brisk breeze and a small amount of sunlight. It cast all manner of odd-shaped shadows in the room, and she could now see more clearly that there was indeed a bed.

Heart pounding, she approached it and gasped upon seeing that someone was in fact lying in it. It was a man who looked absolutely skeletal. She had come looking for an old man and instead, apparently, found his remains.

She drew closer still and wondered why there was not more of a rotting smell. Could he possibly have been mummified?

"Well, Grandfather," she said with forced bravado. "At last we meet. It looks like I'm a little late, though. I think someone forgot to tell Judith you died."

She studied the face. It was gaunt and yellow, but there was no sign of decomposition. Could she be certain he was actually dead? The absolute stillness of the body argued that he was, yet she still had a slight doubt. She held out her hand and positioned it above his mouth—not too close—just to assure herself there was no respiration. She held it there for several moments and was surprised to see it trembling. Was it because of nervousness or caffeine withdrawal?

His hand seized her wrist without warning, and her heart all but stopped.

It happened with incredible suddenness, and Lola wondered if this was how a mouse felt when caught in a trap.

She wanted to scream, but her throat froze. She tried to pull her hand away, but Grandfather's grip was surprisingly stubborn. She panicked and tugged harder. It was enough to get her free, and she fell backward onto the floor. Her intention was to get up and flee down the stairs as fast as she could, but instead she sat there and stared. She wondered if she had witnessed some kind of delayed muscular reaction having to do with rigor mortis. She watched the body intently, ready to flee at the first sign of movement.

Several fraught seconds passed, and she nearly convinced herself it was some sort of natural phenomenon—or even that she had imagined it. Then she saw his arm move slightly and heard a faint, croaking sound. Some instinct told her she was not in immediate danger. She was also very curious.

"Are you trying to speak?"

"Please."

He tried to extend his arm in her direction. There was something pitiful in his sunken face and the frustrated attempt to move. Against her better judgment, she reached over and touched his hand. A chill went through her entire body. At the same time, his hand began to feel less cold. Subtly, his appearance somehow seemed less cadaverous. His eyes opened and glanced in her direction.

"Thank you."

"Grandfather?"

"How...?"

He could not finish his question.

"I'm no medical expert, but I'd say you definitely need a doctor. I need to ask you if there is any way to get off this island."

The longer he held onto her hand, the better he looked. Lola found his hand's grip uncomfortable, but he was not inclined to let go.

"How...?"

"I don't know what you are trying to ask. Are you trying to say 'How am I?' 'How are the children?' 'How did a crazy woman like Judith get control of me?' What is it? Sorry, I tend to ramble when I get nervous. And I am definitely nervous right now."

"How did you find me?"

"Oh, that's easy. I just searched the upstairs of the house until I finally discovered where you were. It wasn't really that hard."

"I mean, how did you get to the island?"

For a man who had appeared to be dead only moments before, his voice, while weak, was now surprisingly smooth and sonorous. He did not sound American. He did not really have any accent that Lola could identify, but if she had to guess, she would have said British.

"We were on a sailing trip. The boat capsized and sank. We all nearly drowned. Actually, one of us probably did drown. Or maybe he didn't. I don't know. It's complicated. Anyway, I thought maybe Judith might have told you."

"Tell me your name."

"I'm Lola. What's your name? I mean, I can't exactly call you Grandfather, can I? After all, I mean, you're not *my* grandfather. Sorry, but I did tell you I ramble sometimes, didn't I?"

His solid black eyes widened, and there was something extremely sad about them.

"I cannot go on the way I have. It has to end."

"Hey, don't give up hope, Gramps. You seem to be improving very quickly. I think you just needed a bit of attention. That Judith would put anybody into a depression. Hang in there. Say, how old are you anyway?"

"I have to let go."

"Hey, don't die on me now. It took a lot of courage for me to come up here and find you, and now you're perking up nicely. Don't talk about dying."

"No, I have to let go of *them.*"

"Of who?"

With considerable effort and Lola's help, the old man managed to sit up on the edge of the bed. The sight of him was astounding. Not only had he looked like a cadaver just a few minutes earlier, but he had looked like the cadaver of a man in his nineties. Now he looked more like a man in his seventies. He closed his eyes and appeared to be thinking very intently. The silence in the room made Lola anxious. There was a strange tingling sensation on the back of her neck.

She turned around and jumped nearly a foot upon seeing Judith's head rising through the trap door.

"I can explain, Judith. I really needed to talk to him. And it's a good thing I did. I think he's been improving since I've been here. It's all right. I haven't done him any harm."

As Judith ascended into the room, she did not acknowledge Lola's presence in the slightest. All of her attention was on the old man.

He said, "I have something to tell you, Judith."

She said, "I know, sir."

"You have served me faithfully for many years."

"Thank you, sir."

"I am afraid, though, I have no further need of your services."

"I understand, sir."

"You have more than earned a good rest."

"Thank you, sir. May I ask...?"

"Yes?"

"The children?"

"Do not worry."

"It is just that..."

"Yes...?"

"Audrey is so young."

"I understand. Do not worry."

"Thank you, sir."

"Thank you, Judith. Farewell."

To Lola's astonishment, the old woman turned transparent. She became fainter and fainter until she had vanished completely.

8
Eliot

"HEY!" CRIED LOLA. "I know she was a bitch and everything, but you didn't have to kill her!"

She dropped the old man's hand, transfixed by the physical changes he was going through. He now appeared another ten years younger.

"I was selfish. I thought all I wanted was my solitude, but I deceived myself. I was lonely. It was wrong. I had no right."

"What happened to Judith? Is she dead? Did you send her somewhere?"

"Oh, she is very much dead. Indeed, she has been dead for many years."

"Okay, this is crazy. Was she even actually real? Are you real? I must be hallucinating."

A cold draft coming from the door made Lola shiver. She turned to see Peter ascending the stairs into the room. Celia and Audrey followed.

"It is so good to see you feeling better, Grandfather," said the boy.

"Thank you, Peter. I hear you have had trouble sleeping."

"Yes, Grandfather. I am so very weary."

"We all are," said Celia.

"I know," said the old man. "I am afraid I have not been very fair to you, but I have good news. You may go to sleep now."

"Really?" said Audrey with a smile on her face. "Will there be dreams?"

"Yes, Audrey, there will be dreams. And you will finally be with your mother and your father again."

"Really?" said Celia. "All of us?"

"Yes, all of you."

"When, Grandfather? When?"

"Now. Immediately. Come give Grandfather a kiss."

Audrey ran to him and put her arms around him.

"I love you, Grandfather."

"I love you too, Audrey. Sleep well, child."

He kissed her on the forehead. Then she stepped back, smiled, and quietly vanished.

"Me too?" asked the remaining girl.

"Yes, Celia," he smiled. "Come to Grandfather for your kiss."

She walked to him eagerly and put her arms around him. He kissed her cheek tenderly.

"Good night, Celia. Sweet dreams."

"I love you, Grandfather," she said, her voice trailing off as she melted into the gloomy air.

He looked over at the boy.

"Your turn, Peter."

He looked uneasy.

"What is wrong, Peter? I believe you are the most exhausted of all."

"I am. It's just that…"

"Just what?"

"I am too old to be kissing my grandfather."

The old man looked at him indulgently.

"Come here. You are never too old to kiss your grandfather."

Peter was indecisive. Finally, though, he rushed to the old man and threw his arms around him.

"Thank you, Grandfather. Will you sleep too?"

"I am afraid not," he replied sadly. "But that is not anything for you to worry about. Pleasant dreams, my boy."

He pushed Peter's mop of hair away and kissed him on the forehead. Peter's lip quivered, and a single tear streamed down his cheek.

"I… I love you, Grandfather."

And then he was gone too.

Lola's mouth was agape.

"What did I just see?"

"I had to let go of them. It was too draining to hold on to them—especially with the addition of you three. Besides, it was time. It was not fair to them."

"Wait, what do you mean about the three of us?"

Her heart beat as if beginning an anxiety attack.

"Are we dead?"

"No, no, my dear girl. Rest assured. You are quite alive."

"What about Maria? Please tell me she's alive too."

"The other girl? Yes, she too is alive. I did have to give you a bit of help, but you mostly managed to survive on your own, and that is to your credit. Not many people would have lived through what you did."

"So can we go? Can we leave this island?"

"You may, of course. I have no interest in keeping prisoners. I will go back to my former solitary life. It is for the best."

"How soon can we go?"

"Soon. I only need a bit of time to regain more strength. Then I shall see to your return home. And you will not be troubled by the memory of this place. Perhaps occasionally in a dream. That will be all."

"Wait. Are you talking about erasing my memory?"

"That is very modern language. I prefer to think of it as the gift of forgetfulness, but yes, I think it will be for the best."

"I don't think I like the idea of that."

"Once you no longer remember, it will not really matter whether you like the idea or not."

"Wait a minute. You said 'you three.' So that means Caleb really is Kyle?"

"The young man from yesterday? Yes, I believe Judith called him Caleb."

"So he survived too? Like me and Maria?"

"No, I'm afraid he succumbed to the water. He put up a good fight, but he did not have the benefit of a flotation device like the two of you."

Lola found herself welling with tears.

"So, he's gone?"

She was devastated, as she tried to make sense of what he was saying.

"But he's not gone," she said, "I mean, we saw him, talked to him. Like Judith and the children. Somehow you can keep people here even though they're dead."

"It is a gift of mine if you want to call it that. It is really more properly called part of my curse."

Lola struggled to work through her confusion and her dread that Kyle was lost.

"So, is he still here?" she asked. "You didn't put him to sleep like you did the others? Please say you didn't."

"His situation is a bit complicated."

Lola jumped at hearing a shout from downstairs.

"Lola! Where are you?"

It was Maria.

"Wait here," she said to the old man. "I have to talk to Maria. She has to come up here and hear what's going on. We both do. I have never been more confused in my life. Just don't go anywhere."

Clearly fatigued, he lay back down and closed his eyes.

"I definitely shall not go anywhere," he murmured. "At least for a while. I am not nearly recovered."

Lola scrambled as fast as she could down the two sets of stairs and found Maria looking very lost in the hallway.

"Thanks be to God, Lola. I was absolutely fearing the worst. Where did everyone go?"

"I found Grandfather. I think everything is going to be okay. I think we will be home soon. Do you know where Caleb is?"

"No, he disappeared around the same time that the others did. Before I knew what was happening, they had all gone back into the house. When I tried to follow, I could see no sign of them."

"Maria, you were right. Caleb really is Kyle. They're one and the same."

"But how did he get to be younger? That is completely unnatural, isn't it?"

"I know. We have to find him. We have to make sure that he…"

"That he... what?"

"That he didn't disappear."

"What?"

"It's all so insane. Please, we just have to find him."

They searched the entire ground floor and then the upstairs. Lola decided to wait before telling Maria about the attic room, as she knew Kyle was not up there and finding him was her priority. They went outside and searched the grounds. The sky had clouded over completely, and intermittent drops of rain fell on them. Gusts of wind made them shiver.

They found the boy sitting on a bench facing the sea. His face had a faraway, lost look. Lola took his hand, and he quietly rose to his feet. She could swear he was a full inch taller than when she had last seen him. His eyes were at the same level as hers. She put her arms around him and hugged him tightly.

"I'm sorry, Kyle. I'm so, so sorry."

He was confused.

"What for?"

"For everything. Just everything."

"You know, you're very pretty."

"Don't start."

Turning to Maria, she said, "We have to keep him away from Grandfather."

"Why?"

"Because he will make him disappear—like the others."

"What do you mean? Where are the others?"

"They're gone, Maria. They just vanished in front of my eyes. Like ghosts. They were actually ghosts—just like you said. And now they're gone."

Maria shivered as the temperature dropped.

"Peter? The girls? They're gone?"

Lola nodded. Maria was surprised at the sudden, profound sense of loss she felt, but her thoughts then turned back to their friend.

"Why would he make Kyle disappear?"

"Because..."

She glanced at the boy and said nothing more.

"But we will need Grandfather's help in order to leave the island."

Lola bit her lip.

"Maria, I'm not sure Kyle is going to be able to leave the island."

"What? Why?"

"It's complicated."

"If it is so complicated, you may as well start explaining then."

"Okay, here is what we're going to do. You and I are going to talk to Grandfather, but I do not want Kyle going anywhere near him. Kyle, you have to stay out of the house until Maria and I come back. Do you understand?"

"But it is getting cold."

"We'll bring you some blankets from the house, and you can wait for us in the gazebo. Do not talk to anyone besides us. Got it?"

"Whatever you say, pretty lady."

"My name is Lola. Please use it."

After taking blankets out to Kyle, Lola and Maria returned to the house. Lola was prepared to climb back up to the attic room, but she did not have to. Looming tall and large at the top of the stairs stood an imposing figure. He looked healthy and middle-aged. His wild mane of hair was black with strands of white. His black eyes were fierce. Lola almost jumped out of her skin. Maria nearly swooned.

"It's him!" she gasped. "The man from my dream."

He was every bit as startled to see Maria as she was to see him. His jaw dropped.

"This is not possible!"

The two of them locked eyes and went silent. Looking at them, Lola felt invisible.

"Uh, so do you two actually know each other?"

The man's look of amazement turned into a scowl.

"Who are you?"

"I am Maria Murphy. Who are you?"

He slowly descended the stairs, keeping his gaze fixed on her.

"Are you some kind of malignant spirit playing a cruel trick on me? Why are you wearing that face?"

"It's my face, the only one I have."

"Can you possibly be who you appear to be?"

"Why should I appear to be anyone other than who I am? Are you saying I remind you of someone?"

"You do not merely remind me of someone. You are her. As impossible as it is, you are truly her—in the flesh."

"Unless you are talking about Maria Murphy from Ballincollig, then you must be mistaken."

"I have been waiting for you for a very long time. After all this time, I did not dream that, of all days, this would be the one. It has been many years since I have experienced the sensation of being surprised. I had nearly forgotten what it was like, but today I can finally and truly say I am taken by surprise."

"Um, I'm a little confused," Lola said. "How old are you exactly? You seem to be getting younger all the time."

"For the moment, I have lost track, but believe me when I say I have lived for a very long time."

"And what's your name? All we have heard anyone call you is Grandfather, and we can't call you that. After all, you're not *our* grandfather. Besides, you're looking less like a grandfather every minute."

"I have used many names in my time."

"Well, just pick one. We need something to call you."

"The last time I broke my solitude, it was to amuse myself by publishing some poetry I had written in my isolation here. That time I used the name Eliot."

"Eliot? Like T.S. Eliot? Wait, you're not telling us you're actually T.S. Eliot?"

He gave her a sideways glance, as she thought about what she had said.

"Wait, your name is Bridge! Eliot Bridge. I studied Eliot Bridge in my English course at U-Dub. A native Washington poet. Are you really him?"

He nodded.

"Not actually a native, but it was simpler to leave that impression."

"But wait. He was early twentieth century. To be him, you would have to be…"

Lola quickly did some rough calculating in her head.

"You would have to be something like a hundred years old or more."

"Yes, well, I did tell you I was very old."

"You definitely looked like you were a hundred when I first saw you, but now you look like my father's age. I mean, the age my father would be if he were alive."

Eliot stood directly in front of Maria. Looking as if she were in trance, she made no protest as he gently took her hand.

"Do you recognize me?" he said to her softly.

"I know you. You were in my dream. You were in many of my dreams."

"I do not know how this can be possible. I do not know if I should be joyful or frightened."

"Myself," said the Irish girl, "I am leaning toward frightened."

"Do you remember those days in Gaillimh?"

"Are you Irish? You do not sound Irish."

"Do you remember anything about our time at Baile an Choirrín?"

"I've only been to Galway a few times. My granny is from Galway."

He held her hand more tightly, stared into her eyes more intently.

"This is so strange, so very, very strange. So unexpected."

"Uh," said Lola. "I don't mean to interrupt, but would this be a good time to talk about us leaving the island? And just to be clear, all *three* of us have to leave together—including Kyle. He goes too. Understand?"

Steadfastly maintaining his intent stare into Maria's eyes, he replied evenly, "You may leave, of course, but now that I have found my beloved Justine again, she will no doubt prefer to remain here with me."

9
The White-haired Girl

"WHAT? NO! SHE'S not staying," said Lola with alarm. "We're all leaving together. All three of us."

"Surely, she can speak for herself," said Eliot, his focus on Maria unwavering.

"Tell him, Maria. Tell him that you are leaving with me and Kyle. You found this place, just like you wanted to, and now that you've satisfied your curiosity, it's time to leave. Tell him."

Looking dazed, Maria said, "I came for answers, and now all I have is more questions. Why does he seem familiar to me? Did I know him before? It makes no sense. None of it."

"It's some kind of trick, Maria. It has to be. How can you possibly know him? He's using some kind of crazy voodoo on you. You have to fight it. I'm not leaving without you."

Drawing nearer still to Maria, Eliot said, "I do actually understand your friend's skepticism, Justine. This really should not be possible. I have to be certain it is really you."

Uncomfortable with how close he now was to her friend, Lola impulsively gave him a shove.

"Don't let him kiss you, Maria! Whenever he kisses people, they disappear."

Eliot's eyes flashed with anger. His voice became a growl.

"Do not do that again! You do not want to anger me. I assure you that I mean her no harm, but you must understand. Everything about her suggests she is the one person I have ever truly loved."

"Except for the fact that she's never met you before."

"Has she not? I think she has, but her memory has been clouded. It has been a very long time. Indeed, most of my damnably long life."

"How old are you anyway?" asked Lola.

"You waste time with irrelevant questions."

"They're not irrelevant to me. I need to understand what is going on. Nothing about you or this place makes any sense. It's like everything I thought I knew and understood is suddenly not true anymore. How can these things be happening? How can you exist?"

"I understand your confusion. If it is any comfort, I myself have pondered those very questions, literally for centuries. I promise to answer all your questions as best I can, but first I think the two of you may prefer to don something other than those terrible dresses."

"Our own clothes are still wet. This place is too damp to dry anything."

"That is not a problem. Please feel free to retrieve your clothes."

Because Maria was still in something of a daze, Lola had to lead her into the sitting room. Logs burned in the fireplace. Lola was pleased to find her jeans, top, and shoes, all bone dry. Maria's clothes were not there. Instead, an elegant ballgown hung on a dressmaker's dummy.

"Does he expect you to wear that?" asked Lola suspiciously.

"I think he does," said Maria with a smile on her face. "It's absolutely gorgeous, so it is."

"I think it's absolutely creepy. How does he do all of this weird stuff? Things appear out of nowhere. Clothes dry by themselves. Does he have us hypnotized or something? What is he after anyway?"

"Perhaps he is exactly what he seems to be," said Maria, as she hurriedly slipped out of one dress and donned the other.

"Hey! Are you really putting on that dress? Have you stopped to think about why he wants you to wear it and what's going to happen next?"

"That's a fair point, Lola, but something about this dress feels like it was made for me. And there has to be a reason he appeared in my dreams. I'm seriously thinking it's possible I did know him in another life."

Despite her concerns, Lola was transfixed by the sight of Maria in the gown. The Irish girl was stunning. Lola only wished that it had not been the strange and mysterious man in the hallway who had provided it to her.

Lola hurriedly pulled off her own dress—tossing it irately across the room—before putting on her own clothes. She then sat on the floor with a glum look and crossed her arms. She had never been so confused in her life.

"Maria, have you actually thought—I mean, actually, really thought—about what all this means?"

"How do you mean?"

"Just think about the implications of everything we have seen and heard. It should be impossible, but it is happening. And if we accept that it is happening, then don't we have to accept that magic—or sorcery or witchcraft or whatever you want to call it—is real?"

"Magic *is* real," said Maria matter-of-factly.

"Really? You believe in magic?"

"Don't you?"

"I believe in science. I believe in what I can see with my own two eyes."

"And are you not seeing this house—and everything that happens in it— with your own two eyes?"

"But it shouldn't be happening. That makes me think there has to be some other explanation. This just isn't the way the world works. It doesn't conform to reality."

"Perhaps you simply have not yet lived long enough to see everything that is possible in reality."

"So, let me get this right. You really believe in magic? You believe in ghosts and sorcery and all of it?"

"All I can tell you, Lola, is that I don't disbelieve anything, and there are certain things I just know to be true—even if I cannot prove it. I believe everything happens for a reason. I know that I have angels that look out for me. I know my dear Granny—God rest her—gives me a helping hand from time to time. I know my cousin Fionn looks over me too. I call him my little angel, and there are times I can feel him near me."

"Okay, I get it. You're religious. But do you really believe that the dead can come back? That man out there says that Judith, Peter, Celia, and Audrey were all dead—even while we were talking to them and even sometimes touching them. Do you think that is possible?"

"I can see discussing whether a thing is possible if it has never happened," said Maria, "but does it make sense to discuss if it's possible *after* it has actually happened?"

"I think I'm going insane," said Lola, bewildered. "That's the only explanation."

"Sure, you're a brilliant girl, Lola, but you cannot solve everything with just your brain."

"That is precisely the sort of thing *she* would have said," said Eliot, startling them as he loomed in the doorway. "I am more convinced than ever that it is you, that you are my beloved Justine whom I knew in Connacht."

"Connacht?" said Maria. "I'm afraid I'm a Munster girl, born and bred. I have always had the feeling I had past lives, but not to be contrary or anything, you are nearly too eager to convince me of it now. After all, I cannot actually recall any of the things you mention. You need to tell me more if I am to figure out if I could actually be this Justine woman. At the moment, all I know for sure and certain is that I am—and always have been—Maria Murphy from Ballincollig."

Eliot sighed as he approached Maria.

"Very well. I shall tell you my story—my entire story—but first I need to put something right."

He ran his fingers through her hair. To Lola's amazement it was transformed, strand by individual strand, from white to a beautiful copper-shaded brown.

"Now you are my Justine down to the last detail. I have missed you so very, very much."

Lola stared. Maria had mesmerized her from the first moment she saw her, but now she was absolutely ravishing.

"Maria," she said, "your hair is so beautiful."

Maria returned her gaze, then gasped in shock.

"Jeepers!"

"What?" said Lola. "What's wrong?"

"Never mind *my* hair. Lola, whatever has happened to *your* hair?"

Lola turned toward the mirror in the corner. She moved closer for a better look and, at first, did not like what she saw.

"No fair," she said. "You made Maria's hair absolutely gorgeous, but you've turned *my* hair completely white! Why on earth did you do that?"

"It is not something I did deliberately," said Eliot. "In fact, I am not certain *I* did it all. I cannot explain why your hair changed."

Lola was on the verge of insisting he make her hair black again, but as she studied it in the mirror, she found her unexpected new look strangely intriguing. She decided to leave it for the time being.

"You said you would tell us your story," said Maria to Eliot.

"Yes, I did. Shall we sit?"

With barely a touch he was able to move the divan closer to the fire. It was no longer old and musty. The fabric was now fresh, clean, and comfortably padded. Eliot and Maria sat on the divan. Lola chose to sit on the floor.

"It is difficult to know where to begin."

"Start at the beginning," said Maria. "Where and when were you born?"

Eliot looked weary, as if summoning old memories was an unpleasant chore.

"I was born on a farm in Cambridgeshire on the 17th of April in the year of our Lord 1620. Well, to clarify, it was the 17th under the Julian calendar. One-hundred and thirty-two years later the Parliament of Great Britain would adopt the calendar of Pope Gregory, shifting the date ahead by eleven days."

"Okay, if you insist on going into this much detail, we'll be here all night," said Lola impatiently. "Try to speed things up. First, though, explain this. How does someone born in 1620 manage to still be alive today?"

"By having his soul damned for all eternity."

"And how did that happen?"

"As with everything to do with me, it is complicated. There may well be more detail to the story than you have the patience for."

"What I want to know," said Maria, "is how someone from Cambridgeshire wound up on this little island on the other side of the world."

"That part of the story is straightforward enough. After the catastrophe that cost me my soul and the only woman I ever loved, I wandered the world lost and alone and, I suppose, more than a little crazed. Cursed with immortality, I sampled every form of depravity and debauchery. With no limits on my wellbeing or my lifespan, I indulged in the worst excesses that the world had to offer. For well over a century, I was self-destructive but without the possibility of the release that would come with actual self-destruction.

"I came to long for a purpose in my life. As a youth, I had wanted to explore the world, but that desire for adventure was quenched by the horrors I had experienced later on as a soldier. Finally, however, I returned to the military life, this time for the exclusive purpose of fulfilling my childhood dream. I wanted to sail to the New World like the early European explorers who had fired my youthful imagination.

"In the year 1791 I joined the Royal Navy crew of the *HMS Discovery* under a 33-year-old commander from Norfolk named George Vancouver. We were about 150 men. The crew included experienced sailors, well-armed marines, and two troublesome 16-year-olds. One was a marquis's son, the other was the prime minister's nephew. And believe me when I tell you, the exploits of that pair are best left un-recounted.

"It was a fascinating year at sea. *Discovery* and its sister ship *Chatham* traveled south to Cape Town, then east to Australia, New Zealand, Tahiti, Hawaii, and eventually to this coast of North America.

"During the bright, warm month of May, we surveyed every corner of the sound. The landscapes were stunning. As we studied the islands and the shorelines at the southern end, we spied some of the native people watching us from the shore. I noticed in particular a woman and small child. Many years later I met the chief of the

Suquamish and the Duwamish, and he claimed to have been that child. He said that, despite being only about seven years old at the time, he could remember distinctly seeing our ships.

"At Admiralty Inlet, Captain Vancouver took formal possession of all the coast and hinterland of the Strait of Juan de Fuca and, in honor of George III whose birthday it was that day, he called it New Georgia. Leaving the *Discovery* and the *Chatham* anchored, we continued our exploration to the north in a smaller two-masted sailing craft that the captain called his yawl.

"We landed at a site which our Second Lieutenant, a Huguenot by the name of Peter Puget, named Noon Breakfast Bluff after the meal we had there. We sailed eastward up an inlet and were met by about fifty local natives in their canoes. They greeted us with great courtesy and civility and offered us a meal of cooked salmon. I was completely taken with these people and wanted to know them better. Not for the first time in my life, I simply chose to abandon my military obligation and go my own way.

"The Suquamish were extremely kind to me. They allowed me to live among them for several months and more or less treated me as one of their own. As different as their culture was from mine, I felt very much at home. At long last I had found peace. While the climate could be wet, wild, and at times violent, the beauty of this corner of the world was unsurpassed. I found myself comparing it to the Garden of Eden. Though their lives could not be called easy, the people lived in harmony with nature and, at that time anyway, were relatively unbothered by interlopers. British and Spanish explorers traveled up and down the coast but were generally respectful of each other and of the natives.

"Over time, however, things changed. It became apparent the ship that brought me was but the vanguard of an invasion of sorts. After the explorers came the fur traders and the missionaries. Waves of people, traveling overland across the width of the North American continent, arrived and established settlements of ever-increasing size. A government thousands of miles away decreed tribal lands would be opened to the immigrants. Sawmills were built to harvest the vast stands of virgin timber, and the Suquamish became loggers to support themselves. In exchange for promises of supplies and services, they signed treaties that extinguished their titles to most of their lands.

"In the British Isles, I had lived through the experience of watching a large, dominant society overwhelm a smaller one. I had no desire to witness anything like it again, so I made the decision to retreat from the world. That is when I made my home here.

"I settled on this island and built this house. I honestly know little of the history of this place—if there is indeed any to know—but I was drawn here by its strange energy. This place has its own strange connection to the beyond. The name is a bit of a mystery to me, though I have reason to believe it was named by the Spanish naval commander Juan Francisco de la Bodega y Quadra. From the day I settled here, I have ventured back out into the world only from time to time, I stopped participating in the regular affairs of society. And these most recent years, I confess, I have become particularly reclusive.

"Thanks to certain abilities I have acquired over the years, I have been able to deter visitors and unwanted attention. At least until you lot washed up." Looking at Maria, he added, "There is no way you could have arrived here by chance alone. You were clearly meant to find me."

"Certain abilities?" asked Lola. "Do you mean magic? How did you learn that?"

"There have always been people out there who have learned to bend nature to their will. Over time these special skills get passed from one master to another. When you have unlimited time, it becomes all the more possible to seek such people out and convince them to teach you. At the same time, though, longevity and knowledge exert a strange burden. Occasionally, threats emerge from the supernatural realm and I find myself in the position of being one of the few able to thwart them. If I chose not to, the consequences would be fearful to contemplate. So that has become my new purpose."

"What about all the dead people?" asked Lola. "What were they doing here?"

Eliot turned reflective.

"As I have told you, I became lonely in spite of myself. Long periods of seclusion darkened my temperament. With the passage of time, I became increasingly aware of—and sensitive to—the wails of the dying. When a life was lost in the water, I heard the cries. Sometimes it was a sinking craft, such as yours. Sometimes it was an unfortunate who fell off a boat. Or someone on a beach swept away by a freak wave. In the beginning, I ignored them. I never felt my unnatural existence gave me the right to interfere with nature's normal course. The most difficult to ignore, though, were the children.

"I mean, it was not as though I could save the poor souls. By the time their cries reached my ears, it was already too late. Indeed, few of these tragedies were recent or nearby when I heard them. They were but distant echoes from the past coming from souls who had not yet been able to find rest. I did my best to ignore them, but when I heard the cries of poor little Audrey, I saved her. Not her body. Her mortal life was long over, but I snatched her soul from the cusp of the afterlife and gave it a physical manifestation.

"It was really more cruel than merciful, but somehow it slightly eased my torment. Then came Celia, then Peter. Make no mistake, they were never grateful. Their fear and confusion broke my heart. The solution I arrived at was to retrieve the soul of a woman who, in a freak accident, was struck by a log while having the bad judgment to walk on a beach in a storm. I needed her to look after the children in a way that I could not.

"What I did not realize until it was nearly too late was that each soul I rescued and kept alive sapped my life's essence. Though unable to die, I can be weakened to the point of virtual paralysis if I attempt to share my life force with too many others. That is the state in which you found me."

Lola gave voice to the fear that nagged her.

"And you swear that Maria and I aren't dead the way the others were?"

Eliot smiled indulgently.

"You need not worry. You two were close enough to me that I could hear you while there was still time to influence the elements and bring you to shore. Rest assured, the two of you are quite alive."

"And Kyle?" asked Maria.

This was the moment Lola had dreaded.

"Maria, I'm sorry," she blurted out. "I didn't know how to tell you. Kyle is dead."

Maria gasped, "What? No, he can't be. He can't."

"I must apologize," said Eliot to Lola with an air of reassurance. "I did not have time to explain fully before. Yes, he did succumb to the water before I was able to bring him to shore. So, yes, he was deceased. Fortunately, the amount of time that had passed was brief enough that I could reverse what happened. He is one of those rare souls who have come back from the dead."

As relieved as Lola was to hear this, she was less than pleased to see Maria impulsively throw her arms around Eliot.

"Thank you. Thank you. I don't know what I would have done if he were dead."

"You should understand" said Eliot soberly, "that he was not brought back entirely without cost."

"What does that mean?" asked Lola.

"You have already discerned he is younger than before. To repair his body I had to reverse his natural physiological progression. It is a complex matter, but simply put, in order to bring him back I had to shave some years off his life. It was that effort which left me completely diminished and helpless in my bed."

"Wait a minute," said Lola. "If you made him younger, wouldn't that make his life *longer*?"

"Yes, I see your point, but no. It is the end of his life that has been cut short, not the beginning. As he recovers, he will soon return to his proper age, but his body will not last as long as it would have."

Maria was crushed.

"How... how many years will he lose?"

"That is hard to say. If he is lucky, perhaps no more than five, maybe ten."

Tears formed in Maria's eyes.

"It is not fair. He has lost those years because of me. I was so stupid. If only I had it to do over again."

"Kyle!" cried Lola. "I completely forgot about him. I told him to wait in the gazebo. He must be frozen by now."

Rushing past Eliot toward the door, Lola eyed him suspiciously and said, "Do you absolutely promise you won't kiss him on the forehead and make him disappear?"

Nearly amused, Eliot replied, "Do not worry. Everything I have told you is true. Your friend is very much alive."

Lola ran out of the house and into the darkness. She raced down the path to the gazebo, her head teeming with all she had heard.

She found Kyle sitting obediently on the bench, staring at the sea. She wondered what he could possibly have been thinking about all this time. When he saw her, he smiled broadly and stood up. To her amazement, he was back to his full six-foot-plus height. His shoulders were again broad, and he had the torso and thighs of a full-grown, athletic man.

"Lola," he said. "Thank God you're here. I've never felt so lost. I'm having trouble remembering things. It all goes hazy after we set sail from Shilshole. Where exactly are we? Was I in some kind of accident? And why is your hair white?"

He was surprised and delighted when she gave him an enthusiastic hug. Lola herself was surprised, but he had definitely earned it.

"The important thing to know is that we're here. We're on Riesgado Island. You got us here. In spite of the storm. In spite of the boat sinking. In spite of everything."

He was devastated.

"The boat sank? Dad's going to kill me. How did we get here?"

"Maybe your memory will come back in time. I don't know. But you should know that you saved Maria's life. If not for you, she would be dead, and she feels terrible because you nearly died because of it. Something else you should know is that she cares about you a lot and you should take that very seriously."

As they walked back to the house, Lola continued, "I'm telling you this because, when we get to the house, you're going to meet a very strange man. He is doing something weird to Maria, affecting her mind. You need to protect her from him. You are the only one who can do it because you are the one she cares about most. You need to remember that."

Kyle stopped and looked into her eyes.

"Lola, you're..."

"Stop. Don't talk. Just listen to what I'm telling you. Maria needs the two of us to protect her. She is the one you need to be thinking about."

"Okay, but I just want to say..."

"What?"

"That white hair makes you look really hot."

When they arrived back in the sitting room, the fire was roaring and hotter than ever. Lola was not at all pleased to see Eliot and Maria sitting together on the couch.

On seeing Kyle, Maria jumped up and threw her arms around him.

"Kyle, you look like you're finally back to yourself. Thanks be to God. I've missed you so much."

Lola watched Eliot's expression as he eyed the two of them.

The two women spent the next several minutes filling Kyle in on everything he had missed, one talking more hurriedly than the other. They even recounted Eliot's tale of the voyage to Puget Sound on *HMS Discovery*.

"Wait," said Kyle, turning to Eliot. "You came here with Captain Vancouver?"

"Yes."

"The guy that Vancouver is named for?"

"Yes."

"And you knew that guy Puget? The one Puget Sound is named for?"

"Yes."

"So are you...?"

"Am I what?"

"Are you the one Elliott Bay is named for?"

Eliot was amused.

"I am afraid not. That was named after a midshipman from a later expedition."

"Okay, Eliot Bridge," said Lola impatiently. "I think it's time you told us your story. I mean, the whole story—from the beginning."

10
Septimus

"AS I HAVE TOLD you, I was born in Cambridgeshire in the year 1620. My parents had seven children, all sons, of which I was the youngest. The first four were named Jacob, Melchior, Balthasar, and Alexander. Having apparently exhausted their imagination, the remaining ones were called, in something of a numeric fashion, Quentin, Sextus, and Septimus."

"So your name isn't really Eliot?" laughed Lola. "It's actually *Septimus*?"

"That is the case."

"Well, I can certainly see why you chose to write your poetry under the name Eliot."

"Shush, Lola," said Maria, "Let him get on with his story."

"We were farmers. It was a monotonous life and one for which I was not well suited. Moreover, I was a lonely child. By the time I was born, my parents were elderly, and my surviving brothers were much older than I was, Quentin and Sextus having died in their infancy. I was bored with our little corner of England and longed constantly to see more of the world. I craved adventure. My nature was totally at odds with the community in which I lived. You see, we were Anabaptists."

"What are anti-Baptists?" asked Kyle.

"Anabaptists," said Septimus. "It was a name originally coined by our detractors—a mocking reference to our custom of baptizing followers at the age of reason rather than at birth. We were among various religious movements born out of the schisms of the Christian church in sixteenth-century Europe. Our people's origins went back to the Old Swiss Confederacy. Because Anabaptists were persecuted in the Thirteen Cantons, many migrated to other lands. Our people settled in England but eventually met with persecution there as well."

"Why were they persecuted?" asked Lola.

"Because, like other sects—such as the Calvinists, the Anglicans, and the Lutherans—they challenged the Catholic orthodoxy. Schisms had occurred over questions like the correct age to baptize a child. More problematic for His Majesty's government was our literal interpretation of Jesus's Sermon on the Mount. We held that the swearing of oaths was forbidden, causing an insurmountable obstacle to certain government demands like paying taxes and serving in the military.

"Over time the Anabaptists were so vilified that the term was loosely applied to any religious group out of official favor. We were slandered and accused of every manner of crime and perversion. There was also a residual fear from a violent rebellion that occurred many years before I was born. In the German city of Münster, a radical Anabaptist sect attempted to establish a ruling theocracy by force, and it did not end well.

"By contrast, all my people ever wanted was simply to be left alone, but the English were incapable of that. A relation of my mother's by the name Edward Wightman had the distinction of being the last person burned publicly for heresy in England. It happened on the authority of King James, the Scottish monarch who united England and Scotland.

"Not only did I have no interest in being a religious martyr, I had precious little interest in religion at all. I thought only of escape. As I matured, I secretly made friends outside of our community and became exposed to other ideas. I was particularly fascinated by the Puritans. They engaged directly and publicly in the great debates of the day. I admired their courage and their willingness to know the wider world. I was enthralled by stories of a separatist Puritan group called the Pilgrims, who sailed across the Atlantic Ocean to the New World. I desperately wanted to follow them, but that would not happen for a century and a half.

"To my parents, I was a complete disappointment. Not only was I of little use on the farm, but I resisted all their efforts to match me with a wife. Moreover, it was obvious I no longer took their faith seriously. I was all but at the point of ostracization when I found my avenue of escape.

"Major political and military developments were unfolding all around us. It had begun when I was five years old, the year King James died and his son Charles succeeded him. Four years later Charles shut down the Parliament and refused to summon it for eleven years. Finally, he was forced to recall it after exhausting the government's funds in the face of a rebellion in Scotland. Tension between the King and the Parliament intensified steadily.

"Of the various figures jockeying for influence, I was most impressed by Cambridge's own Member of Parliament. He was a farmer from Huntingdon, who had undergone a major religious conversion. He now called himself an Independent Puritan, and his name was Oliver Cromwell."

Maria's face darkened.

"Well, sure and that is a name I know all too well," she said with a graveness Lola had not seen in her before.

"It surprises me not at all," said Septimus, "that he would be remembered in Ireland to this very day."

"'Remembered' doesn't quite cover it," said Maria evenly.

"I hope that you will forgive me for my part in what happened subsequently," he said, "just as you did all those years ago, my dear Justine."

"Could you please call her by her correct name?" said Lola.

"I don't mind, really," said Maria, running her hand over the folds in her gown. "I actually rather like the name Justine."

"Nice dress by the way, Maria," said Kyle, who had begun to doze off but was now awake again.

Lola jabbed him in the arm with her elbow and glared.

"Get on with the story, *Septimus,*" she said.

He continued, "After two years of political rancor, things turned violent. The King and the Parliament formed separate armies, and vigorous debate descended into outright bloodshed. My imagination was set afire by the Parliament's purpose. They actually dared challenge the divine right of kings. They were willing to fight in the

92

people's name against a dictator whose authority was derived entirely by the circumstance of his birth. In the heat of the moment, I renounced my religion altogether and became a Puritan. For the first time in my life, I took up arms. I joined the cavalry headed by Cromwell.

"I saw my first action in an operation that blocked a shipment of silver plate from Cambridge meant for the King. During the four years of the Civil War, I would be tested many times in battle. I fought in East Anglia and later took part in the Battle of Gainsborough.

"Being a soldier had an immeasurable effect on me. For the first time in my life I was surrounded by young men from all over England and from all walks of life. There was a heady camaraderie—a feeling of joint purpose and shared vision—I had never experienced before. For the first time in my life, I felt part of something that truly mattered. I made friendships more intense than I had ever known. A shared look, a pat on the back, a knowing glance—it all felt so very heroic. I knew I had found my real family.

"My closest friendship was with a fellow soldier named Valentine Walton, who happened to be Cromwell's nephew and also the son and namesake of Colonel Walton. In the heat of battle we formed a bond that made him more of a brother to me than any of the four with whom I was raised. During the rare quiet moments between training and fighting, we talked of anything and everything. There was nothing I was not willing to share with him—nor him with me. This attachment to another person was new to me and, strangely, gave my soul peace in the midst of war and violence.

"Everything changed, however, at the Battle of Marston Moor.

"Three years into the war, I was twenty-four years old and regarded as a battled-hardened veteran. That summer we laid siege to the city of York, and we should have taken it with little trouble. Lieutenant-general Cromwell, however, was outfoxed by his rival cavalry commander, the King's nephew, Prince Rupert, who swept up from the south, fresh from a victory at Newark. By sheer audacity, the wily prince convinced Cromwell and the other leaders that he had us outnumbered, so we withdrew. Not content with that success, Rupert pursued us. By late afternoon we found ourselves facing his forces across the moor of Long Marston.

"Despite it being the beginning of July, the weather that afternoon was cold and damp. We waited. Thick clouds turned the sky dark. We were shaken by loud claps of thunder and then drenching rain and hail. That was the moment when our left wing charged. Then our entire line moved in. Two hours later the sun had set and the battle was all but over. The carnage on the battlefield was illuminated by an exceedingly bright harvest moon. It was the biggest battle ever fought on British soil. Burial pits were dug for 4,000 of the enemy. The story among the troops was that Prince Rupert had eluded capture only by hiding in a beanfield. The Parliament's supremacy in the north was assured.

"Sadly, our side was not without its casualties, though at about 300 they were many fewer than the enemies'. Devastatingly for me, one of them was Valentine, who was struck by a cannonball early in the battle. His death was painful and drawn-out. Though he had the rank of captain, he was only twenty-one years old. His uncle, the lieutenant-general, was with him when he drew his last breath, which was fitting and appropriate. I confess, though, I was consumed with jealousy and despair not to be the one at his side to hear his last words. From that point on, war was no longer an adventure but rather a dark and grim way of life.

"Subsequently, we became part of what would be known as the New Model Army. Cromwell rose to second-in-command, and we defeated the King's army in the Battle of Naseby. I now look back in horror, recalling my part in the slaughter of a full third of the Royal Garrison at Basing House, the Catholic fortress that fell to us.

"The war was over but for some mopping up in Devon and Cornwall. It ended officially with the King's surrender.

"The political deadlock, however, continued. Two years later there was a Second Civil War. By that time, Cromwell was calling our army 'God's chosen instrument.' In Wales we put down a Royalist uprising, and in the north we fought the pro-Royalist Scottish army.

"It was now clear there would be no accommodation so long as the King remained on the throne. In 1649, amid much controversy, it was decided to do something that had never been done before. The King of Great Britain was charged with treason, put on trial, found guilty, and sentenced. With one clean stroke from the executioner, his head was severed, and a republic—the Commonwealth of England—was declared.

"We had made history by following what we knew without doubt to be God's own will."

Lola noticed that Kyle was now completely asleep. She was about to jostle him when Septimus gestured that she should leave him be.

"Let him rest," he said softly. "After what he has been through, his body will need quite some time to recover completely."

Septimus placed his hand gently on the younger man's head. It occurred to Lola that Septimus would have been little older than Kyle was now when he experienced the horrors of war.

"I have muffled his hearing." said Septimus, "so that I may continue my story without disturbing him."

Curious to see if it was true, Lola clapped her hands loudly. Kyle did not stir. Despite all the strange things she had witnessed, Lola found each new instance as difficult to believe as the previous one.

Maria paid no attention to Lola and Kyle. She was mesmerized by Septimus's account.

"How strange," she said, "that England, at least for a brief time, was actually a republic."

"The ironies multiply," said Septimus. "Not only was there an English republic but the greatest threat to it came from Royalists based in Ireland, specifically the alliance between the Irish Confederate Catholics and the English Royalists."

She replied, "I'll surely need some time to get my head around that one."

The parallels with modern British and Irish history were lost on Lola. Instead, it was the root causes of the fighting that quickened her reaction.

"Did it not occur to you at any point," she asked pointedly, "that all this religious fervor of yours was the reason for so much bloodshed? Did you not see a disconnect between your religion—which I'm sure claimed to be all about peace and heaven and the Golden Rule—and all the killing that went on?"

"At the time? No. There was only right and wrong, and our side was right. But later on? Yes, I have pondered this at length for many years. In the end, it is pointless to blame religion for war. Religion and politics merely provide a pretext for what would happen anyway."

"How can you say that? Every time there's a major war, religion is involved."

"So are people. And weapons. And speeches. Do all those things cause war as well? Correlation does not prove causation. Besides, what is religion anyway and how would you propose to neutralize it so that it causes no more wars? Religion is merely a way of seeing and understanding the world. How do you eliminate *that* from the world? Tell me, what beliefs do you yourself profess?"

"I just try to live my life as a good person. I refuse to hurt anybody. I always try to help other people. And I'm an atheist. I don't need any God to tell me what is right and wrong."

"And how do you know what is right and what is wrong?"

"I just know. I mean, everybody knows the difference between right and wrong. You don't have to have a church for that."

"I accept that we all have a sense of right and wrong, but is everyone's the same? Are there not people who disagree with you about right and wrong?"

"Some things are just obvious. Like murder. Everybody knows that's wrong."

"Do they? Then why are there wars in which people are killed if 'everyone' knows it is wrong?"

"Because bad leaders get people to do things that are wrong, like starting wars."

"If that many people can be convinced to do something that 'everyone' knows is wrong, is there really a consensus on right and wrong? Are you not then just one more person trying to impose *your* view of things on other people?"

"That's why we need education. People need to be taught what is right and wrong."

"And how is that different from religion?"

"Because you don't need to have all the God stuff. That just confuses things and brings up old, outdated ideas of right and wrong."

"So you are not really against religion. You just want a different religion—one without God."

"I guess, if you want to call it that. 'Education' and 'religion' are just labels. What matters is that people are taught the right things."

"Yes, exactly how I saw it when I converted from being an Anabaptist to a Puritan. I wanted people to be taught 'the right things.'"

"You're twisting my words."

"Am I? When you have lived as long as I have, you realize the arguments are always the same. Only the details and the labels are different. And when the argument gets heated enough, people die."

"Lola," said Maria impatiently, "would you ever please let him go on with his story?"

"Yes, sorry," said Septimus. "I became distracted.

"As I was saying, the Royalist forces re-grouped in Ireland. In the summer after the King's execution, Cromwell and his army were dispatched there to extinguish the resistance. A previous attempt to re-assert England's control over Ireland had been made two years earlier. Now Cromwell was bringing a much larger army.

"For him this campaign was as much about faith as politics. He was virulently opposed to the Catholic Church and what he saw as its persecution of Protestants throughout Europe. His views had become cemented by the Irish Rebellion eight years earlier. The massacre of Protestant Scots and English, in his view, demanded vengeance. For him the hated enemy was the Catholic alliance of native Irish, Scottish Highland settlers, and the *Seanghaill,* the so-called 'Old English' descendants of Norman settlers. They would be shown no mercy.

"We departed from Bristol at the end of July, landing at Ringsend in Dublin in the middle of August. Cromwell's methods were relentless, and this is where any romantic notions of war I may still have held turned to pure horror. The numbers speak for themselves. Thousands were killed in sieges of Drogheda and Wexford. Not all of the dead were combatants, nor did the killing stop when the towns were captured.

"If there was a silver lining to the early carnage, it was that other towns became more prone to surrender than to fight to the bitter end. Thus Kilkenny, New Ross, and Carlow submitted to us, as we expanded our control. In Cork our enemies ended by actually coming over to our side.

"The conquest did not slacken after Cromwell was called back to Britain, where the Royalists had crowned the late King's young son. When he left, I truly wished to go back with him. There was nothing to look forward to in Ireland save more sieges and more attacks on us by insurgents in the countryside. The bloodshed was horrific. Before it was over, two-fifths of Ireland's population would be annihilated."

Lola looked at Maria. Her face had gone deathly pale, and there was a dead look in her eyes.

"I grew up my whole life with the story of Cromwell. We all did. How he pushed the true Irish west of the Shannon to make way for a new Protestant ruling class. 'To hell or to Connacht' was the choice he gave them."

"Indeed," said Septimus softly, "and as you will learn from the rest of my story, I myself have personally seen both hell *and* Connacht.

"The fairest way to describe my state of mind at that point was, well, I had gone quite insane. The levels of violence, the inhumanity, and the complete breakdown of civilized behavior left me in a persistent state of shock. Finally, I could bear no more. In the aftermath of a particularly vicious battle, I found myself looking upon the bloody corpses of Irish country lads much younger than myself. Little more than children and not even part of any regular army, they had taken up arms in a hopeless fight against a superior enemy. They had not done it because of any romantic quest for adventure but simply to hold on to their land and their way of life. I could no longer bear my role in the conquest.

"While I froze in horror, my fellow soldiers moved on, little noticing that I was no longer keeping up with them. In a daze, I cast down my weapon, numbly stripped off my uniform, and stole the clothes from one of the corpses. Then I walked aimlessly through the fields, losing track of where I was. All I knew was that we were in Connacht and that we had been working our way toward Galway, the last Catholic-held town not yet taken. Directionless, I wandered for days across farms and through forests with no regard for my safety.

"Eventually, hunger and exhaustion took their toll. I was at the point of physical collapse, when I came upon a large country house near the shore of a massive lake. I prowled through the buildings looking for anything I might be able to eat. All I could manage were a few raw eggs in the chicken coop. As the end of the day drew near, I sought shelter under a pile of hay stored in a shed for the horses stabled nearby. My intention was to nap a few hours and then leave before sunrise.

"What happened instead was that I woke well after the sun had risen, surprised by a young man beginning his morning chores. Despite my best efforts to stay quietly concealed, he sensed something was amiss. I had to reveal myself to avoid being punctured by a pitchfork. He yelled something, but I could not understand him. He spoke in the native language, presumably thinking I was an indigent from the countryside. I said nothing, knowing that to speak would immediately give me away as an Englishman and an enemy.

"He was tall and lanky with ragged black hair and an over-large jaw. As I got a better look at him, I saw that, despite his size, he was callow and unsure of himself. His hairless face was dotted with freckles and pale from the long winter. When I gave no response, he came at me with the pitchfork. Knocking his implement to one side, I easily overpowered him. After all, by this point I had been a trained soldier for ten years and was his senior by a good fifteen years. I wrestled him to the ground and, while he struggled frantically beneath me, I pondered what to do. His wild, intense, blue eyes bore into me, as he writhed desperately against me. His heart pounded so hard I could feel it as if it were in my own chest. It would have been easy to kill him then and there with my bare hands. He certainly would not be the first lad I had killed, but now I was sick of death. I hesitated.

"A figure suddenly appeared in the entrance of the hayshed. Her form was silhouetted by the morning sun.

"'Fearghal?'

"She stepped inside for a better look.

"'Jesus, Mary, and Joseph!' she exclaimed. 'Whatever are you doing there with my stable boy?'

"I sat back and let the lad go. He jumped up, grabbed the pitchfork, and pointed it menacingly in my direction. I paid him no attention. I could look only at her. Unafraid, she drew closer to have a look."

Septimus took Maria's hand and looked into her eyes.

"She had the most beguiling green eyes."

He touched Maria's hair.

"Her hair was a resplendent mix of gold and brown."

"It looks more like copper and brown to me," said Lola.

He caressed Maria's cheek.

"She had *this* exquisite face."

"Okay," said Lola, losing her patience, "you really have to stop that. It's inappropriate, and it's creepy."

"I actually don't mind, Lola," said Maria. "Honestly, it's all right."

"Well, it's making *me* uncomfortable. Yeah, yeah, we know. You think Maria looks like her. We get it. Now what happened next?"

"In that moment when I saw her first," said Septimus quietly, "I knew only two things for certain. One was that, during the previous two years, I had truly seen hell. The other was that, now, I had finally seen heaven."

11
Justine

"'DO YOU THINK he could be a spy, ma'am?' asked the lad.

"'We shall know soon enough, Fearghal,' she replied sensibly. 'We shall know once he speaks.'

"I held my mouth shut and stared at her in helpless paralysis, but not because she or the adolescent with his rusty pitchfork posed any real threat to me. I was in thrall to her. She drew nearer still.

"'I would not be getting too close if I was you, ma'am,' said the boy nervously. 'He is fierce violent that one, so he is.'

"She studied me with intense interest. She showed no fear whatsoever.

"'Is that right? Are you violent?'

"I held my tongue.

"'Are you unwilling to speak,' she asked, 'or unable?'

"I said nothing.

"'Fearghal, attend to the horses. I shall be all right here for a while.'

"'I do not think that is a good idea, ma'am.'

"'I assure you it will be grand. I shall call if I need assistance.'

"Reluctantly, the lad slunk out of the shed. She waited until she heard the sound of the stable door across the yard before speaking to me.

"'Now that there are but the two of us, please tell me your story. Why do you trespass on my property?'

"I held my tongue still.

"I guessed she was about my own age or, perhaps, a few years older."

Lola interrupted, "So she was something like ten years older than Maria."

"Yes," said Septimus, "that would be about right."

"So she and Maria can't be the same person."

"I assure you there is no difference between this woman here and the one I met that day so long ago. Hers is a beauty independent of age. In any event, the question is irrelevant. Justine has clearly been reborn and been given the chance to live her entire life over. But please, allow me to continue the history.

"I judged from her appearance that she belonged to the provincial aristocracy. That meant she was very likely one of the so-called 'Old English' families that had for years dominated life in the walled port town of Galway, or Gaillimh, as the Irish speakers called it. Called the Twelve Tribes, these families were of venerable Anglo-Norman stock and known to have settled so comfortably in Ireland that they were said to have become more Irish than the Irish themselves. If I was correct, that meant she was most certainly a Catholic and a supporter of the Confederacy that had held sway over much of the island since the 1641 Rebellion. As such, I further calculated, she was likely a Royalist, although of that I could not be completely certain. I had heard of divisions within the Confederacy over whether or not to support the British Crown."

"Jeepers," said Maria. "That does not sound at all like the Ireland I know. Irish Catholics supporting the monarchy? English republicans? How did it all get so turned around?"

"Indeed," said Septimus, "If one lives long enough, one will see everything. In any event, I realized that the woman before me represented everything I was against, all things that I hated. Yet I was bewitched by her. I had not experienced anything like it before. I fought to keep my mind focused on my self-preservation. I had every reason to expect, once she understood who and what I was, that I should be turned over immediately to the nearest garrison. She continued to study me.

"'So what am I to do with you?' she asked. 'You are filthy and quite rough-looking, yet there is something civilized in your eyes. Pray speak to me. Are you *Gaeilgeoir*? Spanish? French? Or are you, as Fearghal suspects, an Englishman?'

"I could see no further use in delaying the inevitable.

"'I mean you no harm,' I said.

"'So English then.'

"'Ma'am, I have been a soldier, but I am sick of fighting and of war and of death. I have no intention of returning to the military campaign or of participating in the siege on the town. You have nothing to fear from me. If you allow it, I shall be on my way and trouble you not again. I have no quarrel with you nor do I have any desire to harm one so beautiful.'

"She laughed.

"'So you think *plámás* will deliver you from this situation?'

"'I do not understand the word you use, but I do know that, were I in your place, I would be frightened. Yet you stand there unarmed, showing no fear whatsoever.'

"'After all I have been through, there is quite frankly no fear left in me. I am only interested in what I can get done on my place. Which brings me to this. I need not hear any more of your story. Simply listen. I have a proposition for you. Tell me, do you have any experience at all with farming?'

"'My dear lady,' I laughed. 'I was born and raised on a farm. It was all I knew until I attained twenty-two years.'

"'Splendid, so. I am in dire need of another man on this farm, and you appear to be quite able-bodied. This is my offer. I shall give you shelter and food in exchange for your honest labor. What say you?'

"'Your offer takes me by surprise. Please explain how this arrangement could work? How would you explain my presence, who I am, how I came to be here?'

"'Yes, it will take some imagination. We could say that you are a cousin of Fearghal's up from the country. I shall ensure that Fearghal goes along with the story, and as we never see any of his people down this way, there will be no one to contradict us.'

"'But I do not have the language. Any attempt to speak would give me away.'

"'Yes, it would. Indeed the first word out of your mouth would surely give you away. That is why you will have to keep silent at all times. I will tell people you are a mute.'

"'Why would you do this for me?'

"'I do it not for you. I do it for myself. Do you know how difficult it is to get help in the middle of this war? Now pray tell me your name.'

"'Septimus Bridge at your service, my good lady.'

"'Septimus? Really? Well, that will not do at all. From now on, my dear Septimus, your name will be Feidhlim. Do you understand? You must be ready to respond to it without fail at any moment. When I call for Feidhlim, you must come without hesitation.'

"'I understand, ma'am. And what shall I call you?'

"She laughed.

"'Nothing at all, of course. You are a mute.'

"'I mean for the times when we are alone. As now. What is your name?'

"'I am Justine de Bruin. That would be Browne in the English tongue. I was raised in Menlough, the castle of my stepfather's family. Then I was married to Lynch. This property was his, but he is dead now. The responsibility for it has fallen entirely on my shoulders. Since the two of us will converse only in private, you may call me Justine, and I shall call you... Is your name really Septimus?'

"'I am afraid it is.'

"'And what do your friends call you?'

"'When I was a small lad, my brothers called me Tim.'

"'So, when we are alone, I too shall call you Tim if that is all right.'

"'It is indeed, and I look forward to our conversations alone, Justine.'

"Her eyes flashed at my impudent comment, but there was no sign of a blush on her cheeks.

"'Welcome to Baile an Choirrín, Tim. *Fáilte.*'

"We proceeded with our plan. Despite my fears, no one was overly curious or suspicious about a new man turning up on the Lynch farm. As it turned out, the house did not get that many visitors. Every so often, someone from a neighboring house would call, but that winter there was much illness about, so people tended to keep to themselves.

"It was a wicked cold winter. I had thought the English climate harsh, but it was nothing compared to the West of Ireland. Storms blew in regularly off the Atlantic Ocean, lashing rain in a horizontal direction and uprooting trees everywhere. The days were nearly as dark as the nights. The one visitor we did get on a somewhat consistent schedule was Father Martyn, the parish priest. He was a kindly old man, who took a great interest in me, mainly because of my supposed handicap. I found that silence suited me quite well. The Irish manner of speaking was invariably confusing to me.

"No one questioned the story of me being young Fearghal's relation. It did not seem to matter that, in my own opinion at least, we looked nothing alike. As for Fearghal, he was clearly not happy with the pretense, but he did not go against Justine's request. Mostly, he ignored me, but there was rarely a moment when he was not keeping a wary eye on me over his shoulder. When the work left him no choice but to address me, in a bitter and sarcastic tone he would call me *Uncail Feidhlim.*

"At the time I wished he and I would have gotten on better. I was actually quite fond of the lad. We were not unlike, both being products of a country upbringing. Also, knowing I had come very close to killing him caused an unexpected feeling of responsibility— something of a bond with him. Moreover, we were of one mind in our affection for Justine. He was devoted to her. I might even say he was, no more than myself, smitten. In my mind, this made us allies. For his part, though, he was clearly jealous—something which was only aggravated by the fact that Justine treated me more as her equal than an ordinary farmhand.

"Fearghal and I took our daily midday dinner together in the house's kitchen. In the evenings we would be back for the tea. One evening, however, I was invited to have tea with Justine in the dining room. Over time, this occasional occurrence became a regular one. She was lonely and enjoyed conversing with me. Although we were from different worlds—in terms of both country and religion—she recognized me as someone with whom she could comfortably exchange ideas. She was curious to know about both the Anabaptists and the Puritans and would debate me vigorously about religion and theology. She was keen to discuss the concept of divine right of kings and contrast it with the idea of republicanism. In my somewhat restricted life up until then, I had had no idea a woman—and a Catholic woman at that—could be so knowledgeable and intellectually curious."

At this point, Lola nearly interrupted Septimus's tale but managed to hold her tongue.

"We had great discussions over the concept of free will, the alleged infallibility of the Pope, and whether the 1611 translation of the Bible commissioned by King James was superior to the 1557 Geneva translation. She also kept me informed of the war's progress. In Cromwell's absence, his son-in-law Henry Ireton had laid siege to Limerick, while his general Charles Coote had surrounded Galway. I knew Coote. He was extremely brutal and virulently anti-Catholic. I would not have liked to be anywhere between him and his military objective.

"As time went on, Justine informed me that the castles of Oranmore and Claregalway had fallen to Coote's forces. Within the walls of Galway, the 10,000 inhabitants were trapped and running low on provisions. The town was over-crowded. During the previous year, it had become the destination and refuge of people fleeing towns throughout Ireland, as each one fell to the English. Galway had become every Irishman's last hope, and now it was every refugee's inescapable prison.

"As well-armed as the Parliamentary forces were, their deadliest weapon may have been the one they brought inadvertently. People in the town were now dying of a plague that had traveled with the English. Memories were all too fresh of the 1649 plague that had killed well over 3,000.

"Justine's nightly accounts became ever more dire. Many of the Royalist defenders, including Galway's commander Thomas Preston gave up and fled to Europe. There was a glimmer of hope when Ulick Burke, the Royalist commander at Portumna Castle, offered to send 5,000 men to help defend Galway. Incredibly, he was turned down, apparently because of old rivalries—or perhaps Galway was simply acceding to the inevitable.

"People in the town became increasingly divided. Some advocated immediate surrender. Others wanted to hold out until the bitter end—or at least long enough to negotiate reasonable surrender terms in the hope of avoiding an atrocity like the ones in Drogheda, Wexford, and Limerick. Food was scarce. Two ships attempted to bring supplies but failed. One was captured by the English, while the other was sunk off the Aran Islands.

"In view of the death and destruction, it is strange—and no doubt obscene—to say this was the happiest time of my entire existence. Despite the war, Justine's farm operated in relative peace and isolation. We toiled hard each day, and in the evenings I had my precious hours with the woman I had come to love. I now embraced and enjoyed the sort of farm work I had detested in my youth. I took pride in every exertion and in every bead of sweat. Being with Justine fed my need for learning, teaching, and mental stimulation. I loved her more than life itself. I had no fonder desire than to continue this way of life until I grew old.

"But the outside world would not ignore us indefinitely. One evening in April, I washed myself and went to tea as normal. I was surprised to find a full supper on the table. It was an elaborate spread, the kind of meal one might expect on Christmas, though there were only the usual two places set. Justine opened a bottle of wine.

"'It is from Spain,' she said. 'A merchant friend brought a case last year from Rioja. I had been saving it for a special occasion, but I realize now that each day we are left in peace is a special occasion.'

"She filled our glasses and raised hers.

"'To what or to whom shall we drink, Tim? King Charles II?'

"'Oliver Cromwell?'

"'Never mind them,' she said. 'Let us drink to ourselves, my dear Septimus. Let us drink to the time we have had together.'

"'To you, Justine. You are my savior, my light, my only reason for existence.'

"'You have gone dramatic on me, dear Tim, and I fear more than a little sacrilegious.'

"'It is true, Justine. I love you with all my heart—and I always will.'

"'Always is a long time, and time these days is precious and fleeting. I have news.'

"She told me that a delegation from the mayor of Galway had gone to Claregalway Castle to sign articles of surrender with Coote and that the documents had been sent to Dublin. We were all too aware our time together was coming to an end. Despite our somber mood, the wine soon turned our melancholy to passion.

"A week later, Coote sent Colonel Stubbers and his regiment into the town. They marched through the gates and down the streets, jubilantly banging their drums and blowing their trumpets. Stubbers would become the new mayor of Galway, and the town would feel his cruel wrath and become his base for self-enrichment. The dispossessed would become his property, with many sent to the Caribbean as white slaves.

"At Baile an Choirrín, we waited to see how the scourge of Coote's regime would affect us. At first, the new overlords left us in relative peace. Regardless of any plans they may have had, though, events overtook us catastrophically and in a way we had never expected.

"I mentioned the plague that had arrived with the English. It was most virulent in the crowded towns, but it also spread in the countryside. By a strange coincidence, around the time when the siege of Galway ended, every house neighboring Justine's—without exception—fell victim to the horrible contagion. In the entire vicinity, her home was the only one spared, and that odd circumstance did not go without comment. It was seen as particularly strange given that Justine's husband, a man in the prime of life, had died of the plague not long before I arrived. She had nursed him for weeks without contracting the disease.

"With spirits flagging and panic rising over the surrender to the English, talk in the vicinity bordered on the hysterical. People asked openly why so many near the widow Lynch's house were dying while she herself was unscathed by the pestilence. Despite her offers of assistance to help care for the dying, all doors were closed to her.

We could sense the fear and mania around us, and it was unnerving. We went about our daily work as usual but slept restlessly. We dreaded something without knowing exactly what.

"One day a group of local men arrived, bearing arms. Never one to cower, Justine confronted them openly. They informed her recent events had provided ample evidence of the devil's handiwork. Only witchcraft could explain it, they said, and the evidence was overwhelming she was the source. They intended to put her on trial.

"I was aghast. I had seen witch trials in England, but it had not occurred to me that the Catholics would have them too. I longed to speak out and tell them how utterly foolish they were, but I knew revealing our deception would only make things worse. If they discovered she had been harboring an English soldier, the mob would hang the two of us immediately or else turn us over to Coote so he could do the job. Escape was impossible. There were too many of them. Our only hope was that a reasonable trial would reveal the ridiculous nature of the witchcraft charge. After all, how could anyone think there was anything the least bit evil or supernatural about Justine?

"The trial was held fairly promptly and in her own house. She was interrogated relentlessly, and it soon became clear the so-called judges were uninterested in facts or logic. Their minds were already made up. I recalled the Puritan witch trials I myself had once attended and now saw them in a completely different light. What a fool I had been.

"The transformation of the neighbors astounded me. People who had been thoughtful and courteous were now agitated and rabid in their insults and denunciations. Most shocking was the change in kindly old Father Martyn. He was now like a man possessed. The veins in his head throbbed as he shouted at Justine, accusing her of being a child of Mephistopheles. The wild look in his swollen eyes haunts me to this day.

"The cook was interrogated and, in fear of her life, gave no answers that contradicted what the judges were seeking. I could not blame her, the poor woman. What else was she to do? I could not, on the other hand, forgive Fearghal. Relishing the attention as he sat before the crowd, he invented story after story about Justine's supposed works of magic, spells, and curses. He claimed to have himself seen her perform the incantation that caused Mr. Lynch to be struck down with the plague.

"'And why did you not report this immediately?' he was asked.

"'Because I did not want to be struck dumb—like him,' he replied, pointing to me. 'She took away his voice so that he could not speak. She did it to him as a punishment, and I feared she would do likewise to me, so I did.'

"The dull-eyed faces all nodded in blank sympathy for what he had gone through. I was appalled by the lad's perfidy and his total lack of loyalty for one who had been so good to him. I could bear no more. I stood and roared.

"'You bloody fools!' I cried. 'Can ye not see that ye only deceive yourselves. The only demon here is the fear clouding your once rational minds. Can ye not see this woman is the best and purest of all of us?'

"They stared in stunned silence. The mute they all had known for months had suddenly spoken aloud, and he was screaming with the voice of an Englishman. For a brief moment, I deluded myself with the thought my words would reach their rational minds and be convincing. What a fool.

"The first to react was Father Martyn. Pale and wide-eyed, he stood and cried, 'I would never have believed it if I had not seen it and heard it with my own eyes and ears. It is as the lad said. She took this poor man's voice away, and now, when it suits her, she gives it back. She uses him as a puppet for her own words—and not with an Irishman's voice but with that of the enemy. No more proof can possibly be required.'

"'No! No! Do ye not see? Have ye lost all of your senses? Your minds are clouded by your fear and your self-delusion.'

"My words fell on deaf ears. Three of the men stood and restrained me. Struggle as I might, there was nothing I could do. Father Martyn looked at me sympathetically.

"'It is all right, Feidhlim,' he said. 'With luck, you will return to yourself once she has been executed. If not, an exorcism can be performed. Trust in God, my son. We shall save your soul one way or another.'

"'No! No! Ye do not know what you are doing! Can ye not see? Will no one help? Will no one stand up for the truth?'

"It was no use. Never did I feel so helpless. When they realized I would not cooperate, I was bound tightly with a rope, gagged, and forced to sit through the rest of that mockery of a trial. When it was over, Justine was dragged, yelling angrily, out of the house. Another group of men hauled me out as well.

"We were taken to the nearby hilltop overlooking the lake. Though by the calendar it was late spring, winter had not yet released its grip on the countryside. The trees were bare, and their naked branches waved forlornly in the chilly wind against a gloomy sky that appeared nearly a dark shade of violet.

"I was forced to watch as they placed the noose around her neck. As I struggled in desperation, my eyes locked with hers. Never have I seen such a look of utter terror. The pain in my heart was unbearable.

"The men hurried with their evil work, as if fearful that any delay might cause them to lose their nerve. I tried vainly to scream as they tossed the rope over the large oak tree's gnarled branch.

"It had all happened so fast. Not only had they not involved the Royalist authorities in Galway, there had been no attempt to seek authority from what remained of the Confederacy. There was not even an attempt at a proper hanging. The men simply pulled on the rope, yanking her into the air.

"I wept in horror as she choked frantically, dangling from the ancient tree's twisted bough. I wished in that moment that she were indeed a witch and that she would come back to life and condemn them all to hell. Sobbing and struggling for breath, I watched her lifeless body swing back and forth in the bitter wind.

"Once there was no doubt she was dead, the horde turned strangely sullen and lifeless. There was no air of victory or vindication. Perhaps they were as much in shock at what they had done as I was. Father Martyn looked at me with sincere concern. He loosened my ropes.

"'Are you sure about what you're doing there, Father?' asked one of the men nervously.

"'He should be free of her power now,' said the priest. 'In any case, there is but one way to know.'

"Liberated from the ropes, I stood dumbfounded. Then I roared at the top of my lungs and rushed toward the swinging body. Several men grabbed me.

"'It is no good, Father,' said one. 'She still has control of him.'

"'A pity,' said Father Martyn. 'Ye shall have to lock him up to protect him from himself. I shall be writing to Rome for guidance on an exorcism.'

"I do not remember much about what happened next. I went into a rage. The men holding me were taken by surprise, as I threw them off with a sudden, violent surge. If only I had been able to summon sufficient strength when it mattered and to save my beloved Justine. All I could think of now was flight. I fought them like a maniac, and they were no doubt convinced I was possessed by the devil himself. I broke free and dashed into the woods. A few pursued, but my mania gave me the speed to outrun them. I knew they—or others—would soon come after me with weapons, so I did not stop.

"I have no idea how long I ran. It may have been hours. Despite my state of exhaustion, I continued on. Finally, I collapsed. I curled up on the ground and wept like a babe. I was inconsolable. I prayed for God to strike me dead then and there."

12
Cnoc Meadha

"I LIFTED MY HEAD and stared at the sky. Night had fallen completely, and the wind was icy. The light of a nearly full moon could be perceived faintly behind dark clouds blowing like billows of smoke across the sky.

"A massive shape towered in front of me, and I immediately understood where I was. From Baile an Choirrín one could see a huge hill on the eastern horizon. No matter where I traveled in the vicinity, the hill was always visible. Justine had told me it was called Cnoc Meadha. Because of the tales passed down since pagan times, people were respectful, if not outright fearful, of its mysterious history and its reputed power.

"After hours of aimless running, that I should have arrived there of all places did not seem pure chance to me, so I proceeded through the woods and up the slope. I took care to avoid the tower castle at the hill's foot, lest I be spotted by any of the Kirwans, who lived there. For nearly an hour I climbed the increasingly steep paths. At the summit I found a small open field.

"The hill's vantage encompassed seemingly endless leagues. It was like being on top of the world, albeit covered by night's shadow. I was awed by the sight, but it did not lift my heart—not after what I had endured and lost. Heedless of the icy wind, I tore the shirt from my breast and fell to my knees. I screamed to the heavens.

"I ranted and raved. I renounced once and for all the Deity I had spent my life worshipping. I cursed and blasphemed. I swore I would ally myself to Lucifer himself if he would only bring back my beloved and end my suffering.

"As if in response to my cries, the sky was suddenly reconcealed by clouds. The moon and the stars were extinguished. The

113

darkness was so complete I thought I had gone blind. The winds ceased, and all was eerily quiet. I held my breath.

"Without warning my eyes were seared by a blast of light. The ground shook, and my ears were numbed by a clap of thunder. A bolt of lightning had struck to my right mere yards from where I stood. I dared not move a muscle, though all was again quiet and still. A red glow burned in the patch of grass where the firebolt had landed. A harsh, smoky odor wafted in the air.

"Realizing how tense I had become, I made an effort to relax. I pondered the likelihood of such a meteorological event occurring at that very moment and in that very spot. Of course, lightning would strike the highest point available, I reassured myself, and that was where I indeed stood. It was not at all strange, and I was fortunate not to have been killed.

"Then it happened again. Once more, my eyes were dazzled and made useless for several moments. My legs nearly buckled from the boom and vibration. The lightning had struck the exact same distance from me as before, this time directly to my left. After two strikes so close together, I was paralyzed with fear. I knew I should seek cover immediately, but I could not budge.

"I opened my mouth to recite the Lord's Prayer but then stopped. I could not say the words—not after all my blasphemous utterances. Instead, for no logical reason, I attempted to calm myself by counting numbers aloud.

"I had scarcely reached twenty when it happened a third time, again striking the same exact distance from me. This time the smoldering clump of grass was directly behind me. My heart pounded in my ears. I stared at the ground in front of me, at the theoretical fourth point in the ring forming around me. I held my breath and braced for another blast. It never came.

"No sooner had I counted twenty, a large figure emerged from the darkness and stood in the spot that completed the circle. In the smoky gloom, the thing appeared to have the shape of a man and stood nearly eight feet tall. It stared at me with two glowing eyes. It wore no clothing and stank of rotting flesh. Beyond that, given the darkness and the state of my thrice-assaulted eyes, I could not be entirely certain of what I saw. I was convinced, though, it had the horns of a goat on its head and a snake for a tail.

"Another man might have thought he had lost his mind, but I was quite accepting of what I saw. After all, I had believed in the devil as a literal entity for my entire life. Though I had never expected or hoped to meet him, I had never doubted his existence or the possibility I might encounter him. It was strangely like meeting a famous personage one has heard about since childhood. It seemed only natural to engage him in conversation.

"'So, you indeed look like every drawing I have ever seen of you. The pictures were not mere fanciful works of the artists' imaginations after all.'

"I did not know whether he would speak to me in return or whether he was there only to drag my sorry soul to hell, but he did speak. I had expected a rough, grating, growling voice, but instead it was oddly soft, calming, and melodious. Strangely, I did not hear it through my ears but rather inside my head.

"'You see what you want or expect to see. I am not of your world, so your puny senses will perceive me whatever way your mind can best manage.'

"'And are you truly he? Are you indeed Lucifer the fallen angel? Mephistopheles? What is the correct way to address you? I am not normally a stickler for formality, but given the occasion, I am quite willing to give the devil his due.'

"He laughed. It was not a dark or evil laugh, as I would have expected. It was oddly pleasant.

"'I am not who you think I am. What you think you know of me and my kind has everything to do with you and nothing to do with me.'

"'So, you are a demon? Not Satan himself?'

"'If seeing it that way helps us to have a conversation, then by all means so see it. What matters is that you have come to one of those rare places in your world where it is possible for us to meet and that you have come with a proposition.'

"I swallowed hard. My entire life of deep and abiding faith had prepared me for this exact moment. The irony was that in my defining moment, I would turn my back completely on everything I had been taught and would embrace what I knew to be evil.

"'The woman I love has been murdered unfairly and horribly. I want her back.'

"'And what can you offer in exchange?'

"'All I have is myself. I offer myself in exchange for her.'

"'Do you make this offer freely and with the competent comprehension of a clear mind?'

"I found it strange he would be compelled to nail down so many specific details and to establish my capacity to enter into an agreement. He was like nothing so much as a solicitor drawing up a contract and covering every possible point of contention. Assuming his powers were indeed sufficient for raising the dead, why would he be concerned by the consent and acquiescence of someone as powerless as I? If he wanted something from me—including myself—could he not simply seize it? Why did he need permission? His power may have been mighty and awesome, but evidently it was not absolute. I too apparently had power here, even if it was only the simple power to agree or to disagree.

"'Yes, I understand what I am doing, and I enter into the agreement willingly.'

"'Let us be clear. I shall restore one Justine Lynch née de Bruin, also known as Browne, of Baile an Choirrín to life. In exchange, you shall surrender your energy, your essence, your soul—however you best understand it—to me and my world in perpetuity. Is this what you agree to?'

"'Yes, this is what I agree to.'

"'You must affirm it three times.'

"'I agree. I agree. If it brings back my beloved Justine, then I agree.'

"'You understand that you shall not be able to be with her? You shall be with me. You shall not see her again.'

"'No, I have to see her. How shall I know that you have kept your end of the bargain? I understand I shall dwell forever in hell or whatever you call it, but I must see her again and be assured I have not been tricked. You must do that for me.'

"'Very well. Your condition is noted. You shall see her in her restored mortal form and converse with her for the minimum amount of time necessary to ascertain her identity. Do you agree now?'

"'Yes, I agree. I agree. With this revised understanding, I do willingly agree.'

"'Very well. Our bargain is made. To seal it, all I require is a drop of your blood.'

"'A drop of my blood?'

"'Yes, you must willingly bleed. Once it touches the ground, the bargain will be sealed.'

"Having no knife or anything else sharp at my disposal, I did the only thing I could think of. I tore into my own hand with my teeth. A trickle of warm liquid flowed into my mouth. I shook my hand so that the drops would fall to the soil below. For good measure, I spat out all the blood and saliva in my mouth.

"Once I had done that, the entire hilltop was bathed in a white light that covered my eyes like a veil. I had the giddy and unnerving sensation of floating. I was no longer cold. I pondered what I had done. Had I been deceived?

"The light faded, and once again I could see the hilltop as before. The demon was still before me, but someone was with him. She was scared and confused. She saw me and ran to my arms.

"She looked exactly as she had before, though her neck had gruesome red marks where she had been strangled by the rope. I could scarcely believe she was with me once again, and my heart soared.

"'Tim, what happened? Where are we? The rope. It was awful. How did I survive it? Are we safe now?'

"'Everything is all right now, Justine. You are safe. Thank...'

"I was about to thank God she was back. Bitterly, I choked on my words.

"'We cannot go back to Baile an Choirrín, can we, Tim? It is not safe. I can never go back there again. Would it even be safe to return to Menlough? What shall we do? Where shall we go?'

"I held her close and kissed her, knowing it would be the final time.

"'My dear, dear Justine. All that is important right now is that you know I love you and I shall always love you. The rest, I am afraid, you will have to work out for yourself. I am sorry I shall not be here to help with whatever comes next.'

"'What do you mean? Where are you going? How can you leave?'

"'I do not know how to explain, my love. What matters is that you are alive and safe. You must look after yourself.'

"I looked in the direction of the demon. He stood silently in the dark. I was not certain whether Justine could see him as I could.

"'I refuse to accept this, Tim,' she said defiantly. 'Wherever you go, I shall go too.'

"'That is not possible. Where I am going, you cannot follow.'

"'Explain yourself. Do not hide in riddles. I shall not be treated like a child.'

"I knew her too well to think she would ever settle for anything less than the full truth. I only wondered if she would be able to believe it.

"'Justine, I have made a bargain.'

"'A bargain?'

"'Yes, a gentlemen's agreement, so to speak. I have traded my life for yours.'

"'What do you mean? What are you talking about? How is it possible to make such a bargain?'

"I looked in the demon's direction. Her gaze followed mine. I could tell from the look on her face she saw him too.

"'Who…?'

"'My love, please forgive me. I have bargained with the devil. You were dead, and now you are brought back to life. I am going in your place. That is what I agreed. That is now the debt I must pay.'

"Her eyes were disbelieving.

"'No, no. *I* do not agree. *I* do not accept this bargain. I refuse to accede to these conditions which were negotiated in my absence.'

"The demon stepped forward. His countenance suggested intense interest in her words.

"'You do not have a say in this,' I told her. 'This is a matter purely between myself and this being. In return for my payment, you will have your life. It is a price I pay gladly. In return, all I ask of you is that you have a long and happy life.'

"'No!' she cried. 'I refuse to be part of this. I refuse.'

"'I am afraid that you have no say. The matter is settled. Please accept my gift and know that I love you and shall love you forever.'

"The demon drew yet closer and spoke.

"'She does have standing.'

"'What do you mean by that? You and I have made our bargain. It is signed and sealed. You cannot go back on your word now.'

"'We require her assent to proceed. This is unanticipated. No mortal has refused the gift in comparable circumstances.'

"'We made an agreement! You took my blood. It is done. You cannot let her undo it now.'

"'You are correct. The bargain was sealed, but you made the arrangement more complex by involving a third party and insisting she be brought here. As a consequence, you effectively gave her a voice in the matter.'

"'What does her voice matter if the bargain is sealed?'

"'She may offer her soul in place of yours.'

"'What? No! She cannot. I shall not allow it. Our arrangement was that you take me in order for her to live. You cannot change that now. You cannot!'

"'If she comes with me, she will live forever. I shall have fulfilled my end of the bargain. Our agreement did not specify whether she live in your world or mine.'

"'No, no, that would not be living. She would burn in hell for *my* sins. That is not what I agreed to.'

"'There will be no combustion or similar chemical phenomena where she will be, so she will not burn. In fact, she herself will be a source of energy in our domain, and her energy will do for our purposes as well as yours.'

"'Justine, tell him that you accept my gift. Tell him that you want your life. Please. It is what I want. I could never be happy knowing he took you in my place. I beg you. Live the rest of your life here on earth as you were meant to. Please!'

"'Do you imagine I would be any less unhappy knowing you had made such a sacrifice for me? Do you think I love you any less than you love me? Having already experienced death, I find I no longer have fear of anything—even this. Demon, I shall go with you willingly. Take me now, and let this man live out his life.'

"The eerily calming voice replied, 'I need a drop of your blood to seal the bargain.'

"'No!' I cried.

"I watched helplessly as she did as I had done, drawing her own blood with her teeth. In my horror, each red drop seemed to take hours to reach the ground. Light flashed each time one landed.

"'It is done. The bargain is sealed.'

"'No! It cannot be! I deny this bargain. I refuse it.'

"'It is too late.'

"'I refuse to accept her sacrifice. I shall negate it by taking my own life. Then the bargain will have no meaning. Nothing will have been exchanged for her soul. I swear it. I shall kill myself.'

"'You may try, but it will be to no avail.'

"'What do you mean?'

"'You have no cause for complaint. You have come out the best in this bargain. You exchanged your eternal soul for her life. She exchanged her eternal soul for yours. You now remain in your own world but without the burden of death.'

"'What?'

"'As things stand, I cannot take you with me nor can your soul be extinguished. You have become one of the rarest of creatures in your world. You are now effectively immortal.'

"'I do not understand. How is that possible? There are so many questions. What will become of me? Will I age like other men? How can I possibly cope with eternity knowing what I have caused to happen to my beloved Justine?'

"'All answers can be found in time, and time is something you now have in abundance. Farewell.'

"'No! Do not go! Do not take her!'

120

"I lunged to grab hold of Justine but found only air. Having fallen to the ground, I looked up and saw the hilltop was again deserted except for myself. Only a few smoldering patches of grass offered any evidence I had not experienced a dream or hallucination. I pounded the earth and wept. If only I had not insisted on seeing Justine one last time! I howled as I thought of her spending eternity in that monster's domain and of me living endlessly so that I could spend eternity regretting my mistake.

"I wandered the countryside, wanting nothing other than to end my miserable existence. When I came to the banks of the river Abhainn an Chláir, I threw myself into its flowing waters. For all my gasping and struggling, I repeatedly found myself back at the surface. Stones in my pockets did not help. No matter how long I stayed underwater, I never wanted for breath.

"I searched the land for someone willing to kill me. Yet because I had the crazed appearance of a madman, most people avoided me. In the instances where I succeeded in making someone listen to me, I declared myself to be an English soldier out of uniform. They were then happy to comply with my request—or at least try to. Many men beat me to within an inch of my life, but that final inch could never be bridged. I could be hurt, but my body sustained no lasting injury.

"I brazenly walked into Galway town and turned myself in to the soldiers of the garrison. I was duly tried and sentenced to be hanged as a deserter and traitor. Brave men who had been hardened by battle fled in terror when they cut me down from the gallows and found me unharmed after dangling for hours.

"Confused and despairing, I became an aimless wanderer. It was the strangest of all possible lives. I could go anywhere but belonged nowhere. As I did not have to fear dangers that other men did, there was little limit on my roaming. Yet certain places were closed to me. It was impossible for me to approach any church, temple, or other place of worship. This constraint was absolute, though it was not clear to me whether it was imposed by the demon or by my own guilty conscience.

"It took years to understand fully what I had become. I think I only finally and fully comprehended the utter loneliness and despair that lay ahead on the night I passed through a country village. It began to snow, and in the distance I could hear a church choir singing a Christmas hymn. My heart sank in a flood of intolerable sorrow, knowing that not only would I never again take part in a holy religious ceremony but I would never in my life celebrate Christmas.

"You have to understand what a devastating realization that was. The Anabaptists did not celebrate the Savior's birth, and as a Puritan, I had been part of a religious movement that strictly forbade, and in fact outlawed, festive Christmas celebrations. I was overcome with an unbearable sense of loss, as I was forced to retreat from that village. As much as my soul now longed to hear the music, it caused my ears to burn as if on fire.

"Gradually, I accepted my existence. I had somehow made myself unacceptable to both heaven and hell. I was no longer—and never would be—like other men."

13
Ceremony

"THAT IS SO incredibly sad," said Maria on the verge of tears.

Exhausted from the telling, Septimus looked at her warmly.

"Perhaps you can understand now," he said, "why it has affected me so much to see you here."

Lola was skeptical.

"Something about your story just doesn't add up for me. I still think it's strange that, when you knew her, Justine was, what, in her thirties?"

"Yes, but I have explained that."

"And Maria is about the same age as me. Twenty-three, right, Maria?"

"Twenty-two."

"Why wouldn't she come back the same age as before?"

"I explained that," he replied impatiently. "Do you not listen? Why are you so preoccupied with age? Have you not seen my own age change before your very eyes? Age is a fluid concept when it comes to the supernatural."

"And according to your story, she's stuck forever in that other world with that demon. How is she supposed to have gotten away from him? How can she be back here now?"

"I do not have an answer for that. All I can tell you is that Justine had the strongest mind and fiercest will of anyone I have ever known. If there was a way to escape, she would have found it. She would not have rested until finding her way back to me. It has only been that faintest of hopes that has given me what little taste for life I have left."

He continued, "You attempt to disprove the obvious. The very arrival of this young woman is the effective proof. What is the likelihood a woman with this exact face should find her way across such a long distance to this remote place—of all places—and to me? Use your mathematical skills to calculate that. The overwhelming improbability of coincidence is your proof. All that remains is to find a way to recover her memory."

"I have a question," said Kyle, raising his hand timidly.

The others were startled to see Kyle awake and joining the conversation. Septimus was amused by the young man's schoolboy demeanor. "Yes?"

"Did you really bring me back from the dead?"

"I did."

"And those kids? They were dead too?"

"They were."

"Well, if you had the power to do that, then why didn't you just bring Justine back?"

Lola, in the unaccustomed position of being impressed by something Kyle had uttered, said, "Yeah. What about that?"

Septimus wearied of questions he considered unknowledgeable and unworthy of his time. "You are speaking of cases where souls had only begun to slip the bonds of the mortal world. With skills that have taken hundreds of years to hone, I have indeed learned how, in limited circumstances, to pull individuals back from the afterlife's cusp. Justine's case was entirely different. She did not merely die. Her soul was transported to the Netherworld and imprisoned there. She has always been beyond my feeble grasp."

He looked at Maria and said, "You are her to the life. I swear it. Did you not yourself say you dreamt of this place and of me?"

Bewildered, Maria replied, "I did dream of this place and, I think, of you. You were younger than you are now, but you do indeed seem to be the man in my dream. But I have no memory of the story you told. The name Justine means nothing to me, but if I am being honest, I think I would like the story to be true. It is such a very sad story, and I would so like for it to have a happy ending."

Lola grabbed her by the arms.

"Maria, snap out of it. He's using some kind of voodoo on you. You're Maria Murphy from Cork, not this Justine person from the

17th century. Can't you see? He's trying to take control of your mind. You have to fight him."

"Maybe it *is* true," said Kyle. "It *is* kind of a cool story."

"Am I the only one here not losing their mind?" said Lola. "Can't you both see what is happening? We have to get away from here. And besides, it isn't actually that good a story. It's so... so... heteronormative!"

Maria ignored her and asked Septimus, "So you never saw Justine or that demon again?"

"I have never laid eyes on my beloved since, though I truly do believe I do so now. As for the demon, I did encounter him again and more than once. I even learned his name. And I have met others from his world. You see, in the nearly 140 years before I joined Captain Vancouver on his voyage around the world, I traveled to every corner of Europe and parts of Asia. I sought out every clairvoyant, seer, occultist, soothsayer, alchemist, and necromancer I could find. I followed up on every tale or rumor I heard. Most were frauds and schemers. Some were merely confused. Every so often, however, I found someone who, like myself, had had a brush with the Netherworld. I gathered all the knowledge I could. I learned all the tricks and the spells that were possible in this world. After all, what is the point of an endless life if one does not use it to acquire all the education available?"

"So what was it?" asked Kyle.

"Eh?"

"His name."

"Whose name?"

"The demon's."

"You want to be very careful when it comes to demons' names, my boy. Names have great power in the Netherworld, but I am safe enough here telling you that it is Astaroth. I recommend you never repeat it, though, especially when you are alone in the dark."

"This has all been very interesting," said Lola, "but I think it's time the three of us left now. There are people out there who are frantic with worry and wondering what's happened to us."

"But we have to find out," said Maria. "We have to find out if I am really Justine. I have to know."

"If you were Justine," said Lola, "you would know it. You would remember all the things he has been telling us. You are obviously not her."

Maria looked at Septimus. "How will I ever know? I mean, for sure and for certain?"

"There is a way," he said.

"How?" asked Lola doubtfully.

"There is a ceremony I can perform. If completed successfully, it will give us the truth about the soul that resides in this body."

"Yeah?" said Lola, "And why should we believe that? You could make up anything and we would have no way of knowing the difference."

"I assure you, if the rite is held, it will leave no doubt in anyone's mind. If I am mistaken, I promise I shall concede it at once. I have no interest in forcing my own hopes and delusions on an innocent party. We shall all know the truth together."

"And what's involved in this ceremony?" asked Lola.

"I shall need to open a small rift in the fabric of reality and make the slightest of connections to the Netherworld. This woman will be under my protection as I ascertain the authentic identity of her soul."

"I don't know, Septimus," said Lola. "Sounds kind of dangerous to me. I don't want anything happening to Maria, understand?"

"Nor do I. Believe me when I tell you I shall not allow any harm to come to this woman."

"I just don't like it," insisted Lola.

"*I* want to do it," said Maria. "*I* would like to know. Maybe I did live before. If there is any chance at all it is true, I want to be able to remember."

"Can you absolutely promise there is no danger?" asked Lola emphatically.

Septimus chose his words carefully. "I shall not lie to you. When dealing with the supernatural, there are always risks. To tell you otherwise would be dishonest, but I assure you all my powers will be employed to keep all of ye safe. I anticipate no danger."

"Yeah, well," said Lola. "You miscalculated pretty badly when you were bargaining with that demon on 'Nock Mah' or whatever it was called back in the 1600s."

"I knew nothing back then. I now have centuries of experience in the dark arts. Little escapes me these days."

"What do *you* think, Kyle?" asked Maria.

"Me? Gosh, I don't know. This is all so crazy. I mean, I guess if I was in your situation, I would want to know for sure."

"Okay so. Let's give it a go," said Maria. "What do I need to do?"

"Maria," said Lola, "please don't."

"You're very good to be worrying about me, Lola, but I'll be grand."

"If anything happens to her," said Lola gravely to Septimus, "you will answer to me and I promise I will definitely find a way to cut your damned immortal life short. Got that?"

"I understand, and I assure you that you and I are of one mind on this."

"So, what do we do, Tim?" asked Maria.

Septimus flinched upon being called by his old nickname.

"We must go to the highest point on the island. I will gather some talismans for the rite. Ye will want to dress warmly. Ye will find jumpers and coats in the wardrobe over there."

"There wasn't anything in that wardrobe before," said Lola, her voice trailing off.

She still had not gotten completely accustomed to Septimus's sleights of hand. She went to the wardrobe and indeed found an assortment of sweaters and jackets. Maria, Kyle, and she made their choices and donned them.

They followed Septimus out of the house and through the woods. It was by now late at night, and the wind coming off the sea chilled their bones in spite of the extra clothing. Septimus carried a large sack, as he led them up a winding trail toward the hilltop.

"So, what's the right word for you," Kyle asked Septimus abruptly.

"Eh?"

"I mean, what are you exactly? Are you a warlock? Sorcerer? Wizard? Necromancer?"

Septimus laughed wearily.

"It is not as though I have ever had a card or *curriculum vitae,* which required me to specify a title. If I were required to have one, I suppose the most applicable one would be 'demon hunter.'"

"Really? Do you actually hunt demons?" asked Kyle, impressed.

"Well, not for sport, as if they were game. More accurately, they hunt me or, rather, they have a way of seeking me out. As it happens, they have surprisingly little power in this world. It is rare for one to cross over from their world to ours, but it does happen on occasion. When it does, they are often drawn to me because of my own personal connection to the Netherworld. Fortunately, I have learned to ward them off fairly effectively. Sometimes, though, they afflict innocent mortals and, if I become aware of it, I do my best to intervene."

"Wow. So you're like a demon cop!"

"I had not thought of it that way, but I suppose the comparison is not inapt."

"And are you the only one or are there others?"

"Yes, there are others. I do not know how many exactly, but I have met a few of them. Each one has his own unique story of where he became connected to the Netherworld and learned his skills. Some even survive to this day."

"Wow," said Kyle. "The world just became a whole lot scarier."

"Do not over-concern yourself. It is rare enough for *me* to see a demon—and nearly unheard of for others, including the likes of you."

When they emerged from the woods at the top of the hill, there was a stunning moonlit view of the sea and the nearby islands. A chill went up Lola's spine, and she wondered if it was anything like what Septimus felt hundreds of years earlier on that hill in Ireland.

"Explain to me again," she said, "exactly what you are going to do and why any of us should go along with it?"

"I shall open a tiny rift in the fabric between this world and the Netherworld. Just for a few moments."

"Why does that sound dangerous to me? I mean, weren't you just explaining to Kyle that you have a way of attracting demons?"

"As I have said, this is not without risk. There are indeed untold perils in the Netherworld, but think of it like venturing into a forest. Although there are dangerous creatures roaming the forest, if you enter it at the margins and then withdraw immediately, there is practically no chance of crossing paths with a deadly threat."

"And what exactly is the point of doing this?"

"If this woman has indeed spent time in the Netherworld, I shall know it instantly once she makes any contact with it in my presence. More importantly, she would then immediately recover her lost memories. That would be our proof positive that she is my Justine."

"But," said Lola, "you said she was reborn. This is a different body, and it hasn't been in your Netherworld."

"It is not her physical body I am testing. It is her true essence, what we usually refer to as the soul. None of us knows all the places our life force may have been in any past lives we may have had."

"And you promise not to tell us she's Justine just because you want her to be?"

"It is Justine I want, not merely someone who looks like her. In any event, you will not need me to tell you anything. If she is Justine, she will tell you herself."

Lola was still uneasy. "Maria, I don't think you should do this. I just don't like it. I have a really bad feeling about it."

"It's all right, Lola," said Maria. "I honestly do want to do it. I need to know whether it is true or not. Otherwise, I think I will spend the rest of my life wondering."

Kyle said, "For what it's worth, I think it should be Maria's choice. If she's okay with it, Lola, then I think you and I should go along with her."

"I guess I'm outnumbered," said Lola, "but I want everyone to remember that I was against this."

"So noted," said Septimus. "Shall we begin?"

"Is this going to be like a séance?" asked Maria.

Septimus sighed. "By séance, I expect you mean one of those ceremonies that purports to allow the living to talk with the dead.

Those are generally only so much theater, but yes, this will be not unlike what I suppose you are thinking of."

Slowly and deliberately, Septimus opened his sack and removed four large iron candle holders as well as four thick white candles. Each holder had a sharp point on the bottom, suited for driving into the ground like a stake. He placed them carefully at equal distances from a center point so as to form points on a circle. He then pulled from the bag a match so large that it nearly appeared to be a stick of wood with an ugly head of sulfur on one end. With a flourish, he swung around scratching the match along the face of a large stone and leaving a trail of flashing light like a sparkler.

Solemnly, he lit the four candles one by one. Each erupted in a surprisingly large flame that danced wildly in the wind. The three observers were spellbound by the display of light and motion.

Maria swallowed hard as Septimus approached and took her hand, leading her to the center of the circle. Heart pounding, she wondered if Lola might have been right about this.

Septimus stepped back and left her standing there on her own. Then, in a language that none of them recognized, he recited an incantation. His voice took on an eerie, otherworldly quality, as if someone or something from beyond was speaking through him. Lola's heart raced. The chanting continued for several minutes. It ceased abruptly. Rolling thunder filled their ears, and as the sound died away, the air became unexpectedly calm.

Lola and Kyle gasped for air when a sudden flash enveloped the entire hilltop. The illumination made everything white. In horror, Lola watched a large scaly arm appear out of nowhere and wrap itself around Maria. The Irish girl looked helplessly in Lola's direction and tried to scream. Before she could, she was yanked backward, melting into the light. In the next moment, everything was pitch dark.

Stunned and blinded, Lola and Kyle fell to their knees. Their ears were assaulted by a piercing scream.

"No!"

Their vision returned slowly. The scream had come from Septimus, who had also fallen to his knees.

"Fool!" he cried.

He pounded the ground with such force that Lola thought he might actually break both of his hands.

"What a fool! I am the biggest fool in the entire history of the universe!"

Lola attempted to stand but fell. Her legs had turned to jelly.

"How can I have been so stupid? How is this possible? How did I not see it? It was so obvious. It was a trap. A carefully laid ambush, and I led her into it. And now I have lost her again. How could I have been so stupid? How is it possible?"

Lola finally recovered her balance. She looked at the pitiful figure prostrate on the ground, weeping like a child.

Overcome by rage, she laid her hands on him roughly and pulled his face toward hers.

She screamed, "You do not get to do this! You do not get to make this about you! I don't know what just happened, but it is obviously not good, and Maria is gone. You do not get to go on screaming about how upset *you* are. Listen to me. You are going to make this right. Right now all I care about is Maria. You understand? Now explain to me what just happened and tell me how we are going to get her back."

Tears streamed from Septimus's eyes.

"It has happened again. And again it is my fault. He has taken her again. He laid a trap and I walked right into it. I gave him what he wanted. I gave him Justine—again. It is over. There is nothing to be done. Nothing."

Kyle watched in astonishment as Lola slapped the demon hunter's face with a fury the young man had never seen in her before. In the heat of the moment, she appeared to be a demon herself.

"Don't tell me there is nothing to be done! Don't you dare say that! We are getting her back, and that's the end of it. Understand?"

"I am sorry," he replied pitifully.

14
The Diabolusbane

ALARMED BY the intensity of Lola's anger, Kyle pulled her away from the demon hunter. While attacking him seemed foolhardy or even dangerous—given the demon hunter's considerable powers—the young man's concern was actually more for Septimus than for Lola. The former Puritan showed no interest in defending himself.

"Lola," said Kyle, "take it easy. We need to understand what happened. Give him a chance to talk."

Understanding her upset and wanting to comfort her, Kyle left his hand on her shoulder, but she pushed him away brusquely.

"I have listened to this jerk tell his stories all night. And now Maria is gone, and I'm not going to listen to him anymore. Because all I learned from his stories is that he's satisfied just to wander the earth for centuries and feel sorry for himself because some demon snatched away the woman he loves. Well, I'm not going to wallow in self-pity instead of taking action. I don't care whether it's heaven or hell where that thing has taken Maria. Because heaven and hell both better damn well get ready because I'm going after her."

The first light of sunrise appeared in the east. The candles' flames had gone out, and the wicks spewed black smoke. Septimus sat up. He appeared to have aged ten years within the past several minutes.

"I am sorry," he said quietly. "You were right. Does that satisfy you?"

"No!" she yelled. "That does *not* satisfy me. This is not about you and whether you were right or wrong. This is about getting Maria back. You have to tell me where she is and how to get her. You have to tell me exactly what just happened."

"He was waiting for her," said Septimus in a low voice. "He knew we would be in this spot. He knew I would attempt making contact with the Netherworld. He knew everything. This was all planned."

"Who had it all planned? Is this the same demon that took Justine?"

"Yes. I call him the Fiend to distinguish him from any other demon and because I do not like to use his real name. He has plagued me for more than three-hundred years. He was not satisfied with taking the only one I ever loved. He has never ceased taunting me in my thoughts and in my dreams. Somehow Justine must have escaped him. Somehow she was reborn in this world but without her full memory. He took advantage of her lack of memory and my ignorance to manipulate us to this time and place so that he could seize her back. History has repeated itself, and again it is entirely my fault."

"What do you mean 'manipulate'?" asked Kyle.

"While the denizens of the demon plane have limited power in our world, they can influence events subtly and remotely. With a dream or a suggestion they give a nudge in one direction or a push in another. Somehow the Fiend succeeded in sending Justine back to me but knowing that I would need to make certain it was really her. That gave him his chance."

"So he caused her to have those dreams about you and about this place?" said Kyle.

"Yes, I now believe that is what happened. It was insidious, and I should have seen it. If only it had not happened while I was distracted and in a weak state. My self-indulgent folly of bringing back dead children for company drained me of my powers. It was my undoing and Justine's. What a bloody fool I am."

"What did you say his name was again?" asked Lola.

Septimus was lost in his thoughts. "Eh?"

"This demon who took Justine and now has Maria. What is he called?"

"Let us not continue this conversation here in this place. We shall go back to the house. I cannot emphasize how careful you need to be with certain names and when and where you utter them."

They walked down the hill in silence. By the time they reached the house, the sun had fully cleared the horizon.

"Any chance I can get a decent cup of coffee today, Tim?" asked Lola as she headed for the kitchen.

Septimus was annoyed. "That is a name used only by those closest to me."

"I think I've earned the right to call you whatever I want, Tim," she replied scornfully, "especially after what you've put us through. Especially after what you let happen to Maria."

Her mood improved slightly when she found a hot latte on the kitchen table.

"Nice," she said, "but this does not even begin to let you off the hook. So start talking. First, what was the demon's name again?"

"He goes by many names, most unpronounceable by the likes of us. To the extent he is known in our world, he is called…"

"Astaroth," said Kyle, proud to have remembered.

"Very good for remembering, young man, although you seem to have forgotten I advised you not to repeat it. To be safe, do as I do and call him the Fiend."

"I don't understand," said Kyle, watching Lola enjoy her latte. "How you can make a cup of coffee appear out of thin air, but you can't just snap your fingers and bring Maria back."

"You are talking about very different things. Justine—or Maria as you call her—is in the grip of a terrible supernatural force. Releasing her from its grasp is beyond the power of any mortal or even myself. Assuming it were even possible, it would require much more than a simple bit of conjuring."

"I don't want to hear how hard it is," said Lola. "I just want you to tell us how we are going to get her back."

"I am not saying it is difficult," replied Septimus. "I am saying it is hopeless. It would require me to enter the Netherworld, to somehow penetrate the demon's native domain. I would have to do this without being detected. I would have to find a way to locate her in a world that does not correspond to any of the natural laws we know and understand. I would have to find a way to somehow free her and bring her back to this world, all while battling the Fiend in his own realm, where his powers are boundless. There is no likelihood that I would return from such a futile rescue attempt."

"This is good," said Lola. "Now that you've laid out the basic framework of a plan, we need to drop the negativity and flesh out the details."

Septimus looked at her with bewildered amazement. "You refuse to grasp the impossibility of what you suggest. For one thing, there is no way I could do this alone. If there is a shred of hope of doing this, it would require me to find other demon hunters and convince them to join me in a suicide pact."

"You said you know other demon hunters," said Kyle. "Do you know any of them well enough to ask them?"

"There are perhaps two who might at least hear me out, assuming I can even find them. There is something about this kind of life that makes one, shall we say, eremetic."

"What's that mean?" asked Kyle.

"Just sounds to me like a fancy word for antisocial," said Lola. "Anyway, this all sounds great. How soon can we go see these demon hunters and ask them?"

"I am afraid, before we can contemplate that," said Septimus, "there is another obstacle to your fanciful rescue plan. I have not yet recovered fully from the state in which you found me. There is no point in even thinking of such an insane mission unless I can return to my full powers."

"And how can you do that?" asked Lola.

He looked in Kyle's direction and said, "I should have to take back a portion of a gift that I gave."

"What does that mean?" asked Lola suspiciously.

"I expended a great deal of energy in rescuing ye three. The largest portion was required to loose this young fellow from the grip of death. That energy now resides in his body. I fear I may now have to take some of it back."

"Exactly what are you talking about? And what does it mean for Kyle? What would happen to him?"

"He would be severely weakened. He would require days, perhaps a week or more, to recover. Most significantly, though, it would shorten his lifespan—more than it has already been shortened."

Kyle said nothing, but Lola saw the apprehension in his eyes.

"No, you can't do that," she said. "That's not right. There has to be another way. Figure out another way."

"There is no other way. Over time, my powers may eventually recover to what they were on their own, but it could take years, perhaps decades. Normally, my patience is vast and this would not be a problem, but if we are serious about me launching an assault on the Netherworld itself, it would be out of the question in my present condition."

"I refuse to accept that. Think of something else."

Septimus shrugged sadly.

"It's okay," said Kyle. "Go ahead and do it. I don't mind."

"Kyle, no," said Lola. "I won't let you. It's not fair. No one should have to make a choice like that."

"How much shorter would my life be?" asked Kyle.

"Because of what you have already been through," said Septimus, "you will have lost five to ten years. If I take back the vitality I require, it would be something like ten to fifteen years."

"So, instead of living to 120," said Kyle with a weak smile, "I might live to only 105?"

"Yes, that is the optimistic way to look at it. Or you may be run down by a street conveyance at the age of thirty, and the length of your natural lifespan would turn out to be irrelevant."

"Stop joking about this, the two of you," said Lola crossly. "This is serious. Kyle, I am not going to let you give up part of your life— even if it is to get Maria back."

Despite her words, internally Lola was torn. She desperately wanted Maria back.

"It's not up to you, Lola. It was Maria's choice to go through with the ceremony, and now it's my choice—and mine alone—whether to do this. And I choose to do it."

"But why? You heard him. He keeps saying he probably won't be able to rescue her anyway? Why would you throw away part of your life for such a slim chance?"

Kyle swallowed.

"I'm not completely stupid, Lola. I know how much you care about Maria. Yes, I'm doing it for her, but I'm mostly doing it for you. I know that getting her back is the only way you'll ever be happy, and I want you to be happy. Besides, it's the right thing to do. It's what people do for each other."

Lola did not know what to say. She had always just about tolerated Kyle because he was so insistent on being friends with her. She now regretted all the times she had regarded him as little more than a borderline nuisance. Maybe he was not the most stimulating conversationalist in the world, but she had to give him credit for being a truly good and decent person.

"Are you sure I can't talk you out of it, Kyle? I can't stand the thought of something bad happening to you. I really can't. You don't deserve it."

"Yeah, and Maria doesn't deserve to be trapped by a demon. I guess life just isn't fair, Lola. Anyway, the way I look at it, every minute since the boat sank has been a gift. I'm living on borrowed time anyway. I guess if you think about it, from the moment we're born, *all* our time is borrowed."

It was the kind of trite sentiment that Lola usually hated, but this time it melted her heart. She wrapped her arms around Kyle and gave him a long and sincere hug.

"I've never told you how great you are," she said to him, "and I'm sorry about that. You're a pretty amazing guy."

Knowing him as she did, she was not the least surprised to see him blush. If Septimus was moved at all by this scene, he hid it well.

"So, what do we need to do?" Kyle asked him.

"It is a relatively simple matter," said the demon hunter. "though not as simple as it was to transmit my life force to you in the first place."

"Why's that?"

"Releasing my life force was straightforward. I could transmit it to you at a distance while you were in the water. To reabsorb it, it must be extracted directly. Physical contact is required."

"What does that mean?"

"The ectoplasmic energy must rise through your throat and pass through your mouth into mine."

"Really? But it's not like our mouths need to touch or anything, right?"

"Well, yes, they will."

"So, would we be, like, kissing?"

"No. Well, not exactly. Think of it more like performing mouth-to-mouth resuscitation."

"Isn't there some other way?"

"Well, there is," said Septimus matter-of-factly, "but trust me when I tell you, you would like it even less."

Kyle appeared unsure. Lola had nothing but sympathy for him but was amused that the idea of another man's lips touching his held more terror for him than having his life shortened.

"Okay, if you're sure it's the only way," said Kyle stoically. "Let's do it."

"Allow me to say," said Septimus, "I am not often impressed, but I have nothing but admiration for your selflessness. Because it is for the benefit of the woman I love, you also have my gratitude and respect."

"Thanks. I guess," said Kyle weakly. "Can we get on with it now?"

Without another word, Septimus drew near Kyle, his eyes only an inch from the younger man's. Septimus's face went blank as he concentrated his thoughts. Slowly, a ghostly glow emanated from his fingers. He raised his hands and placed them on Kyle's shoulders. Within moments, Kyle's entire body shimmered with light. Deliberately and almost tenderly, Septimus's mouth drew near the younger man's. As their mouths joined, Kyle's body went quickly limp, as if he had fainted. Septimus held him upright as the light encompassing his body shifted in the direction of his head and then passed toward Septimus. Within moments, the demon hunter's body grew visibly taller and glowed brightly. Kyle slumped to the floor like a rag doll.

Seeing him motionless on the floor, Lola panicked and dropped to her knees. She ran her fingers through his tousled hair. It was surprisingly soft, like a child's. She ran a finger along his cheek to feel for a sign of life. His skin was unexpectedly delicate. She could not tell if he was breathing. She pressed her hand on his chest and could not feel a heartbeat. She hoped it was only because of the thickness of his sweater. Seeing her athletic friend now so helpless—and with no apparent sign of life—upset her. She leapt to her feet and turned angrily to Septimus.

The demon hunter, meanwhile, had gone through a startling transformation. He was a full two inches taller. His shoulders were broader, and his waist was trim. Though the texture of his face was rough, the deep lines had vanished. His aquiline features were sharper than before. His black hair and bushy eyebrows showed no trace of gray. His shoulder-length mane was thick and full, and his severe countenance was intimidating. In that instant, Lola knew she gazed at the same Puritan soldier Justine Browne Lynch had beheld unexpectedly on her Irish farm more than 350 years earlier. And that he was also the same "fine, tall fella" Maria had seen in her dreams.

He stood unsteadily, as if in a daze. He did not speak. Not caring about his wobbly state, Lola pounded his chest angrily with both her fists.

"You greedy bastard! You couldn't help yourself. You had to suck all the life out of him, didn't you? You killed him."

"What? What's that you are saying?"

"Look at him. There's no life left in him. You weren't supposed to kill him!"

Slowly, he focused his thoughts. He knelt beside Kyle and laid a hand gently on his forehead.

"I did warn both of you there would be a price for him to pay if I were to regain my full powers. It was necessary if there is to be an attempt at rescuing Justine."

"You didn't say it would kill him!"

"And it has not," said Septimus calmly. "He is still alive. He will, however, need much time to recover. Help me take him to the bed upstairs."

The demon hunter reached under the younger man's arms and lifted him, while Lola carried his legs. His body was as solid and muscular as ever, but it felt inert and devoid of life.

"Are you sure he will be okay?"

"Trust me. He should be fine—eventually."

As they struggled up the stairs, Lola said, "This is a lot of work. Isn't this the sort of thing you could make happen with a snap of your fingers?"

"He is not the only one weakened by the transfer. It will take me some time to recover as well. Once we have laid him on the bed and I have regained more strength, I will create a protective spell so that no harm will come to him in my absence. You, of course, are welcome to stay and mind him."

"Stay? Does he actually need someone to take care of him?"

"No, his body will be in a state of suspension. He will have no biological requirements, and he will be under my lingering protection. I only thought you might prefer to remain by his side."

"Well, you thought wrong. I'm going with you."

"With me? Really?"

"Yeah, really. I'm getting tired of watching my friends make sacrifices. Maria did what you wanted, and now she's gone. Kyle did what you wanted, and now he's like this. Now it's my turn. I'm going with you. I'm going to help get Maria back."

For the first time, Lola heard Septimus laugh heartily. "Absolutely out of the question."

"I wasn't asking for your permission."

"If you actually grasped what you are proposing..."

Having reached the top floor, they settled Kyle onto the bed. Septimus quietly said an incantation over his still form, and Lola watched as he was slowly enveloped in a dimly golden glow.

"He is safe," said Septimus. "The rest is up to him now."

In silence, they spent several minutes watching him rest peacefully. Then they descended the stairs.

"You said yourself you were going to need help to rescue Maria. You said you'd need other demon hunters. So, teach me to fight demons. I could be, like, you know, your apprentice."

"While this mad plan of invading the Netherworld did indeed begin as your idea, it is now my duty. I rarely change my mind, so you should be flattered to know I now concede you were right. I now accept I must do this for Justine even if there be no real chance of success. I shall take it on and see it through. And if you wish to see this mission carried out in your own natural lifetime, do not insist on coming along. Do you have any idea what is involved in fighting supernatural creatures?"

"No, I don't. That's why you have to teach me. Don't underestimate me. I'm pretty athletic, if I do say so myself. I was top in my Tsun Jo class, and I even paid for my own Bushido training until I was entitled to wear the black belt."

"Impressive," said Septimus with a slight trace of mockery.

"And I'm not completely ignorant about fighting demons."

"Oh?"

"Yeah, well, I…"

Lola's voice dropped to a mumble.

"I am sorry. I did not hear. What did you say?"

"I said I learned a thing or two about demons from, uh…"

"Yes?"

"In high school I went through a serious phase of, um, playing video games."

"Game playing?"

"Yeah, and I know what you're going to say next."

"And what is that?"

"You're going to say that hunting real demons is not a game."

"Yes, that is precisely what I was going to say."

141

"And you want to know how I knew you were going to say that?"

"Very well."

"Because that's what an avatar in the video game says."

Septimus could not contain his amusement. "I have nothing but admiration for your good intentions, but a bit of physical training and game playing will not be sufficient preparation for the supernatural realms. You may remain here with your friend or I can send you back to your own home, but any other choice is absolutely out of the question."

"Humor me, Tim."

"I have asked you not to call me that."

"This is all I ask. Just show me some of the things I would need to know. Let me show you my stuff. Give me a fair chance. If, after that, you still think it's a bad idea, I'll give up and not argue. But just give me a chance. That's all I ask. Just a chance."

Septimus sighed heavily.

"Yes, I suppose that could be the most effective way of convincing you. You have to agree, however. If and when I tell you this is beyond your mortal capabilities, you must accept my judgment without qualification or protest. Do you understand?"

"Understood. All I want is a shot."

"Very well. This will not take long."

He extended his hand. Lola was startled by a bright flash of light. When her eyes refocused, Septimus held what appeared to be a long iron lance with intricate ornamentation on either end. He held it out to her, and she took it.

"This is the diabolusbane. It is the only instrument that, in the hands of a mortal, has any effect against a supernatural creature. It works by drawing on your own body's energy and is controlled by the trained concentration of the mind."

"Hey, that's not fair. How am I supposed to know how to do that? You have to teach me."

"That part cannot be taught. It has to be learned through experience with the Netherworld and from many years of practice.

Do you understand now why your proposal was futile from the beginning?"

Lola held the lance up in front of her.

"Just give me a clue. What am I supposed to do with it?"

"If you were an experienced wielder of the diabolusbane, you would be able to refract your energy through it and direct it at a target. Either you know how to do it or you do not."

Lola closed her eyes. She imagined energy flowing out of her and into the lance. She opened her eyes, then closed them again. She banished all other thoughts from her mind and attempted to imagine more vividly. She opened her eyes again. Septimus smiled wearily, and that made her angry. She shut her eyes tightly and imagined a lightning bolt striking the man in front of her. The picture in her head delighted her so much that she could feel her pulse racing from excitement. In her mind she saw multiple bolts of lightning strike him, one after another.

Her heart rate increased to the point of no longer being under her control. She could not calm herself and thought she must be having a panic attack—if not a heart attack. A violent shudder coursed through her body. Frightened, she threw the lance to the floor. Before it left her hand, however, an intensely bright ball of light formed and streaked from the lance in Septimus's direction. It struck him with such force that he was thrown several feet in the air before landing on the floor. A smell like gunpowder permeated the air.

He looked up at her with wide eyes and a dazed expression. When he finally spoke, his voice quivered.

"So, Lola, my young friend, it turns out this is not your first lifetime."

15
Sapphire

WARILY, SEPTIMUS FOUND his way to his feet and eyed Lola with apprehension.

"What kind of trickster are you? You have been deceiving me, Lola Blumquist. How did I not detect this before?"

"I honestly don't know how I did that. Just beginner's luck, I guess."

"That was no luck, and you are no beginner. That was fine-honed skill—though carelessly employed—and beyond the capability of most mortals. That skill must have lain dormant your entire brief life. It did not simply happen spontaneously. It must be inherited from a previous life. Do you truly have no memory of any other existence?"

"I swear. I have never been—and never wanted to be—anyone except me, Lola Blumquist from Ballard. Okay, when I was a kid, I sometimes fantasized that I was a Viking warrior princess, but that was just playing. At least I thought it was. Hey, do you think I could have once really been a Viking warrior princess?"

As she rambled, Septimus drew near and stared deeply into her eyes.

"Who are you really, Lola Blumquist?" he mused.

"So, does this mean that I can be your apprentice after all?"

"One thing at a time. We have a mystery to solve. We must find out who you really are—or were. If you have no past-life memories, then what about dreams? Do you ever have extremely vivid dreams that make no sense to you? Dreams in which you are a different person?"

144

"Well, I have had some pretty strange dreams in my time all right, but I usually don't remember them. As far as I can remember, when I'm having them, I've always been me."

"I am going to try something. With luck I may be able to free your occluded memories. Remain perfectly still and look into my eyes."

Lola did as she was told. The sudden prospect of learning something new and unexpected about herself made her nervous, but she was also intensely curious. The irises in Septimus's eyes appeared to grow and draw near until they passed through her own eyes. She could actually feel him rummage around in her thoughts. She experienced random childhood memories. It embarrassed her that the demon hunter might be experiencing them along with her. She did not like the helpless feeling that had overcome her. She wanted to tell him to stop, to get out of her head, but she was unable to speak.

Finally, he looked away, and she began to feel normal again.

"So," she asked apprehensively, "did you find anything?"

"No. Do you remember anything more than before?"

"I remember my whole life. I remember that I was born in Ballard, and I remember growing up there and never living anywhere else. I remember every day I went to school. I remember the day my parents died."

"You need to remember more."

His frustration was palpable.

"The memories are either buried too deep or else..."

"Or else?"

"I do not know. It is unusual that your ability to wield the diabolusbane would pass from one incarnation to the next without being accompanied by some memories. It is as though something supernatural is at work in your mind."

"Or maybe I just never lived before. I mean, I don't feel like I've ever lived before. Couldn't I just have been born with some natural talent for using this thing of yours? Maybe I just have a gift."

"No one is born with a gift like that. No, you definitely lived before, and you were almost certainly a demon hunter."

"That is so weird. I wonder what my name was. I just hope it wasn't Buffy."

"I seriously doubt your name was Buffy. In our attempts to solve this mystery, there is something you should probably bear in mind."

"What's that?"

"In your former life, you could have been anybody. You were probably nothing as you are now, and…"

"And?"

"And I am afraid what I am about to say could make you angry."

"I'll be the judge of what makes me angry. Just say it."

"If you were a demon hunter—and taking into consideration your, ah, apparent romantic inclinations—well…"

"Yes?"

"There is every chance that, in your previous life, you were a man."

Lola considered this for a moment and said, "Yes, actually you are definitely right."

"So you agree you were probably a man?"

"No, I mean, you were right that what you said made me angry. Very angry. I'm a woman, and I know I've always been a woman. For my whole life and in any other lives I may have had. There is no doubt in my mind. One of the first things I ever told Maria was that I hated that song where Lola turns out to be a man."

"Yes, you feel that way now, but in your previous life, you may have felt just as strongly that you could never be a woman."

"You don't know that. You don't know anything about me. You and I only met, like, five minutes ago. On your time scale, that's probably only one nanosecond ago. Don't pretend to know me better than I know myself."

"You are, of course, right. I was presumptuous. I apologize."

"So, let's get back to the important thing. Are you going to train me now or what?"

"Well, in light of this new information, your proposal no longer appears completely insane. Yes, let us proceed with some education and see how it goes. Even if your memory is blocked, your skills and powers do not seem to be."

Lola could not stop herself from an impulsive hop and a cry of "Yippee!"

"Yippee, indeed," said Septimus dourly.

"This is exciting. I feel like I'm, well, I guess The Chosen One."

"Chosen? Chosen by whom? Certainly not chosen by me."

"This can't be a coincidence. Maybe my coming was foretold by some prophecy or something?"

"Prophecy? I am confused. I seem to recall that you are an atheist."

"Well, yeah, that's true. I was. I mean, I am. But I might reconsider my belief system if it means I'm The Chosen One. If I know now that I'm someone really special."

"Yes, well, that is really the point of organized religions—and political parties, for that matter—to make the believer feel 'really special.' I can assure you, though, you will not feel particularly special when your heart is consumed by the ice-cold dread of a demon's presence—or the fiery incandescence of its unholy power in your mind. Consider that carefully, and tell me, whether you are serious and still insistent on being tested for a suicide mission in the Netherworld. Because, if not, you can save us both a great deal of time and trouble."

"Oh, I'm still up for it all right. And you need to understand something from the get-go. I am doing this to bring Maria back. And I'm bringing her back for me, not for you."

"That will be her choice. Now that she has returned to the Netherworld, she will by now have most definitely recovered all her memories—just as you surely will. When we see her again, she will be the one to tell us what she decides."

"That's right, and I think she will be more than happy to go on being Maria. I never believed she was this Justine person anyway."

"There is really no point in having this discussion since the overwhelming likelihood is that the mission will fail spectacularly and you will die a horrible death while I am imprisoned in the Netherworld for all eternity."

Lola's enthusiasm waned.

"You know, you really need to work on your motivational skills, Tim. No one is going to want to follow you into hell after a speech like that."

"And one would be right."

The demon hunter was as good as his word. For the next several days, he instructed her in the uses and powers of the diabolusbane. He also had her demonstrate her martial arts skills and then instructed her on the usefulness of certain maneuvers for confronting a supernatural presence directing its energy toward her.

For the first few hours, her enthusiasm was high—especially after Septimus conjured her a black, form-fitting catsuit. She was surprised to find it was much more comfortable than the loose-fitting karategi she had worn for her Tsun Jo class. It was light and flexible and never made her sweat, no matter how hard she exercised. Despite the thinness of the material, it was virtually impermeable. Septimus assured her no earthly blade or arrow would be able to pierce it.

"How do you do it?"

"Do what?"

"How do you make clothing and coffee and food appear out of nowhere? I mean, that's impossible stuff. If you can make things appear out of nowhere, then there must not be anything you can't do. I still don't understand why you can't just snap your fingers and bring Maria back."

"Everything is mysterious when we do not understand it."

"But for example, this outfit you made me. Where did it come from? How was it made?"

"It is complicated to explain."

"I'm not stupid, you know. I have a bachelor of arts degree from the University of Washington."

"I do not question your intelligence. I simply acknowledge the difficulty of comprehending information entirely outside of one's own lived experience. You must understand the world you think you see is nothing more than a collection of images, sounds, smells, tastes, and sensations that your brain has generated in reaction to outside stimuli. Once you understand that—I mean well and truly understand that—then you are on the path to being an actor in the universe's reality rather than a mere receiver through your limited human senses."

"Okay, now you're getting a little deep. I still don't understand how you make things appear out of nowhere."

"Very well. I have an alternate explanation that may work better for you."

"Okay."

"It is magic."

"Yep, that works for me."

"Good. Now let us return to the task at hand."

Lola found Septimus relentless as a teacher. He insisted on beginning the lessons each morning before sunrise and continuing until late into the evening. She came to feel trapped in a constant state of exhaustion.

Much of the training was not unlike her experience in martial arts, but Septimus showed her techniques different from anything she had ever known before. He said she needed to be prepared for opponents much larger and stronger than her—and with abilities beyond any human. He conjured frightening hallucinations of phantom demons that she was obliged to fight. The illusions were frighteningly realistic, and she found there was no point reminding herself none of it was real. Her body's and mind's natural reactions were no different than if these images had actually been real. The apparitions came at her tenaciously and incessantly. The punishing pace wore her down.

"I need a break!" she cried as she collapsed to the ground.

"I assure you," said Septimus, "the Fiend's hellions will not withdraw politely and give you respite simply because you say you are a bit fatigued."

"You think I don't know that? When the time comes, I'll be ready, but right now I'm burnt out. I mean, it's not like this is real. It's just training. Cut me some slack."

"The legions of the Netherworld will not..."

"Yeah, yeah, I know. The legions of the Netherworld won't cut me any slack." She forced herself to stand and then said, "Okay, start up the magic sparring partners again."

Pain coursed through her body as she compelled herself to continue in spite of the agony. In her mind, she promised herself that, once she had proved to Septimus she could get through this particular day, she would quit and go back to her life in Seattle. She would make herself forget that any of this had happened.

She then thought of Maria and imagined what she must be going through in the Netherworld. She thought of Kyle, lying helplessly upstairs. As much as she hated it, she knew she had no choice but to keep going and do the best she could.

Though time had dragged the first two days, her persistence was rewarded. On the third day, while the work was no less taxing, she found it easier going. Moreover, she felt better about herself. For the first time in her life, she had a goal in front of her that really mattered and was worth working toward.

She began the fourth day full of confidence but was disappointed to find herself once again tiring of the repetition and constant physical exertion. She realized there would be no magic breakthrough moment—just slow and uneven progress. At least, however, she now knew what success looked like, and she could see it slowly getting closer.

In the evening, as she and Septimus ate their spartan supper, she peppered him with more questions.

"So, you have all the answers, don't you?"

"Answers? Answers to what?"

"You know, everything. I mean, after all the years you have lived and all the experiences you have had, you know firsthand what the rest of us can only wonder about."

"I am not certain I follow you."

"You are familiar with the supernatural. You know, for example, whether or not God exists."

"As do you—at least according to what you have said."

"Yeah, yeah, I know. I said I was an atheist, but that was just my opinion. It wasn't like I actually knew definitively that God doesn't exist. That was just what seemed like the truth to me. It wasn't like I could prove it one way or the other."

"So you have discovered the paradox of atheism."

"Paradox? What paradox?"

"It takes as much blind faith to disbelieve in God as it does to believe in God. In any event, you should more properly refer to yourself as an agnostic."

"Whatever. The point is that, like everybody else, I'm just guessing at these things. You actually know. You have talked to the devil himself or at least one of his assistants. You know what's out there, what the truth is. I mean, you can tell me, for example, whether Jesus is real. What about Buddha? Or Mohammed? Can they all be real? Is everything in the Bible true? What about other holy books?"

"Do you remember what I said the other day about our senses and the limited way we perceive reality?"

"Yeah."

"Did you grasp the implication of what I explained to you?"

"I don't know. Maybe. Kind of."

"When you speak of God, you are speaking of absolute truth. If our only grasp of reality is through such limited senses as we have, what hope have we of understanding absolute truth? Asking whether God exists is, in the end, pointless. The real question is, do *you* exist?"

"That's a silly question. Of course, I exist."

"How do you know?"

"Because I couldn't even ask the question if I didn't exist."

"Exactly. And could the world, the universe, this reality exist if you did not exist?"

"Yeah, I suppose."

"How?"

"Well, everything would be here except for me. It would all go on without me?"

"How do you know?"

"I don't know. I mean I wouldn't know. I wouldn't be here."

"So I ask you again. If your only evidence of the existence of the universe is your own perception of the universe, how could you say it exists if you did not exist to perceive it?"

"You're just playing mind games with me. There's no answer to that."

"And so you begin to understand. If you are looking for proof of what you call God, you need look no further than your own existence. When people argue over the existence of God, they really argue over their own existence, and that is pointless. It is the one question that answers itself. People's time would be better spent arguing over the *nature* of God."

"Okay, this is getting kind of deep, and I'm tired."

"Yes, I suggest you sleep while you can. Another day will be here soon enough."

That night Lola had a strange dream. Since she did not usually remember her dreams, she was surprised it still played in her mind the next morning. In the dream, she had stood on a high hill, holding the diabolusbane and surveying a fantastic landscape. It was entirely alien, although in the dream she seemed to be familiar with it. A rugged desert wasteland under a dark sky was illuminated by frequent lightning strikes on the horizon. Smoke rose from distant mountaintops. Standing there, she was filled with dread. Something terrible was coming for her. Something dark and evil.

Lola shivered at the memory of it and did her best to put it out of her mind.

Before beginning the usual instruction and exercises, Septimus said, "I must compliment you."

"Really? Compliment me on what?"

"Do you see no difference between your first day of training and yesterday?"

Lola thought about it and realized what he meant. At some point during the previous few days—she could not pinpoint precisely when—something had changed. The constant struggle to merely keep going had gradually become a routine that she embraced and accepted as second nature. The work was still hard, but she was no longer discouraged.

"Thank you for saying that. Maybe you're not such a bad teacher after all."

"And now you need to choose a sobriquet."

"A what?"

"A *nom de guerre.* Something for me to call you after we leave this island."

"Why? Can't you just call me Lola?"

"As I have told you, names have great power. Anywhere in the vicinity of the Netherworld, you must never utter your own name or mine. That would risk ceding power to the demon. This is very important. In fact, it is so important that a demon hunter trains himself to avoid, to the extent possible, even thinking his own name. Consequently, he never shares his name with another demon hunter."

"But *I* know your real name."

"Yes, you do, and you must keep it secret at all costs. I never dreamed you might ever become a demon hunter. Now I must trust you not to reveal it to anyone else we might meet. As for your own *nom de guerre,* take some time during the day to ponder what name *you* wish to use."

Lola thought briefly and said, "Sapphire."

Septimus was impressed.

"Well, that did not take long. And not a bad choice at all. As a gem, the sapphire is quite durable and has excellent luster. Its toughness is impressive in that it does not break easily. Tell me, how did you arrive at that name so readily?"

"It's, um…"

Lola mumbled something.

"I am sorry. I did not hear."

"It's, well, it's…"

"Yes?"

"It was my supermodel name," said Lola, embarrassed.

"Your what?"

"When I was a little girl, I used to dream that I would grow up to be a supermodel. That was the professional name I chose for myself."

"Yes, well, I see."

"Hey, don't judge me. I was just a little kid."

"I do not judge. Regardless of its origin, it is a perfectly functional name for an apprentice demon hunter. I shall henceforth call you Sapphire."

"So what should I call you? What's your demon hunter name?"

"I long ago chose a name from Greek mythology, but I shall wait to share it with you."

On the sixth morning, Lola was distracted.

"Clearly," said Septimus, "there is something on your mind, and it is affecting your performance. Tell me."

"I was thinking about what you said the other day, about maybe I was a man in a previous life."

"We do not know that. I should not have said anything, as it obviously upset you."

"Are there no women demon hunters?"

"My knowledge on the matter is not infinite, but given the span of my life, I would have known—or at least heard of—most of my kind. Based on my experience, the large majority of them have been men."

"But not all of them?"

"No, not all."

"Because I was wondering. You were so hesitant to train me until you found out I could use the diabolusbane. Was it because I'm a woman?"

"It was because, as far as I knew at the time, you were young and inexperienced. I did not think you understood the danger of what you wanted to do. I am still not certain that you do. But if I am honest, there may have been another reason. You are not the first woman I have trained in the mystical arts. And that experience did not end well. Indeed, to this day I wonder if I did not make a huge mistake in taking her on."

"Really? Who was she?"

"You will find out. Indeed, with any luck you will meet her tomorrow."

16
Orpheus

"TOMORROW? REALLY? Is she coming here?"

"No. We must go find her. Normally, finding a demon hunter is quite difficult, and she will not want to be found. She is skilled at avoiding detection, but as I said, I trained her, so I have something of an advantage in this situation."

For a moment Septimus was lost in his thoughts. "Anyway, enough about that. Let us make the most of what remains of this day."

They continued the training for several more hours. As the afternoon wore on, they stopped to rest.

"I have prepared you as best I can," said Septimus, "but there is simply not enough time. What you have learned from me in addition to your own inherited abilities will have to suffice. This will all end in doom anyway."

"Hey, Tim, we've talked about this. You really need to stop with the negative talk. It doesn't help."

"Very well. Let us continue for another hour or two. Then get a good night's rest and be prepared to travel in the morning. First, however, I have something for you."

"A present? For me? Aw, you shouldn't have."

As if out of thin air, he produced a curved blade with an ornate handle. Lola was not certain if it was a long knife or a short sword.

"Carry this with you always. You must be ready to protect yourself at all times."

"Am I going to use this to fight demons?"

"No, it is for something nearly as bad—people."

"People? What people would I need to fight with this?"

"Not all our adversaries will be of the supernatural kind. I am confident your skills are sufficient to ward off any mortal threat, and this weapon will augment your advantage."

"It is kind of awkward, isn't it, you know, to be carrying around?"

"That will not be a problem. You will find it fits easily into your pocket."

"This suit doesn't have any pockets."

"It will when you need one."

"But it's so big. I'm liable to stab myself with it if I have it on me all the time."

"Trust me, that will not happen."

Lola placed the blade at her side and was amazed when it melted into the fabric of her suit. When she reached for it, it was in her hand again.

"This is cool. Do I need to give it a name?"

"Why would you need to give it a name?"

"I don't know. I just have trouble keeping track of all the ground rules."

"Come. We shall spend the rest of our time instructing you in the use of your weapon."

When Septimus had mentioned travel, Lola presumed he would produce a boat or maybe even a light airplane, so what actually happened was unexpected. When the time came to depart, he asked her if she was ready to leave and, when she said yes, simply put an arm around her, covered her eyes with his hand, and muttered a few unintelligible words. Her bones were chilled by a cold breeze, and she had a momentary dizzying sensation of floating.

A moment later he removed his hand from her eyes, and she looked around in astonishment. They were standing on a street in a large city.

"Just like that?" she gasped. "That's all you have to do to take us to a whole other place? I was right. You really are a wizard."

"As it happens, this is quite near the place where I first met the Suquamish, though it has certainly changed a great deal since."

"Wait," said Lola. "I know where we are. This is Vancouver. You took me to Canada. We're in Gastown."

"There is no time to waste. Do you see that establishment across the street?" he asked, pointing to a nineteenth-century red-brick building.

"The pub? Yeah."

"She is inside, and this will be a bit tricky. You see, if we do not surprise her, she will be gone in an instant, and it could take a very long time to locate her again. On the other hand, if we do surprise her, things could turn violent."

"So what do we do?"

"I propose you go in alone and engage her in conversation."

"By myself? I thought you said she was dangerous."

"You need not worry. She will not find you threatening. She will be off guard. You must distract her."

"What do I say to her?"

"You will think of something. I believe this is what you are good at. Make small talk. You know. Do a bit of flirting."

"Flirting? Wait a minute, I think you may have gotten the wrong impression about me."

"This is no time to act coy. Just put her at ease. Once I see that she is at ease with you, I will appear. With luck this will go well and there will be no incident."

"I'm getting a bad feeling about this, Tim. Maybe you should just go in first."

"Trust me."

"My natural instinct is to never trust anybody who says, 'Trust me.'"

"Go."

"How will I know her?"

"You will know her."

Lola took a deep breath, crossed the street, and entered the pub. As she looked around, she did her best not to appear nervous. How did Septimus expect her to recognize someone she had never met, someone who had not even been described to her?

Her gaze settled on a woman sitting by herself at a small corner table. She had jet black hair tied tightly behind her head in a long ponytail. Narrow, well-defined eyebrows made semi-circles above black, almond-shaped eyes. Poring intently over a book, she took a sip of white wine from a small, tall-stemmed glass. Lola knew immediately this was the one she was meant to find.

At the same instant Lola spotted her, the woman's eyes jerked in Lola's direction and did not waver. Self-consciously, Lola looked away and approached the bar counter. She was about to order a beer when it occurred to her she had no Canadian money—or any money for that matter. She wondered if perhaps Septimus had thought to put money in an invisible pocket that would magically appear when she needed it. She put her hand on her hip and was horrified to see her long knife. She hurriedly put it away again, looking around nervously to see if anyone had noticed. To her relief, she saw no reaction.

She felt completely ill-at-ease approaching the woman, but she reminded herself that chatting up people in bars was actually something she was good at. She remembered how she had walked right up to Maria and Sinéad in the U District and joined them in conversation with no problem whatsoever. She turned and walked toward the woman at the corner table.

The woman stared at her. Lola flashed her friendliest smile. The woman's impassive face did not change. Lola did her best to maintain her smile and make it sincere. The woman's face still did not change. The relentlessness of her stare was a bit unnerving.

"Hello," said Lola in her warmest, most ingratiating voice.

She had a reasonable story all worked out that would explain why she, a complete stranger, was approaching a woman in a pub in Gastown. She had even worked out the kind of details that would make the story sound convincing. She was confident she could pull this off.

The woman sprang to her feet. "Damn! He's here, isn't he? Damn!"

She charged Lola and pushed her to the floor. Scrambling to her feet, Lola turned to see Septimus standing in the doorway, blocking the exit. Everyone in the pub looked on in astonishment as the woman extended her arms and shot a burst of bright energy in the demon hunter's direction.

He wobbled but did not fall. "Impressive. You've learned a new trick since we last met."

"Out of the way. I'm warning you."

"We need to talk."

"You need to move."

"Five minutes. That is all I ask."

"So you found another sucker," she said, nodding in Lola's direction.

"I swore I would never take on another apprentice, but this is different."

"Get away from him while you can," she said to Lola. "Do not believe any of his lies. He is not to be trusted."

"Five minutes. Please. You know how difficult this is for me. Something has happened."

"I don't want to hear it!"

She thrust another bolt of energy toward him, and this time its force made him drop to one knee.

The bartender carefully reached for his telephone, but as Septimus stood up, he caused it to fly from the barman's hand. Then in an instant, demon hunter was across the room and pinning the woman against the wall.

"There is no need to fight," he said.

"You're right," she replied as she flung him backward, sending him sprawling.

She leapt into the air and came down on him with the full force of her body. Lola knew she should do something but did not know what. The woman shot another burst of light from her hands, this time focusing the energy on the demon hunter's neck. He appeared unable or unwilling to resist.

"Stop it!" yelled Lola, grabbing at her and pulling her away. "Just listen to him. Just give him his five minutes."

She looked at Lola coldly.

"You touched me. No one touches me."

"You were hurting him."

"There is no way I can hurt him—unless he wants me to. I don't know what he has told you, but believe me, I know him much better than you, and he is a snake. You need to get away from him before it's too late."

"I found her, Izanami," said the demon hunter, struggling to get his voice back. "I found Justine."

"Still on about your Justine, eh? I thought you said she was gone forever."

"I believed she was. I do not know how she escaped, but I have seen her. She was in my house on the island. She was there in front of me, just as you are now."

"So, what's the problem then?"

"I lost her again. I was foolish. I made a terrible mistake and lost her all over again."

"What did I tell you?" she said to Lola. "He is bad news. It never ends well for anyone who crosses his path. Why are you still here?"

"Hear me out, Izanami."

"What is there to hear? It sounds as though nothing has changed. You say you found and then lost her again. It sounds to me as though nothing is different than it was before."

"It is different. I am going after her. I am going to get her back."

"What? You've completely lost it, old man."

Lola took note of the nervous witnesses and saw a couple of them recording the encounter on their phones and one or two others hurriedly typing.

"Uh, guys? Do you think we should take this somewhere else? I think you're freaking out the customers."

Septimus looked to Izanami for a response.

"Five minutes," she said reluctantly. "Not a second more, understand?"

"Thank you," he said with relief. "Take my hands, the two of you."

Lola felt the same strange sensation as before. When she got her bearings, the three of them were now on the side of a high mountain with a spectacular view of the city below. The wind was freezing on her face and hands, although her suit kept her body surprisingly warm.

"This is fantastic," said Lola. "Where are we?"

"Grouse Mountain," said Izanami impatiently. "Talk, Orpheus. The clock is ticking."

"Orpheus?"

"My *nom de guerre*," explained Septimus.

"Do you want to know *my* demon hunter name?" Lola asked Izanami.

"No. We're wasting time. What's this nonsense about going after Justine? I thought that was impossible."

"It is. I mean, yes, it probably is, but I am going to try anyway. I thought it was impossible for her to escape the Netherworld, and yet she did. Obviously, my understanding of these things is not infallible. If she was able to escape once, then it is theoretically possible for her to escape again. I am going to make certain she has the opportunity."

"And what does any of this have to do with me?" said Izanami, looking at her watch.

"You know I cannot do this alone."

"I know you cannot do it—full stop. Besides, you are not alone. You have her."

"She has had all of six days' training."

"Where did you find her anyway?"

"She washed up on my island. She is a mystery. She was able to wield the diabolusbane on her first attempt."

Izanami took a good look at Lola—and with something akin to respect.

"So what's your story anyway?"

"I… I don't really have a story. I'm just a girl from Seattle. My name's…"

"No names," interrupted Septimus.

"Sorry. For the record, you know, the woman he thought was Justine, well, I don't actually believe she was Justine. She was my friend Maria Murphy from Ireland, and I love her. I miss her so much, and that's why I am going with, uh, Orpheus on this rescue mission. And I wish you would come with us because we could really use the help."

"What's in it for me?"

"I don't know," said Lola. "Nothing, I guess. Unless it's the satisfaction of knowing you are doing something good for someone else. I mean, you're a demon hunter, aren't you? What's in it for you any other time you fight demons?"

"I fight demons because they invade my world. Invading their world is a whole other matter."

"But they are holding one of us prisoner. Maria is in their world, and she should be in this world. Isn't that more or less the same thing?"

"No, it's not the same thing. When I fight them here, I actually have some reasonable chance of surviving. Going into their domain is just plain suicide."

"So, do you want to live forever?" asked Lola.

"Well, yes."

"This guy's living forever," said Lola, pointing at Septimus, "and it hasn't made him happy. He says he's miserable. He would be happy to die. Isn't that right, uh, Orpheus?"

The demon hunter was amused.

"She has a point. Immortality is overrated."

"That's fine for you, but some of us are still living out our natural lifespans."

"Natural? How old are you now, Izanami? Eighty? Ninety?"

Lola's jaw dropped. "He's kidding, right?"

Izanami had every appearance of being in her twenties if not a teenager.

"Contact with the Netherworld," she said by way of explanation, "tends to slow down one's aging process. It is one of the few benefits of this way of life. If I ever get to know you better, I will show you my scars to illustrate the downside."

"Well," said Septimus, "if you value your precious life so much, just think how much this little jaunt will add to your years. You might actually reach my age."

"I think your five minutes are up."

"What's the matter, Izanami? Are you afraid? Not up to the challenge?"

"Don't waste your feeble attempts at psychology on me, Orpheus. Now, are you going to take me back to Gastown or are you going to make me walk?"

"Can't you transport yourself to places like he can?" asked Lola.

"No. Can you?"

"I could teach you that, Izanami," said Septimus. "I am sure, after a journey to the Netherworld, I could coax that power out of you. You would be as nearly powerful as I."

"So you're really going to make me walk all the way back?"

"I have not managed to tempt you? Well, here is something that may convince you when nothing else does. If you come with us, there is every chance you could see me die. Or at least burn in hell for eternity. How about that?"

"Now that sounds good. Except I would be burning along with you. No thanks."

"So that is it then?"

"That's it."

"Fair enough. You cannot blame me for asking."

"Yes, I can."

"Thank you for hearing me out anyway. Now I need to ask someone else, who might be more inclined. Do you have any idea where I might find Koschei?"

"Koschei?"

"Yes. You remember him, don't you?"

"Koschei won't help you."

"There is no way to know until I ask."

"You shouldn't even ask him. I don't know why he would help you."

"He is not nearly as preoccupied with his own safety as you are. I have always admired his nihilistic streak. Have you seen him lately?"

"No, of course not. Not since that time in the Nullarbor. The time Ragnar was pierced through the heart by a haladie made of

Damascus steel. God, that was a horrible way to die. No, I don't think Koschei will help you."

"So you have no idea where I should look?"

"Look, there is no way I am going on this crazy quest of yours, but I might tag along for a while, you know, just to help you find Koschei. I wouldn't mind seeing him again. Ragnar and I used to have great drinking sessions, and we would place bets with each other on what Koschei's real name was. And how old he was. God, I miss Ragnar. He was a lot of fun."

"So, it is agreed. You will join us—at least until we find Koschei."

"Okay, but don't get any funny ideas that you will be able to convince me to go all the way to the end with you. I may be crazy, but I am not certifiably insane."

"Thank you," said Lola gratefully.

Izanami looked her up and down again.

"So, white-haired girl, what should I call you?"

"Oh, my demon hunter name is Sapphire."

"Sapphire, eh? That's a pretty name."

"Why, thank you. I…"

"I hate pretty names."

17
Izanami

"COME BACK to my island, Izanami," said Septimus. "We shall spend the night there while we work on tracking down Koschei. He may not be as easy to find as you were."

"Your island? Honestly? You've never invited me there before, Orpheus. Are we going to become friends now? And was I really that easy to find? I guess I need to do a better job at not being found. My carelessness is going to get me killed one of these days."

"With luck, though, not before we succeed in our quest."

The three joined hands and were quickly back at Riesgado Island. Lola was still not accustomed to this easy but unsettling way of traveling. For a few moments she thought she might get sick. Even Izanami, who Lola imagined would be well used to such things, seemed a bit dazed.

"Will you really teach me how to teleport, Orpheus?"

"Of course, just as soon as we return from the Netherworld with Justine."

"So never then. I should have known."

As they walked into the house, Izanami said, "So this is your home. I'm flattered to finally be invited."

"You really must excuse the untidiness," said Septimus. "I am afraid I had to let the housekeeper go."

"Frankly," said Lola quietly to Izanami, "she wasn't really much of a housekeeper."

Later, as they had their supper, Lola said, "Izanami is such a cool name. Where does it come from?"

"She is the Japanese goddess of creation and death."

"Are you Japanese?"

"I'm Canadian. My parents were Japanese. They have been dead a long time now."

"Well, I suppose that's to be expected," said Lola, "when you are... how old are you again?"

"I don't like to talk about my age."

"My parents are dead too, and I'm a lot younger than you."

"Well, well, so we are all orphans here. How sad. Do you have anything to drink, Orpheus?"

"You know my feelings about that, Izanami."

The demon hunter closed his eyes and went silent. He was now oblivious to the other two.

"Ah, yes. Once a Puritan, always a Puritan. Now I remember why I was in no hurry to see him again."

"Why are you so mad at Orpheus?" asked Lola. "What did he do to make you so hostile?"

"I don't really want to talk about it. He always said that I was the problem, that I couldn't get along with him because of some unresolved issues with my father. Can you believe that? Where does a seventeenth-century Puritan get off lecturing me about daddy issues? I had a great relationship with my father. Orpheus was the problem. He was never satisfied until he had complete control over me. He and I were always a bad combination. It makes me wonder what I'm doing back here now."

"Maybe you and he can talk through your problems with each other. I mean, you're both old enough, you should be able to get past it."

"You sound like someone who's been to college," said Izanami somewhat sarcastically. "Did you major in psychology or something?"

"Well, I do have a BA from U-Dub. I didn't major in psych, but I did take a psychology course for one quarter. Maybe I could help the two of you work through your issues."

"You're kidding, right? Hey, Orpheus, are you sure we can't have something to drink?"

He appeared to be in a trance.

"He could conjure up a bottle of vodka for us with a snap of his fingers, you know," said Izanami wistfully.

"I do not snap my fingers," said Septimus, suddenly breaking his silence. "You are thinking of stage magicians. While you two have been prattling, I have been concentrating my consciousness on finding Koschei. I think we should look for him in London."

"London is a very big city, Orpheus," said Izanami. "We are hardly going to run into him by strolling around Trafalgar Square."

"No, but if we get within a few miles of him, I may be able to locate him more precisely."

"I think you just want to go back to your old stomping ground."

"Believe me, I have no particular desire to return to England. The very thought disheartens me."

"Are you sure that Koschei has not gone back to Russia?" said Izanami. "That would make more sense to me."

"Perhaps, but I do not think so. No, London is more his style now."

"So, how come you want to see this Co-Skay so much?" Lola asked Izanami. "Were you and he an item or something?"

"An item? Do you mean, were we lovers? Ha. I think Koschei was only ever in love with himself. The first time I met him, I thought he was a woman. God, he was beautiful. Come to think of it, maybe he was a woman at one time. Who knows? I guess that's part of the mystery. Anyway, he sure knew how to drink—unlike certain other people." She looked pointedly at Septimus.

"I think we should go to sleep now," said Septimus, rising. "I shall want to be well-rested for my long-deferred return to perfidious Albion."

As he left the room, Lola said, "I'm going upstairs to sit with Kyle for a while before I turn in."

"What?" whispered Izanami to her with concern. "There's someone else here? How did I not sense it?"

"He's my friend," said Lola. "Sep... he put him under some kind of spell to protect him."

"Who did?"

"Orpheus."

"You started to call him something else."

"Did I?"

Izanami's jaw dropped.

"Do you know Orpheus's real name?"

"I don't know. Maybe."

"How do you know his real name? Why would he tell you that?"

"I guess I'm just special. Anyway, I'm sworn to secrecy."

"Tell me."

"No."

"Come on, tell me."

"I can't. It's a rule."

"It's just Orpheus's rule. It's a stupid rule."

"It's still a rule."

"Show me your friend."

Izanami followed Lola up the stairs to the room where Kyle lay still as death on the bed. The dull golden glow continued to shimmer faintly.

"My," said the Canadian. "He is nice-looking, isn't he?"

"Is he? I suppose that's a matter of opinion."

"What happened to him?"

"He drowned. Orpheus saved him and gave him most of his life back, but then he had to take some of it back again. Now poor Kyle needs time to recover."

"That's Orpheus, all right. Giving you something and then taking it back again. And you believed everything he told you?"

"Yeah, I guess so. It's not like I have a way to fact-check him about any of this stuff."

It bothered Lola to see Izanami run a hand through Kyle's hair. "I don't know if you should be touching him."

"Yes, he's very nice-looking. You know what this is, don't you?"

"What?"

"He's Sleeping Beauty, and you're his Prince Charming."

"No, not really. He will wake up when he's ready. He doesn't need someone to kiss him."

"Are you sure?" said the Canadian, leaning close to him. "I would be willing to kiss him to see if it wakes him up."

"Let's go. This isn't right. It's wrong to be here looking at him and talking about him when he's asleep and so helpless."

As they walked down the stairs, Izanami asked, "Are you sure he is going to wake up?"

"Orpheus said he would."

"You really need to be more skeptical."

"At this point, I don't have much of a choice."

"You always have a choice. You should never forget that. It's Orpheus and his manipulation that make you feel like you don't have a choice."

"All I care about is rescuing my friend Maria, and he's my only hope of doing that. So, for now, I choose to believe him."

"I hope you don't regret it. Everyone else has."

That night Lola had another disturbing dream. This time she was in an underground cavern completely engulfed in flames. In the distance she saw Maria bound to a large rock with heavy iron chains. Lola struggled to reach her, but she found it difficult to move. After much exertion, she was finally close enough to call out to her.

"Maria! It's me, Lola. I'll get you out of here."

The Irish girl looked at her with a strange expression on her face.

"I remember now," said Maria. "It has all come back to me. He was right. He was right about everything. I am Justine Browne of Menlough, and my one true love was Septimus Bridge. I was hanged as a witch, and now this is my fate. Go. Save yourself. I will burn here for all eternity. Flee while you can. Go!"

Lola woke with a start, her heart pounding. It had seemed so real. It upset her so much that she was afraid to go back to sleep.

Outside the wind howled. Another storm had blown in. She lay there for what seemed like hours unable to stop thinking about the dream. Then, seemingly only an instant later, she opened her eyes and saw the morning sunlight.

She joined the others for breakfast.

"Delicious coffee," said Izanami. "When did you start making coffee, Orpheus?"

"She insisted."

"She did, did she? You never made coffee for me. All the times we traveled together, you always made me drink your tea. Why is that?"

"I did not know it was important to you."

"And do you want to know *why* you didn't know?"

Lola could not stand to hear any more. "Will the two of you please stop bickering? It's getting on my nerves."

"She's right," said Septimus. "We have more important things to discuss. Did either of you dream last night?"

Lola bit her lip and said nothing. She did not feel like sharing her dream. She did not want to tell Septimus that her own dream seemed to confirm his own belief about Maria.

"I only had my usual dream," said Izanami. "The one where I see the blade piercing Ragnar's heart. I have that one nearly every night."

"Nothing else?" he asked, looking at the two of them. "Well, I had an extremely vivid dream, and in it I saw Koschei. He was in London."

"You saw that in a dream?" asked Izanami.

"Yes."

"You know what that means, don't you?"

"Indeed."

"What does it mean?" asked Lola.

"There are only two ways that knowledge could have come to me in that way. One is if Koschei himself had sent it to me."

"And that is impossible," said Izanami. "He would never do that. That is the last thing he would do. Certainly not after the way the two of you left things."

"That is true, and in any event, for him to do that now would be too much of a coincidence."

"Definitely," said Izanami.

"So what's the other explanation?" asked Lola.

"The only other way that information could have come to me," said Septimus, "would be through the Fiend's intervention. He has the power to influence my dreams."

"Couldn't it have just been a dream?" asked Lola. "I mean, do dreams *always* have to have some meaning or be some sort of message? People dream all the time, and it usually doesn't mean anything at all."

Septimus looked at her curiously. "You never mentioned whether *you* dreamt last night. Did you?"

"I... I don't think so. I mean, I don't remember. Not exactly anyway. It's hard to remember."

"If you had a dream—especially a particularly vivid one—you should tell me. It could well be significant."

"There's nothing to tell. All right? So why do you think the Fiend made you have that dream last night?"

"There can be only one reason."

"Yes," agreed Izanami. "Only one reason."

"Yes?" said Lola.

"He wants us to find Koschei," said Septimus.

"Why would he want that?"

"It is a trap."

"Yes," said Izanami. "Definitely a trap."

"So what do we do then?" asked Lola.

"There is only one thing we can do," said Septimus.

"I hope you're not going to say what I think you're about to say, Orpheus," said Izanami.

"We shall go to London. We shall find Koschei, and we shall march deliberately and forthrightly into the trap the Fiend has laid for us."

"That's what I was afraid you were going to say," said Izanami.

"Why would we do that?" asked Lola. "Why would we walk into something we know is a trap?"

"Because the Fiend will surely know that I know it is a trap. We have few options here, but walking heedlessly into the trap may be our only hope of having any element of surprise."

"More like disbelief you would be so stupid," said Izanami.

"If you have a better plan," said Septimus, "please do share it with me now."

For once the Canadian woman remained silent.

"So it is decided," said Septimus. "Let us make ready to depart for London."

"Hey," said Lola. "What do you mean 'decided'? I didn't see any vote."

"There's never a vote," said Izanami.

"There must be other options," said Lola.

"If so, I am still waiting to hear them," said Septimus.

"Just so you know, Orpheus, I will go as far as London with you. I will go to see Koschei, but after that, I am out of this. You two will be on your own then."

"We two and Koschei," said Septimus. "That will make three of us."

"Koschei will not join you. I concede he does not always have the best judgment, but he is not completely stupid either. He won't have any part of this."

"At least he is no coward."

"Really? Do you really think that will work on me?"

"Stop making excuses, Izanami. I am actually looking forward to being rid of you. Now, I must take some time to prepare. London is a long way to travel. Let us meet outside in an hour."

Lola went upstairs to say goodbye to Kyle. As she sat next to the bed, she looked at him and tried to work through all the doubts the Canadian woman had planted in her mind.

"I guess you have the easy part, Kyle," she said softly. "You just have to lie here and sleep, but I wouldn't trade places with you for anything. I'd rather be doing something—even if it's dangerous and foolish and suicidal—instead of lying there, not knowing what is going on. I know you can't hear me, but if you could, I would just want you to know that I think you're a really good guy. I'm sorry I wasn't a better friend to you when I had the chance. If things don't work out and I never see you again, well, I hope you have a really good life. I really do. Goodbye."

Lola joined Septimus and Izanami on the grassy area in front of Bridge House.

"It's a bit trickier getting all the way to London, as opposed to making the hop to Vancouver," Septimus explained to Lola. "We shall need to have some momentum to get started."

"What does that mean?"

"It means you have to trust him," said Izanami, "even when all your instincts say not to. It's something I've never gotten used to—and never will."

"Take my hands."

The demon hunter led the two women to the bluff's periphery, right up to the edge where they looked down and saw waves crashing into the rocks below. The wind was so strong that Lola feared losing her balance and tumbling over.

"She is right, you know," he said. "I am afraid you do have to trust me."

Then he walked right over the brink, taking the other two with him.

18
Koschei

THEIR PLUNGE through the air had caught Lola by surprise. She flailed in panic, then blacked out. When she woke, she lay on a sidewalk on a busy city street. Looking concerned, Izanami stood over her while Septimus knelt at her side.

"I am sorry about that," he said. "I never know the best way to prepare someone. In the end, the best preparation is no preparation."

It was nighttime, and Lola smelled diesel exhaust from a passing truck. It was followed by a red double-decker bus on the left-hand side of the street.

"You did it," said Lola. "This is London, isn't it?"

"Can you stand? We need to move away from here. We are drawing too much attention."

Passers-by had begun to stop and ask if they needed any assistance.

"The English are always so damned courteous," said Izanami, sounding annoyed and taking no care not to be heard. "They get on my nerves."

Septimus helped Lola to her feet, and the three of them made their way down the street slowly.

"This is Camden, isn't it?" said Izanami.

Lola stared at the funky shopfronts. She had never crossed the Atlantic before, and everything looked so different.

"Yes, Camden," said Septimus. "We need a strategy for approaching Koschei. I cannot sense him, but I know from the dream he will be close by."

"Maybe closer than you think," said Izanami staring upward. "Take a look at that, Orpheus."

Septimus and Lola followed the Canadian's gaze. Atop a five-story building was a billboard with the face of a young man with shoulder-length, straight, blond hair. He had extremely high cheek bones, and the photograph made his skin look exquisitely smooth— apart from a few very short black whiskers dotting his lower face. His cobalt blue eyes stared straight ahead, as if coveting something in the far distance.

"I don't believe it," said Izanami. Her tone was half-disgusted and half-amused. "He's turned himself into a freaking fashion model. How perfect."

"That's Koschei?" said Lola, her mouth agape. "He looks too pretty to fight demons."

"I always thought his *nom de guerre* should be Lucifer," said Septimus, unimpressed. "He always did fancy himself the light-bringing morning star."

"Does this make it easier to find him?" asked Lola. "Or harder?"

"Izanami, do you have one of those devices that tap into information stored somewhere? Everywhere I look people seem to be staring at them constantly."

"You mean, my phone? It's dead. When you ambushed me in Gastown, there wasn't quite enough time to go home and get my charger."

He looked at Lola.

"I lost mine when the boat sank," she said. "I don't think I had international roaming anyway."

"Let's wander around," said Izanami. "We might get lucky and find a late-night internet café, but you are going to have to generate some pound sterling."

They had no luck in Camden Town, but they eventually found a small, rather seedy 24-hour internet café after taking the Underground to Leicester Square. Izanami was annoyed when Septimus asked her to use her credit card to buy time on a computer.

"You're definitely reimbursing me for this," she grumbled as she searched the web. "And with interest."

"Now, this is *truly* magic," said Septimus, impressed by the quick results.

"Thank goodness for the online tabloid press," said Izanami. "Everything we need is here, including the name he uses for modeling and all the latest gossip about him. He calls himself Alexei Mikhailov and—can you believe this—he actually bought a castle in Sussex. Shall we go visit?"

"Yes," said Septimus. "Show me the location on the map. I shall do the rest."

The surly proprietor of the café dropped his jaw when they vanished in a flash of light.

They found themselves standing next to an imposing four-sided stone tower. Light emanated from two narrow windows above them. A much bigger rectangular window at ground level was dark.

"Is this it?" said Izanami, as they walked around to the large wooden door. "Somehow I thought it would be more impressive."

"Were you expecting Buckingham Palace?" said Septimus. "This is a renovated Norman castle. It was already old when I was a child. He—or a previous owner—must have gone to great trouble to install that large window."

"Do you think he answers his own door?" said Izanami. "Do you think he is even home?"

"We shall know soon enough," said Septimus, touching his temples with his fingertips. "If he is here, he is more than close enough to receive the message I am sending."

They waited silently for five minutes or so. Then they heard the sound of a latch. Very slowly the heavy wooden door opened inward. Lola was thrown to the ground by a sudden blast of light. The other two had moved deftly out of the way.

"Go away!"

"Koschei!" called Izanami. "It's us. Your friends."

Lola barely managed to roll out of the way of another blast of energy. Her training had finally kicked in.

"You are not my friends. Go away."

"Koschei," said Izanami. "don't be like that. I promise, you'll have a great laugh when you hear why we've come."

They waited several minutes to see what would happen next. Finally, Izanami said, "We're coming in now, okay?"

There was no response. Cautiously, the Canadian pushed the door open further. She stepped aside as another blast of energy rushed past her.

"Now you're just being childish. Let us in. For old time's sake."

"I do not want to see you. Things are different now. I have left that way of life behind me. Things are good now. Go away."

Despite the brusqueness of his words, Lola found the sound of his voice—British-sounding with just a hint of a Russian accent—smooth and melodic.

"Fifteen minutes," said Izanami. "That's all, and then we'll go. Fifteen minutes."

"That is how it always begins. Fifteen minutes. Ten minutes. Five minutes. Then before I know it, my life goes to hell—literally. No thank you. Go away."

"It is different this time. I swear. Wait until you hear what Orpheus has in mind. I promise you, this will probably be the last time you see him. He won't be back after this. Not if he really goes through with it."

"Why? What is he doing?"

"Let us in, old friend," said Septimus, "and I will tell you myself."

"What does any of this have to do with me?"

"Perhaps," said Septimus, "I merely want to say goodbye to an old comrade. As Izanami says, I shall probably not come back after this."

The door opened fully, and a slender yet imposing man stepped forth. He looked exactly like the billboard but more impressive because of his height. Lola judged him to be six-and-a-half feet tall. His light hair flowed around his shoulders. His eyes were even more piercing than in the photograph. Most amazing to her was his skin. They had not needed to airbrush his face at all, she thought to herself.

"I will regret this. I always do. Come in, but do not make yourselves too comfortable."

Izanami reached up and gave him a hug.

"It's so good to see you, *solnyshka.*"

"I regret ever trying to teach you Russian, Izanami."

"What's the deal with all of you?" asked Lola. "I have never seen so much passive-aggressive behavior in one group of people before."

"Who is this?" asked Koschei. "She sounds like a psychologist—and a mediocre one at that."

"She took psychology at Washington State," said Izanami.

"It was University of Washington. I'm Orpheus's new apprentice. My name is Sapphire."

"Sapphire? Really? I almost chose that as my modeling name. Come, everyone. We might as well have a drink. I will open a bottle of kvass."

"Now that is more like it," said Izanami happily.

Koschei filled glasses for everyone.

"*Za vstrechu!*" said the Russian.

"*Kanpai!*" said Izanami.

"*Skål!*" said Lola.

Septimus's glass sat untouched.

"So what is this all about? I do not mean to be inhospitable, but I have a photo shoot in the morning, and I need my beauty rest."

"Orpheus is no longer content to hunt demons in this world," said Izanami. "Now he is going after them in the Netherworld."

"What? Are you crazy, man? You may be immortal, but that is not the same thing as being invincible. You will never come back from there."

"I do not care about coming back. I only care about freeing the one person I have ever loved."

Koschei looked at Izanami. "Himself?"

"Justine," she said.

"Oh, yes. Her. But why now? That all happened centuries ago. I thought you decided a long time ago it was hopeless."

"I was wrong. Something happened. She escaped. If she could do it once, she could do it again. I have wasted too much time."

"So you will rescue her, even if it means you yourself do not come back?"

"I owe it to her."

"Well, good luck to you, my friend. And farewell. That did not even take fifteen minutes."

"You know I cannot do this alone."

"I know more than that. I know you cannot do it at all. No one can."

"I know you think it is impossible. Just as I thought it was impossible that she could escape—and I was wrong about that."

"As I said, good luck to you."

"You used to be braver, Koschei."

"Perhaps. And you used to be smarter."

The Russian turned to Izanami.

"Are you going along with this foolishness?"

"No. I told him the same as you."

"What about you?" he asked Lola.

"Yes, I'm going with him."

"Why on earth would you do that, pretty white-haired girl?"

"Because… because I don't believe it's Justine we are going to rescue. The woman we are going after is my friend Maria Murphy, and I love her and I would do anything for her. That's why."

Koschei laughed. "You need to get some things straight, Orpheus. Are you certain you are even going to rescue the right woman?"

"Sapphire and I agree on who we are rescuing. We only differ as to who she actually is."

Koschei laughed more heartily than before.

"This is the craziest thing I ever heard. I would nearly go along just to see how it all ends."

"You would be very welcome, my friend."

"I am sure I would be. You know, it might be worth it to finally see you meet the end you deserve. The only problem is that I might meet the end I myself do not deserve."

"That is what *I* said, Koschei," said Izanami. "But there is something else about it that tempts me."

"What is that?"

"How old are you?"

"You and I agreed a long time ago not to discuss age."

179

"I am making a point. Orpheus brought up an interesting aspect before. You know how, every time we get near the Netherworld, our lifespans get longer?"

"Yes."

"Well, he suggested, logically enough, if we were to penetrate all the way into the Netherworld, we might become virtually immortal—or at least add several centuries to our lives. Our other powers would probably be increased as well. He even said he would train me to teleport. I could sure have some fun with that ability."

Koschei took another sip of his drink and stroked his perfect chin.

"You know, I wouldn't mind adding a few years to my life. Do you know I actually found a gray hair the other day? And a few wrinkles around my eyes. It was devastating. But a longer lifespan would not be worth much if we are dead or trapped in the Netherworld forever. I have never heard of anyone going there and returning."

"You have now," said Septimus. "As I told you, Justine returned. And she will return again."

"Yes, but there seems to be some question whether it was actually Justine at all."

"It was her all right. Believe me. I knew her even if she did not know herself."

"I think the kvass is affecting my head. I am actually starting to be intrigued by this proposition, now that I see there could be something in it for me."

"It is very high-risk, Koschei," said Izanami.

"You know I always liked long odds."

"Are you seriously thinking about doing this?" she asked.

"If I am being honest, lately I have been getting a little bored. Sitting around waiting on photographers can get tedious—especially when compared to the thrill of a feverish struggle with a monster that wants to kill you. Besides, I do not enjoy all the attention as much as I once did. Sometimes I feel like a piece of meat. Nobody in the industry appreciates my intellect. They only want me to look right. It drains your soul being a sex object all the time. There is definitely no worrying about that in the heat of battle. You really feel alive in the midst of the fight."

"So you will join us?" asked Septimus.

He looked at Izanami. "I will if you will."

"You brat. You know I've never been able to resist a dare from you. This is crazy."

"Do you want to live forever?" he asked.

"Yes. That's the problem."

"Well, this might turn out to be our best opportunity to achieve that. It may turn out to be the best bet we ever made."

Lola had never witnessed a conversation like this in her life, and she did not know exactly what to make of it. All she knew was that, based on everything she remembered from her course on statistics and probability at U-Dub, Koschei and Izanami were engaged in some seriously dodgy decision-making.

"That's it then," said Koschei. "I'm in, but I need a very exacting promise, Orpheus, for all the things you are going to do for us in return. Understand? We are not charity workers. Not for a fool's errand like this. Do you agree, Izanami?"

She stood up and said, "Where is your bathroom, Koschei? Sapphire, come with me."

Lola followed her to the bathroom but was annoyed at being dragged along. The Canadian's attitude had made her feel like a child.

"You know, Izanami, I don't actually need to go."

"I don't need to go either. I didn't bring you in here so you could pee, you nitwit. If you want me to go along on this disaster of an operation, you and I need to make our own separate bargain."

"Bargain? What kind of bargain?"

"I need something in exchange for risking my life to rescue this woman you care so much about."

"What do you want?"

"Just one specific piece of information."

"Yes?"

"Tell me Orpheus's real name."

"I... I can't do that."

181

"Yeah, yeah, I know. It's a rule. Screw the rules. This is just between you and me. He'll never know that you told me."

"But what are you going to do with it? Why do you need to know?"

"Because I need to have something over him. In the entire time I have known him, he has always had the advantage. The balance of power has always been on his side. I just want to know that I have some crucial piece of information that matters to him."

"And you won't help us rescue Maria if I don't tell you?"

"No."

"You have to promise never to tell him that you know. You can't ever tell him I told you."

"Don't worry. This will be between just the two of us. Now spill it."

Lola swallowed hard. "Okay. His real name is…"

"Yes?"

"It's Septimus Bridge."

"What? No. That can't be right. You made that up, didn't you? Look, if you're not going to tell me, just say so instead of making up joke names."

"No, I swear. That's his real name. He was the youngest of seven sons. That's where his name comes from."

"Well, well, who would have thought?" said Izanami smugly.

"You're going to keep your word, aren't you? You're still going to come with us to rescue Maria?"

"Don't worry. I wouldn't miss it for the world. And I would have gone anyway—even if you hadn't told me."

19
Cultists

"A TOAST to the success of this mission," said Koschei. "May we all come back alive and in one piece."

"I'll drink to that," said Izanami.

"You will drink to anything," said Septimus.

"Be nice to me, Orpheus. For once, you need me more than I need you."

"I have kind of a basic question," said Lola. "How do we actually get to the Netherworld?"

"I confess," said Koschei, "I was wondering that myself. As often as I have been witness to demons penetrating into our world, I have never before worried about how one would penetrate into theirs."

"We shall have to go back to where it all began for me," said Septimus. "We must go to Cnoc Meadha, the very spot I first encountered the Fiend three-and-a-half centuries ago."

"Ireland, eh? This sounds good already," said Koschei. "Irish beer is always better in its own country. I wonder if the same is true of the whiskey."

"The drink can wait until this is over, Koschei," said Septimus.

"Of course, I would not have it any other way."

Feeling restless, Lola went to the large window. There were no curtains, presumably because the grounds were sufficiently secure that Koschei did not worry about privacy. It was very dark outside, but she was certain she saw movement.

"Uh, Koschei," she said, "were you by any chance expecting company?"

"Besides the three of you? No, and I was not expecting you either."

Lola could definitely see figures running.

"Do you have people working for you outside at this time of night?"

"What are you talking about?"

"Somebody else take a look and tell me I'm not crazy."

Izanami and Koschei rushed to the window.

"She's right," said Izanami. "There's someone out there."

Septimus had remained seated with his eyes closed. "I sense them. There are five of them—so far. We are under assault."

"So much for my idyllic country life," said Koschei with a sigh, as he drew a long knife. "I should have known, once you two showed up, trouble would not be far behind."

"If I'm being honest," said Izanami, also producing a knife, "I've been itching to hurt someone for a long time now. This is just what the doctor ordered."

Lola fought the urge to panic. "Who are they? Are they demons?"

"No," said Septimus, getting to his feet. "They are worse than demons. They are human beings—and the worst kind of human beings. They are cultists."

"Cultists? You mean, like the people who hang out at the airport?"

"Not precisely. The Fiend preys on those with weak minds, and he has no trouble finding simple intellects who can be duped. There are always those who will happily follow the tenets of his false religion and become warriors and agents for a cause they do not understand. There is never a shortage of aimless souls willing to be recruited and follow blindly."

"Sounds to me like you're describing Puritans," said the Canadian.

Septimus ignored her. "Someone once called these sorts useful idiots. But being idiots does not make them any less dangerous. Indeed it makes them more so. Do you have your blade at the ready, Sapphire?"

"Oh, right, yeah, I do."

Remembering her training, Lola produced her shiny weapon. "I've got trusty old Shieldbreaker right here."

"Oh my God," said Izanami with disgust. "She named it. I can't believe she actually named it."

"We shall be more than a match for this lot," said Septimus, adding, "Having said that, we should take care not to be *overly* confident. Let us go out to meet them before they barge in and trample Koschei's beautiful rugs."

"The bloody philistines!" cried the Russian, as a large stone crashed through the window.

A loud male voice bellowed from the dark, "We live for Belial!"

The words were echoed by others, as the light of flickering flames pierced the darkness.

"They have torches!" yelled Izanami.

She had no sooner said it when a flaming baton sailed through the window, igniting the Persian carpet where it landed.

"That's just wrong!" screamed Koschei, as he leapt through the shattered window, heedless of the remaining shards.

The others went out through the door. By the light of the torches' flames, they could make out a crowd of at least twenty.

"I thought you said there were *five,* Orpheus," said Izanami.

"The situation is clearly dynamic," he replied.

As far as Lola could tell, they were all men—and large ones at that. Many had beards or mustaches, and all of them were bald. They wore black tee-shirts bearing various examples of satanic imagery.

"You have offended Belial!" yelled one in a distinctively East London accent, as he swung a club at Lola.

She blocked it by embedding her blade in the wood, but the brute then pulled the club back, taking her weapon with it.

"Hey!" she yelled. "Give that back!"

Angered by the attack, she took two steps backward, sprang into the air and somersaulted. Her feet struck him in the jaw, and he fell to the ground unconscious, allowing her to retrieve her knife. Curious that the mob had become quiet, she looked around. Everyone had stopped to stare at her.

"Where did you say you found her?" asked Koschei, looking rather impressed.

Septimus too was admiring. "It is increasingly obvious that she is the one who found me."

"Hey, Orpheus," said Lola, fending off another attacker. "Why do we have to waste time fighting these guys anyway? Can't you just wave your magic wand and put them to sleep or send them somewhere else?"

"So you might think," he replied, contending with another attacker of his own. "My powers draw on my mind's own energy and its link to our common perceived reality. That means it relies as well on the minds of others, making my gifts frustratingly limited when it comes to unthinking fanatics like these."

"Sheesh," muttered Izanami. "It's bad enough he doesn't break a sweat, but he even has enough breath to give us an entire lecture."

By now several of the cultists had swarmed around Lola. Taking no time to think, she picked up the dropped club and began rotating her body faster and faster. Any man who came too close was immediately knocked to the ground by her rapidly moving bludgeon. One brute, slightly smarter than the others, hurled his club at her from a distance, but she simply knocked it away with her own cudgel.

Fed up with what he saw, a particularly large thug threw the entire bulk of his body at her, sending the two of them sprawling on the ground. Before she could recover, he had crawled on top of her. His body smelled of sweat and grime, his breath of cabbage.

"Get... off... me!" she screamed, straining against his weight.

Izanami rushed to help. When he proved too heavy to pull off, the Canadian sank her blade into his upper arm. He barely flinched.

"These damn cultists are completely hyped up on drugs," muttered Koschei to Septimus, as the two engaged in their own fights. "They seem to feel no pain at all."

Taking advantage of the knife embedded in her opponent's arm, Lola gave it a yank, forcing his body to roll over. Unhappily for Izanami, the bulk of his weight landed on her.

"Hey!" she cried. "I was helping you. You should show some gratitude. I hardly ever help anybody."

Lola slipped out from under the barbarian and seized his ankle in order to drag him off the Canadian. She then pulled Izanami's blade from his arm and used it to pierce his Achilles tendon.

"That's me saying thank you. Anyway, he won't be doing much walking for a while."

As Lola helped her to her feet, Izanami gaped at her.

"Did Orpheus really teach you all that in a week?"

"I... I don't know where all this is coming from. It's like I've done this all before, but a long time ago. I don't remember. Let's talk later. Right now we still have a fight on our hands."

Some of the brighter members of the mob had already fled, leaving only the most stubborn and mentally unstable to continue the assault. A strange elation came over Lola as she found herself sailing from one opponent to another as if in some celestially choreographed ballet.

As she glanced around, she saw the other three heavily engaged in their own elegant and savage dances. They whirled and maneuvered to knock their opponents into submission. As easy as they made it look, she could see countless years of training and experience behind every move. Yet somehow it was all coming to her seemingly without effort, as if she were born knowing how to do it. It made no sense. She knew a large chunk of herself was missing.

Lola also envied the others for being able to emit bright bursts of power from their hands, making their battles easier. She made a mental note to ask Septimus to teach her how it was done.

Before long the last of the cultists were chased away, rendered unconscious, or immobilized by injuries.

Lola panted with excitement as much as exhaustion.

"So what do we do with them? Should we call the police?"

"It is generally best," said Septimus, "not to trouble local law enforcement with these matters."

Koschei looked in despair at the lingering flames in his sitting room. "It is destroyed! I had some valuable paintings in there. You better make this right, Orpheus."

"I will do what I can to sort you out, Koschei, but there is something else to tidy first."

The demon hunter went from one cultist to another, kneeling by each one to whisper something in his ear. One by one, they each stood and plodded—or limped—away.

"The one good thing about true believers is that they are, by nature, easily open to suggestion."

"What were they doing here?" asked Lola. "Did they really come here after us?"

"There is no question," said Septimus. "The Fiend is clearly aware of our every move."

Izanami said to Koschei, "Did Orpheus happen to mention to you we are deliberately and purposefully walking into a trap?"

"We are? Is that wise?"

"Is the best course of action," said Septimus. "The Fiend will be expecting us to be clever. Our only hope of wrong-footing him is not to be clever."

"Is Astaroth really clever enough," asked Koschei, "to take into account whether or not we are clever?"

"In truth, no. In the end, our cleverness—or lack of it—will not be particularly relevant. Still, walking into the trap is the best course of action. Being clever would end up distracting us more than him."

"How does he get so many people to fight for him anyway?" asked Lola, still concerned about the cultists. "Don't these people have minds of their own?"

"There are always people more than willing to follow someone blindly. Historically, they have fallen prey to flimflammers peddling alluring religions. Lately, however, it seems more to be political ideas that seduce them. The older I get, the more I tend to believe that the Anabaptists were right in proscribing participation in civic affairs."

"I want to know more about this Sapphire of yours," said Koschei, taking a good look at Lola. "What she did was very impressive. Where did she come from again?"

"Ballard," said Lola, beginning to feel self-conscious under the stares from him and Izanami. "And you can ask me directly. I like to speak for myself."

"If you say so," said the Russian, "but who were you before you were in that Ballard place?"

"I… I don't know. I didn't think I was anyone before, but I'm starting to think that maybe I was. I guess I must have been. I wish I could remember."

"Your mind will clear," said Septimus, "and all your memories will come together once you pass into the Netherworld. That is where the mystery will be solved."

"But at what price?" mused Koschei. "No one has returned from the Netherworld."

"Incorrect," said Septimus. "Justine returned."

"The truth about that," said Izanami, "has yet to be settled conclusively."

"Well, we will not settle this tonight," said Koschei. "Orpheus, will you repair my sitting room now or wait until morning? And how soon do we leave for Ireland?"

"The truth is," said Septimus, "I am feeling strangely weak. I may have been exerting myself too much and too soon since coming back to my full powers. Moreover, my expenditure of energy is clearly making it easier for the Fiend to track my movements. Given what lies ahead, I think I should be prudent and avoid displays of power for the time being. I may have to leave your sitting room, Koschei, until we return from our quest."

"In other words, never."

"If we do not return, then your sitting room will not matter anyway. This also means that we shall have to travel to Ireland by conventional means. Fortunately, it is not that far away."

"Will we go by plane or by train?" asked Izanami.

"Definitely by train and by ferry," said the Russian.

"It would be much faster by air," said the Canadian.

"I know," said Koschei, "but I prefer to travel by land."

"Why?"

"I do not like to fly. It makes me nervous."

"Let me get this straight," laughed Izanami. "You are planning to go with us to the Netherworld and confront all the worst demons in their own native domain in what is almost certainly going to be a suicide mission, but you're scared to go on an airplane?"

"It is not funny, Izanami. It is something I have struggled with my whole life."

She laughed heartily. "Well, now I have heard everything. You should take the plane anyway and hope it crashes so you don't have to go to the Netherworld."

"Despite all this amusement," said Septimus, "I suggest we go to bed. It sounds as though we have a long journey ahead of us. Koschei, can you accommodate overnight guests?"

"I suppose. If you do not mind a little smoke."

Given the number of suitable beds in the castle, Lola and Izanami were told they would have to share one.

"I see Orpheus and Koschei do not have to share a bed," grumbled Izanami, as they settled into their room. "Orpheus always makes the decisions, and the rest of us are expected to follow. Why does he get to make decisions for me?"

Lola shrugged. "I guess because he's the one who sold his soul to the devil."

"Well, aren't you the profound one. Anyway, I don't mind sharing if you don't. I just hope you don't snore."

"If you're half as tired as I am, snoring won't keep you awake."

As they settled into the bed, Lola said, "I really do appreciate you going along to get Maria back. I know you don't know me or her, but for what it's worth, I'll be grateful to you forever."

"This Maria means a lot to you, eh?"

"She means the world to me. She's wonderful. When I first met her, she had the most beautiful blue hair. And had the coolest Irish accent. And she is just the nicest person. And she has this wonderful sense of humor. And she... she... she makes my heart beat like a subway train."

"And what if it turns out that she actually *is* Justine? If she is, then she will have her memory back by now. She will know that she and Septimus are the ones who belong together."

"The one thing I know for sure is that she and Septimus do not belong together. Even if Maria and Justine were the same person, he let her go to hell in his place. There is no way she could ever forgive him for that. I sure wouldn't. Anyway, she isn't Justine. It's just a coincidence she looks like her. They are two different people. I know they are."

"Then why did the Fiend take her?"

"I… I don't know. Maybe for the same reason that Septimus wants to make her Justine. Because of the way she looks. Men just have trouble looking beneath the surface."

"The Fiend is not a man," said Izanami. "Demons have no gender, but I take your point. All *I* know for sure is that, between you and Orpheus, before this is all over, one of you is definitely going to be *very* disappointed. Say, can you move over a little? You're on my half of the bed."

That night Lola had another dream. She stood in the same rugged alien landscape as before, and she felt the same overwhelming dread as before. This time, however, she heard a low, ominous voice bellowing in the distance. It echoed through the black sky like thunder. She clutched the diabolusbane tightly and peered in the distance. In the gloom she could just about make out a roiling cloud moving toward her. She heard wails, as if the souls of all the damned were trapped in the cloud and crying for release. Their cries made it difficult to clearly hear the bellowing voice, which grew increasingly loud. Finally, she succeeded in making out the words. They were in an ancient forgotten language, which she was somehow able to understand. They threatened her. They prophesied her inevitable doom. The voice called her by name, but it was a name that was neither Lola nor Sapphire. The voice grew louder and more distinct. It was not merely with her ears that she heard it. It echoed in her mind. It grew so loud it made her body ache. She feared her head would split in two. She tried to stop listening but could not.

Lola woke with a start and sat up, covered in sweat. She struggled to breathe.

"What's the matter with you?" grumbled Izanami, annoyed at having been wakened.

It took Lola more than a minute to be able to talk. The Canadian sat up and watched with concern. Finally, the white-haired girl caught her breath.

"I remember now," she gasped. "I remember the name I had before."

20
Journey

"THE NAME YOU had before? Before what?"

"I remember the name I chose as a demon hunter."

"It isn't Sapphire?"

"No, I mean the name I used in my previous life. You see, I only found out recently that I lived before. I never had any idea about it, but now I'm remembering things. I didn't believe it when Septimus…"

"Orpheus."

"I mean, Orpheus. I'm definitely not very good at keeping secrets, am I? I didn't believe it when Orpheus told me I was reincarnated, but I'm pretty sure now he was right."

"So what's your 'true' demon hunter name?"

"I don't know if I'm supposed to tell you."

Izanami sighed impatiently. "That rule only goes for your *real* name in *this* life. There's no reason not to tell me your *demon hunter* name in a *previous* life."

"Are you sure? I already blew it when I told you Orpheus's name. I think I better check before I give away any more secrets that I'm not supposed to."

"Suit yourself. I'm not really that interested anyway. I mean, who cares what you were called in a past life?"

Izanami fell back and closed her eyes. She quickly sat up again.

"Unless you were someone famous. Were you someone famous?"

"I don't know. I don't think so, but then I never heard of any demon hunters at all until lately."

The Canadian fell back again.

"Then who cares? Please don't wake me up again."

Lola did not sleep for the rest of the night. She could not get the sounds and images of the dream out of her mind. It was a relief when, finally, she heard Septimus's call for everyone to get up.

She remained silent during breakfast as Septimus outlined the day's journey. Determined to travel by traditional means, he said they would take a commuter train to London, where they would then board a train at Euston Station for Holyhead. Then a ferry for Dublin followed by another train journey. It would be a long day of travel finishing with their arrival in Galway at around ten o'clock at night.

"That seems like forever," complained Izanami. "Your teleporting has me spoiled."

A mobile phone on the table buzzed. Koschei picked it up and looked at it nonchalantly. He then dropped it to the floor and smashed it with his foot.

"I do not feel like making up a story for why I will not be at work today. Perhaps it is time to disappear mysteriously and cement my legend. If I happen to return from the looming disaster we are about to undertake, I can always establish a new identity."

Later, as she watched the passing countryside through the train's window, Lola pondered the strange course her life had taken. She had always planned to travel to Europe someday, and Britain was at the top of her list of countries to visit, along with Sweden and Norway, where her grandparents had come from. Now she was unexpectedly on a train in England. On her way to Wales and the Irish Sea and then to Ireland. It was unreal. She knew she should be afraid, but something had switched off inside her. Too many things had changed too fast to even worry about any of it.

"You have been very quiet," said Septimus.

"Did Izanami say something to you?"

"Izanami is always saying something to me. I've learned not to listen."

"I mean, did she tell you anything about me? About last night?"

"Do I really want to hear this?"

Lola stared straight ahead and said nothing for a full minute.

"I've read all your poetry, you know. The poetry you wrote under the name Eliot Bridge."

"Have you?"

"Yes, I had an English professor at U-Dub who was a big fan of yours. She made us read everything."

"Made you? You have my sympathy."

"I didn't mean it like that. I actually liked it. For a while I was really into it. It seemed so profound, as if he... you really understood the true meaning of life."

"I assure you that impression had as much to do with your own imagination as with any of my words."

"It felt like you were speaking to me directly. I felt this strong, personal connection. Now that I actually know you, I don't feel that at all. It's as though you are not the same person as the one who wrote the poetry."

"I am not the same person. We all change constantly. I have had enough time to go through more changes than most."

"Why did you write that poetry? And why did you stop?"

"The best way to explain it, I suppose, is that I was trying to work through my anguish. Does that sound overly melodramatic? I have carried so much guilt for so long. It has never been easy."

"I can't imagine what it's like to live so long. Your life just keeps going on and on, but at least you know who you are. You have always been the same person even if you have gone through changes."

"Are you trying to tell me something?"

"I had a dream last night. Actually, I've had a few dreams lately."

"I suspected as much. Do you want to tell me about them?"

She whispered, "I know who I am, Septimus. I've begun to remember."

"Yes?"

"It still doesn't quite make sense. I don't recall everything, but the pieces are starting to fall into place."

"That is good. We shall have more hope of success if you can draw on your full experience and memories. Tell me, who were you?"

She smiled slyly.

"Demon hunters do not share their real names with other demon hunters."

"Yes, but tell me your *nom de guerre*. I surely would have known you or heard of you, but I cannot imagine for the life of me who you were. It vexes me that I cannot work it out."

"I have no memory of knowing you before, but I think I was somehow aware of you."

"What name did you fight under?"

"It's very strange."

"Yes?"

"I called myself Eurydice."

"But that's…"

"I know. English and psych weren't my only subjects at U-Dub. I also studied Greek mythology. She was Orpheus's wife."

"How did you come to choose that of all possible names?"

"I don't remember. Maybe it's just a coincidence."

"Perhaps. That is certainly possible. But if it is mere coincidence, it is an awfully strange one. Do you remember what your actual birth name was?"

"No. Not yet. I have a vague sense of it, though. It was something foreign. Definitely not a name I am familiar with. I think it began with 'T.'"

Septimus studied her intently.

"I am beginning to wonder if the Fiend has somehow planted false memories in you as a way of taunting us."

"He certainly didn't give me my fighting skills."

"No, no. Those are definitely your own. I have no doubt that you lived before and have special gifts. It is the fact that I never heard of you and that you chose that particular name which has me perplexed. Something does not add up. I wonder if you were a demon hunter at all—or perhaps something else?"

"What else could I have been?"

"I do not know. I need to ponder this. The Fiend is crafty, insidious. It would not be beyond him to mold a mortal human into the perfect weapon and keep her ultimate purpose hidden until the time is right. Is it possible you were always meant to lead me back to the Netherworld—without consciously realizing that you are doing the Fiend's bidding?"

"Wait. You think I'm a spy? A double agent?"

"Frankly, I do not know what to believe. As I say, I need time to think this through. It might be best if we do not speak for the remainder of the journey."

Lola was dejected. Until now all she had cared about was rescuing Maria, and she knew she could not do it without Septimus. She did not really care what he thought of her, so she was surprised how much it wounded her that he now questioned her trustworthiness. Moreover, she now wondered if she could trust herself. What if his suspicions were correct? What if, without knowing it, she had been programmed to take Septimus back to the Netherworld and trap him there?

She found another seat on the train, one where she could sit completely alone while watching the scenery. She saw Izanami and Koschei sitting together a few rows ahead of her. They talked and laughed incessantly. She envied them for not having to question who they were. She longed for a time when her life was simple. She held onto the hope that, if she could just be with Maria again, everything would make sense and she might even be happy.

The crossing on the Irish Sea was rough.

"They should have canceled the sailing," complained Koschei, his complexion turning a faint shade of green as the vessel shifted in one direction, then another.

"We are lucky they did not," said Septimus. "It is better for us if there is no delay."

"Are you sorry now that we didn't fly?" teased Izanami.

"No," said Koschei. "That would have been worse."

To the Russian's relief, the ferry terminal at Dun Laoghaire had finally come into view. His ordeal was nearly over.

At every step along the way, Septimus had handled the situation when tickets or passports were required. He was able to produce identification that satisfied the staff and plastic cards that they accepted for payment.

"Where does the money come from," asked Lola, "that pays for the tickets?"

"From the banks ultimately," explained Koschei. "It will show up as an error and they will be unable to track down the cardholder. The bank will end up taking the cost."

"Isn't that basically stealing?"

"I suppose," said the Russian, "although some would accuse the banks of the same thing. I would argue it is not good for the banks' business if demons succeed in invading the world, so the banks actually benefit in the end. It's like paying insurance to the government."

As they boarded another train, this time at Heuston Station in Dublin, Lola reflected on the fact she was now in Maria's country. She wondered briefly whether she should try to make contact with Maria's family in Cork but realized immediately there was no point. What could she possibly tell them? By now they would be frantic with worry, having learned she disappeared during a weekend visit to Seattle. Perhaps Sinéad had been in contact with them to tell them of the planned sailing excursion to Riesgado Island. Of course, everyone would naturally assume the worst. The reality was certainly no more hopeful, and attempting to tell them the truth would only provoke questions she had no way of answering.

Septimus advised them to try napping while they had the chance since it would be a late night. The plan was to arrive at Cnoc Meadha for the stroke of midnight. Izanami and Koschei paid no heed. They continued their chatter unabated. Lola leaned against her window and closed her eyes but could not rest.

As the train rumbled through the Irish midlands, she regretted it was too dark to see anything. She promised herself she would someday come back to Ireland as a tourist. Perhaps she would come with Maria, and her friend would take her all over the country and show her all her favorite places. They would visit the ruins of old castles and drink in quaint old pubs. As much as she enjoyed thinking about such a holiday, she feared it would never happen. She dreaded the thought she might never see Maria again.

Only slightly later than scheduled, the train pulled into Ceannt Station in Galway a few minutes after ten o'clock. They strolled out of the building and were chilled by a brisk wind blowing off the Atlantic Ocean. They walked down to the street bordering a large, grassy square. A line of taxis waited in front of a hotel. Septimus leaned over to speak with the driver of the nearest cab.

A shiver ran through Lola's body, and she tapped Septimus on the shoulder.

"Something about him gives me the creeps," she said quietly. "Can we take a different taxi? I just have a bad feeling about him."

"It is bad form," said Koschei, "not to take the taxi at the head of the queue."

Septimus took Lola's instinct seriously. "It is all right. What do you think of that man?"

The driver of the next car was an amiable, middle-aged fellow with a wide grin and a twinkle in his eye.

"Yeah," said Lola. "I like him better."

To the annoyance of the first driver, Septimus approached him and asked, "Sir, would you be so kind as to take us to Cnoc Meadha?"

"Where? Oh, Knockma? Off the N17 about twenty miles from here? You want to go there now, like? Tonight?"

"Please."

"Sure, and I don't know why you'd want to be doing that. It's a funny place for a ramble in the dark."

"I shall happily make it worth your while, my good man."

"Well, the customer's always right. That's what I say anyways."

He cheerfully hopped out of the car and opened the rear door so that Koschei and the two women could squeeze in. Septimus took the front passenger seat. As he headed out of the city, the driver did his best to engage them in chat.

"Are ye here on holidays?"

"I suppose you could say that."

"First time in Galway?"

"As it happens, I was here before," said Septimus drily, "but that was very many years ago. It has changed a great deal since then."

"I do not doubt it."

They traveled down a wide, two-lane highway for about fifteen minutes, and the lights of the city gave way to dark countryside. The driver slowed and made a turn to the left onto a narrow, twisty road with tall trees on either side. The car climbed steep hills and descended into small valleys. Lola was struck by how few homes they had seen. It seemed very remote, considering how near it was to the city. The driver pulled over next to a small field.

"Is this it?" asked Izanami skeptically.

"Everything has changed so much," said Septimus. "Nothing here looks familiar."

The driver hopped out of the car and opened the rear door. Septimus peered into the darkness.

"Are you certain this is the right place?"

The driver walked behind the car and opened the trunk. As if it were the most natural thing in the world, he carried a large box made of oak wood over to Septimus and set it on the ground in front of him. The demon hunter watched all this, quizzically at first and then with alarm. The driver's countenance had changed completely. His face was now grave and purposeful. He opened the lid of the box and released plumes of purple smoke with glittering sparks.

"All hail Belial!" he shouted.

"Aw, no," cried Izanami, drawing her weapon.

"And he seemed like such a nice man," said Lola with disappointment, producing her weapon as well.

"What is that bloody thing?" yelled Koschei, as the strange cloud grew larger, enveloping Septimus. "Orpheus, get away from there!"

The Russian's warning was to no avail. The driver, having covered his nose and mouth, fled, and the strange vapor quickly filled the car and expanded to surround them all. Panic set in as they became increasingly disoriented.

"What is this, Orpheus?" cried Koschei. "What manner of devilry did that man unleash on us?"

"I do not know," coughed Septimus. "Try to hold your breath. Try not to breathe the fumes."

As quickly as the strange cloud had billowed around them, so it rapidly dissipated and left only a sweet, burning odor in the air. The four looked at one another apprehensively.

"I do not like the sensation it has left in my head," complained Izanami. "It's making my heart pound like I'm going to have a heart attack."

A look of shock came over Koschei's face as he stared at Septimus.

"You! Here?!"

Septimus, for his part, appeared equally dismayed. "How is this possible? How can you be here? Now?"

"What's going on?" asked Lola. "Why are they acting so strange?"

To her alarm, though, Izanami did not answer. She looked at Lola as if she saw a ghost.

"Not you! Anybody but you!" cried the Canadian.

To Lola's horror Izanami came at her with her blade, giving every indication that she meant to use it.

"Izanami! Stop! What are you doing?"

Lola was left with no choice but to defend herself. She used her own blade but only to deflect her friend's attempts to cut her.

"Please stop!" she cried. "Try to fight whatever that stuff did to you. You're fighting the wrong person. It's me. Sapphire."

As she continued to defend herself, Lola did her best to follow what was going on between Septimus and Koschei. The Russian attacked him, but at least Septimus did not seem as crazed as Koschei and Izanami were. Still, he appeared confused in a way that was not at all characteristic of him. If he had a solution to their dilemma, he showed no sign of revealing it.

Izanami's blade swiped against Lola's upper arm and drew blood. The woman from Ballard winced at the pain but refused to let it slow her. She knew the Canadian had an advantage over her in terms of fresh experience, but Lola took heart from the fact that whatever enchantment had seized her friend had also seemed to dull her instincts and slow her reactions—perhaps enough to give Lola a fighting chance.

The Canadian swung wildly with her blade. Lola succeeded in knocking it from her hand, but before the American could take advantage, Izanami leapt at her heedlessly, causing Lola's own blade to fall to the ground. As Izanami wrestled her on the grass, she shouted, "I'll kill you, Mackenzie! You'll never treat me like that again!"

"Who's Mackenzie?" yelled Lola, struggling frantically against her assault. "Izanami, it's me, Sapphire! Snap out of it!"

"I was little more than a child! You'll pay for what you did!"

Completely confused, Lola continued to grapple with the crazed Canadian. She glanced over at the other two and saw that Koschei was no less hysterical than Izanami.

"Rasputin! They say you cannot be killed, but I will prove them wrong!" shouted the Russian as he swung his blade wildly at the demon hunter.

"Please!" countered Septimus, as he levitated Koschei's weapon out of his reach. "You are closer to me than any of my brothers. I do not want to fight you!"

Enraged, the Russian pushed Septimus to the ground and clamped his hands around the demon hunter's throat. "Do not dare try your evil magic on me, mad monk! Your time is over!"

"You've all gone crazy!" shouted Lola, still tussling violently with Izanami. "Can't you see? This is what the Fiend wants! He is making us kill each other!"

The Canadian's hands tightened around Lola's throat, cutting off her air. Struggling vainly for breath, the white-haired girl searched her memory for anything from her former life that might help. Time was short, though, and she felt herself losing consciousness from strangulation.

As everything grew dark, Lola entered a sort of dream state. She felt as though she were leaving her body and floating into the sky above. She wondered, is this what it feels like to die?

She found herself again in her dream, standing once more in the alien landscape. As before, a huge cloud in the distance rolled in her direction. This time, however, the black billows were gorged with moisture. As they neared her, she saw them releasing torrents of water onto the land.

"Water," she murmured. "Water is the ultimate purifier."

Her eyes popped open to see Izanami's wild face an inch away, close enough to feel and smell her hot breath. Lola's lungs ached, her mouth still helpless to draw breath. She no longer fought the horror of death. She embraced it. She thought of the day her parents died. She thought of Maria trapped in the Netherworld and the terror she was experiencing. She thought of every bad thing that had ever happened to her and to everyone she ever loved.

As her heart pounded, her eyes welled with tears. A single drop fell and landed on Izanami's hand. The Canadian pulled away as if its wetness had burned her. Lola gasped with relief, and her tears flowed more freely.

"Stop blubbering, Mackenzie!" yelled Izanami angrily. "Don't pretend you have a heart!"

Now that her opponent's grip had loosened, Lola moved her head in every direction she could, smearing her teardrops on Izanami's hands and wrists. She craned her neck upward and rubbed her moist cheek against the Canadian's.

Izanami sat up, confused. She stared at Lola in disbelief.

"Sapphire, what are you doing there? What happened to…?"

"To Mackenzie? Who is that? Who did you think I was?"

Lola's voice cracked as she spoke. Her mouth felt like sandpaper.

"I… I… I don't want to talk about it. It was a long time ago. In Hastings Park. What the devil is happening to us anyway?"

"I don't know. We'll figure it out, but first we have to separate Orpheus and Koschei. Slap me as hard as you can."

"What? Have you gone insane too?"

"Don't ask questions. Just do it. Hit me in the face as hard as you can!"

Lola was so insistent and Izanami was so disoriented that the easiest thing to do was what she was told. She slapped her hand across Sapphire's cheek as hard as she could. The side of the white-haired girl's face glowed red, as tears flowed from her eyes.

"Good job," Lola sobbed. "Actually, too good, but never mind."

She grabbed Izanami by the wrists and forced the Canadian's hands against her face. "We have to get Orpheus and Koschei as wet as we can."

The Russian was on top of Septimus, who appeared strangely reluctant to defend himself. Koschei pounded him in the head repeatedly. Coming up behind her friend, Izanami put her hands on Koschei's face and smeared it with Lola's tears. As he rolled to one side and off Septimus, Lola did the same to the demon hunter. Gradually, they came to their senses.

"What on earth happened to all of you?" asked the shaken Lola, as she collapsed into a sitting position on the ground.

"It was an enchantment," said Septimus groggily, "and a very powerful one at that. If not for you, Sapphire, we would have killed one another. That was a very lucky escape."

"But why were you killing each other?" asked Lola. "Who did you think you were fighting?"

"I'm not going to talk about it," said Izanami bitterly. "Let's just say, I had a very bad experience in an internment camp during the war."

Koschei's eyes were still wide from the experience. "Orpheus, I could have sworn you were Rasputin."

"Rasputin?" said Izanami. "*The* Rasputin? Did you actually know him?"

"Yes," said the Russian evenly. "As a child. He healed me, saved my life, but I was not grateful. Not after what he did later, but that is my own affair."

"And who did you think Koschei was, Orpheus?" asked Izanami.

Septimus stared grimly into the distance. "I was attacked by the one person I never wanted to fight, the one man who was more of a brother to me than any other. You were the image and personification of my beloved friend Valentine Walton."

"I have a more urgent question," said Koschei. "Why was Sapphire unaffected? What protected her from the enchantment? Even Orpheus was not immune to it."

"That's a very good question," said Izanami. "And don't forget, she was the one who picked the cabbie who drove us out here and unleashed the enchantment on us. Say, where did he go anyway?"

"He is long gone, you can be certain," said Septimus.

"I'm not a spy if that's what you're all thinking," said Lola defensively. "Don't forget, I'm the one who saved you."

"Yes, that was very convenient as well," said Izanami. "How did you know to do that anyway? It's like you're a split personality, sometimes leading us into traps and sometimes saving us."

"The important thing," said Septimus, "is that she did save us. She is much too valuable not to have with us, so for now, she is one of us. Whatever doubts we may have, we must not let the Fiend sow division among us."

He noticed the blood on Lola's arm and instinctively put his hand on the wound. "I'm afraid this suit is little protection against our own weapons, but at least I can mend it."

As his fingers touched her blood, a strange look came over his face. He stared intently into her eyes, trying to fathom the mystery behind them, but it was no use. Her wound, though, was promptly healed, as was the tear in her suit.

"I am tired of fighting cultists and dealing with enchantments," said Koschei. "I want to fight an actual demon."

"Be careful what you wish for, Koschei," said Septimus.

"Well, so much for arriving at your magical hill all rested and ready for battle," said Izanami. "Where are we anyway?"

"I do not know," said Septimus. "I suppose I shall have to resort to my powers to determine our location."

"Save your energy," said the Canadian. "I can handle this. Luckily, the driver ran off on foot and left his taxi here. He wasn't going to hang around and get exposed to his own devil smoke."

She sat in the taxi and activated its GPS system.

"We're in luck. We're actually not too far from the hill. It's just a few miles down the road. Hop in. It's been a while since I drove a stick shift, let alone with my left hand, but I'll manage."

Septimus looked at the GPS display in astonishment. "Amazing," he said. "And people think what *I* do is magic."

Izanami's first few attempts at driving resulted in the taxi jerking and stopping, causing Koschei no end of laughter, but she soon had the hang of driving the car. The others were unnerved by her tendency to weave from one side of the road to the other but said nothing. After several minutes she pulled into a small unpaved parking lot.

"This is it, according to the GPS."

"Yes," said Septimus, stepping out of the car. "It does look familiar. I see there is now a proper walking trail up the hill. Let us go."

Spotting an ivy-covered stone structure nearby, the demon hunter paused and stared.

"Castle Hackett," he murmured. "The last time I saw it, it was home to one of the most prominent families in Galway. Now it is but an ancient ruin. And it seems to have happened in the blink of an eye."

They followed the winding path up one side of the hill and then across its face to the other side. As they climbed, the trees surrounded and sheltered them in darkness. When a bend in the path took them past a gnarled sessile oak, Septimus stopped to gaze in wonder.

"I remember this tree. I swear I passed it on my previous ascent all those years ago. It has not changed at all, but that is impossible, isn't it? Does an oak live that long? Who knows? If not the same one, then another that took its place."

Their climb ended after clambering up a pile of rocks to reach the summit. They found themselves on a grassy area with unimpeded views to the south and west. The flat plain below was black save for a few pools of shimmering light indicating towns and villages. A long, narrow trail of lights traced the road on which they had traveled. It ended at the horizon where a golden glow marked the city of Galway.

The lights below were not strong enough to obscure the spectacular display in the sky above. There was no moon, and the stars shone bright as in a planetarium. They numbered in the thousands. Familiar constellations, such as the Big Dipper, the Little Dipper, and Orion's Belt, were clearly identifiable.

Lola gasped. "Definitely no problem with light pollution here."

"I have been to Ireland before," said Koschei, "and it is not known for its clear skies. This, I have to say, is impressive."

Septimus wasted no time looking at the sky. He walked to a specific spot and stood perfectly still. He closed his eyes, extended his arms, and began an otherworldly chant. When he finished, he lowered his arms and remained motionless. The others held their breath. Nearly a minute passed before they were blinded by a sudden burst of light.

When their eyes were able to focus again, before them stood a creature nearly ten feet tall. Its bright yellow eyes had irises in the shape of diamonds. It stood on cloven hoofs and had horns like a ram. Its slithery tail and spitting tongue were both forked. It swiped in their direction with angry claws.

"Koschei," said Septimus, "your wish has been granted. You have a demon to fight."

21
Hell's Guardian

"WHAT A MONSTER!" exclaimed the Russian. "He is particularly nasty. I have not seen one like him before."

"You have never been at the gate of hell before," said Septimus. "Arm yourselves!"

By now it was second nature for Lola to produce her blade when threatened. This time, however, she found herself holding the diabolusbane. The others were similarly armed.

"For the record," shouted Izanami, "these creatures are androgynous. You should use neutral pronouns."

"Do not start," replied the Russian. "Your stupid English language is difficult enough as it is. Besides, Orpheus uses the male pronoun."

"I advise you to take this deadly seriously," shouted Septimus severely. "We must get past this hellion if we are to enter the Fiend's realm—indeed if we are to survive."

"No one is saying they think this will be easy, Orpheus," muttered Koschei darkly. "And I am not the one distracted with using the correct pronouns."

Slowly, the demon leaned backward, paused for a moment, and then forced itself forward again with breathtaking speed. As it did this, it extended a claw forward, surprising the demon hunters with its arm's full length. Light emanated from its shoulder, traveled the length of the arm, and then burst through the claw as a fiery ball of searing energy. The four felt its intense heat as they leapt out of its path. It left a gaping charred gash in the grass, billowing black smoke.

Izanami sprang heedlessly in the creature's direction, landing at its feet. With a quick smooth motion, she planted the sharp end of her diabolusbane in its enormous hoof. Its roar was deafening, though it sounded to Lola more like extreme annoyance than pain. With increased fury it cast another fireball, this time in Septimus's direction. Lola knew people in nearby towns and villages must be able to see the storm of lights atop the hill, and she wondered what they made of the nighttime spectacle.

The white-haired girl joined the fray, bounding forward and planting her feet on the creature's thigh. She alighted only momentarily, just long enough to plunge her weapon into its leg and then spring away again. A swipe of its claw caught her on the back and sent her sprawling ungracefully to the ground. She jumped quickly to her feet and rapidly backed away. The beast let out a roar louder than before. The wave of sound nearly knocked her off her feet again.

"Explain something to me, Orpheus," she said. "Doesn't the Fiend like sucking people into its world and trapping them there? Why is it making it so hard for us to get in?"

"Mortals entering his realm of their own volition is unheard of. In such a case he would have less control over them than if he had taken them himself. Yes, that is something that surely frightens the Fiend. There is nothing he loathes more than free will—especially when wielded by a mortal."

"So is this the trap that you were talking about?" asked Lola. "Is this the snare the Fiend set out for us?"

"I honestly do not know, and in this moment it does not matter. I have to concentrate all my efforts on finding Justine."

"You mean Maria," Lola muttered under her breath.

Izanami and Koschei had begun a two-pronged attack. The Russian drew the monster's attention by circling it. The Canadian, sprinting in the other direction, brazenly seized its tail, and wrapped it around her diabolusbane. She tugged with all her might, while Koschei gave a shove from his end. It was all to no avail. The demon screamed, this time with an unmistakable sound of pain. Yet it continued to hold its ground with apparent ease. It yanked its tail—along with Izanami's weapon—from her grasp. It batted the diabolusbane away, wincing slightly as if the merest touch of it had injured its claw. In a rage, it kicked the Russian's body like a soccer ball, sending him flying for several yards. It tried to step on Izanami, but she quickly rolled out of its way.

In the midst of all this, Septimus stood motionless with outstretched arms and concentrated his thoughts. His hands gripped the diabolusbane in a horizontal position. Lola watched in fascination, as a bright yellow glow enveloped the demon hunter's head, then flowed to his shoulders, arms, and finally, into the weapon. It grew increasingly bright until Lola had to avert her eyes. The light then shot like a fiery cannonball in the beast's direction, hitting it squarely in the chest. It tottered and stared dumbly at Septimus.

Regaining its balance, it leaned its hideous head back and let out a deafening howl. The ball of light, which had continued flickering on its breast, regained its blinding brilliance and was thrust back at Septimus. They all felt its intense heat. Panicked, the demon hunter flung himself out of the way, barely evading the fiery ball. It landed on a clump of bushes which burst immediately into flame.

"This is ridiculous," muttered Koschei, still trying to catch his breath. "We need to be coordinated. This every-man-for-himself approach is not working."

"What do you propose?" asked Izanami.

The Russian displayed his diabolusbane before him. "Four of these together—right in the heart. With everything we've got."

"I don't think it has a heart."

"We have to aim somewhere."

They looked to Septimus. He was still catching his breath, but he nodded in agreement.

The four raised their weapons. Three pairs of eyes looked to Koschei for a signal.

"*Odin... dva... tri...* go!"

They rushed forward, paying no heed to the flailing claws. One of the pincers brushed Lola, sending her off course, but she quickly corrected herself. The tips of all four weapons were plunged into the middle of the monster's breast. While none pierced its scales, their combined impact did elicit a shriek, and the sound of it was horrible.

The creature tried to rid itself of its attackers by spinning. When that did not send them flying, it waved its claws more violently. Koschei and the two women dropped to the ground to avoid them, but Septimus succeeded in digging his weapon into the creature's chest and twisting it.

The roars were like thunder. Lola was certain they would be heard for miles and miles. She gasped to see her mentor whipped back and forth like a rag doll as the monster twisted and writhed in one direction and then another. Septimus finally lost his grip and was flung through the air. The beast roared in pain, unable or unwilling to touch the diabolusbane lodged in its breast. It lumbered in Izanami's direction, forcing her to scramble away. Then it turned to Koschei, and he too made a retreat.

It was then Lola's turn. Heeding some long-buried instinct, she sprang high into the air, making an arc in the beast's direction. Pounding its torso with her feet, she plunged her weapon into the hole made by Septimus's diabolusbane. The monster's cries were all but unendurable. She did her best to imitate Septimus by clinging to her weapon, but the whiplash of the beast's frantic movements made it difficult to maintain her grip. She finally had no choice but to let go, flying through the air to a painful landing.

For several minutes the demon stood motionless except for the violent heaving of its chest. Then it raised its claws high in the air in apparent reaction to the pain inflicted by the two weapons lodged in its breast. It shook itself violently. The shaking continued for several moments until the two weapons were finally dislodged and fell to the ground. The creature raised its head and let out one final, ear-splitting howl. A hole opened up in the air behind it and grew slowly larger. Its interior was completely black, as if absorbing and obliterating any light around it. The monster turned and lumbered into the hole, quickly slipping from view.

The four demon hunters, still lying on the ground, watched the hole intently to see what would happen next and whether anything would emerge from it. The hole did not shrink or disappear. Everything had gone eerily quiet except for the panting of the exhausted quartet. Several minutes passed before any of them spoke.

"That's it?" gasped Izanami. "I don't even know who won that fight."

"The point," said Septimus, "was not winning or losing. It was to exhaust us as much as possible before we enter the Netherworld."

"Wait," said Lola. "You mean, now Astaroth *wants* us to go in?"

"Please do not use that name here," said Septimus, looking stricken. "But yes, we are clearly expected. There is nothing barring our way."

"So this is it then," said Lola. "This is the trap. The Fiend is waiting for us in there."

"And we're just going in?" said Izanami. "Like lambs to the slaughter?"

"This was always the plan," said Septimus. "This would be your final opportunity to turn back."

"Why has he left the door open like that?" mused Koschei, mesmerized by the gaping black hole. "He wants to trap us in there, doesn't he? We will never come out again, will we?"

"In the end," said Septimus, "that will be up to us. I am going in. Who will join me?"

"I'm in," said Lola. "I'm not leaving without Maria."

Izanami looked doubtful.

"Did you mean it when you said that we could come back from this with much longer lifespans? Maybe even immortal?"

"If you survive," said Septimus.

The Canadian and the Russian looked at each other, one nearly daring the other with the looks in their eyes.

"I'm in," said Izanami.

"I'm in," said Koschei.

In a manner that was neither rushed nor hesitant, Septimus stood, retrieved his diabolusbane and walked into the waiting void. The suddenness of his disappearance startled Lola. It was as though his very existence had been extinguished like a candle's flame blown out by a wintry breeze. She swallowed hard and followed.

As she stepped through the portal, a bone-numbing chill went through her entire body. In the blink of an eye, everything went black as if she had gone blind. The sensation was the reverse of seeing Septimus disappear into the hole. Now it felt as though the earth and the sky and the world had been extinguished. It was the most solitary feeling she had ever experienced. This must be what it's like to be dead, she thought.

She stood, waiting for something to happen. A feeling of vertigo overtook her, leaving her afraid to move lest the wrong motion send her plunging into an abyss. She dared not speak, fearful the sound of her voice might cause something terrible to happen. She suddenly lost track of time. She wondered if she had been there a few minutes or whether she had always been there. Conscious thoughts drained from her mind, making her feel she would soon have no memories or even a language. It was as though she were ceasing to exist.

A light appeared. She could not make it out at first. Thoughts came to her with frustrating sluggishness. Gradually, her brain kicked in and began making sense of things. The light was from the glowing tip of Septimus's diabolusbane. She could see the outline of his black mane by way of his flickering weapon. It occurred to her to illuminate her own lance. She could now see that Izanami and Koschei were there and had done the same. She looked to Septimus's face for some kind of reassurance and got none. He was as grim as death.

She wanted to say something but could not. It was as though, in this place, there was nothing worth saying, as if language and coherent thoughts no longer mattered.

And there was something else. Her brain was now increasingly overloaded. Memories flooded into her mind. In an instant she relived every second of every minute of every hour since she was born. There was not a moment she could not recall, and it overwhelmed her. And there was more. There was another life. A whole other life lived in another country, speaking another language. A life much longer than the one she had lived in Ballard. A life full of struggle, battles, violence, victories, and defeats. It engulfed her, and her mind could not contain it.

"Orpheus," she managed to whisper.

He was distracted. He appeared to be having a similar experience, perhaps reliving all of his three-and-a-half centuries on earth. She saw him struggle for control of his thoughts. Eventually he turned to her.

"I remember now," she said. "You were right. My memory has come back. I definitely did live before. I can tell you my true name now."

"Do not mention your name here," he admonished her with alarm.

"It will not matter," she said. "My true name belongs to one who is long dead. It cannot give the Fiend any power over me."

"What were you called then?"

"My name was Tyra Knagenhjelm, and I was indeed a demon hunter. In fact, I fought many demons, and I defeated most of them. At least I never ended with worse than a draw when it mattered."

"So you were…"

She smirked. "Yes, I was a woman, just like I always knew I was."

"When did you live?"

"Not that long ago really. In my lifetime Haakon VII was the king of Norway. As I recall, George VI was on the throne in Britain."

"That is less than a century ago," said Septimus, astonished. "How did I not know of you?"

"I was aware of you. I actually knew who you were. That part is still kind of fuzzy. I remember knowing somehow that, if you and I ever met, it would result in some kind of catastrophe. I lived my whole life avoiding you, making sure we never crossed paths."

"But why? What possible reason was there for us not to meet?"

"I don't know. Maybe we were always destined to end up here together, and I somehow knew it and was trying to avoid it. Who knows? It will eventually come back to me. What I do know for sure is that the Fiend hunted me relentlessly. I was on the run for so many years. Eventually, I realized he would never let me rest until he had tracked me down. There would never be any respite as long as I lived. The only way to be free of him was to die and be reborn. I had to be reincarnated as someone else with absolutely no memory of my prior life. That was the only way certain to keep him from finding me again. Now here I am, back in his grasp. The only question is… does he even realize he finally has me?"

"With luck he may be yet unaware of who you are. If that is the case, then he will also be unaware of your skills and powers. This may be what gives us the advantage we desperately need to rescue Justine."

"You mean Maria."

"So your recovered memories have not changed your, ah, perception of things?"

"Not in the least. She continues to be foremost in my mind and my heart."

Izanami and Koschei had taken longer than Septimus and Lola to adjust to this plane of existence, but they too now could focus their senses.

"So this is the Netherworld," said the Canadian. "Not exactly my idea of a tourist destination."

"I cannot make heads or tails of this place," said the Russian. "How do you plan to go about finding your long-lost lady friend anyway?"

"I shall rely on the powers acquired in my previous exposure to this place," said Septimus. "In the end, though, I fear I am as blind and lost as the rest of you."

"I know what we must do," said Lola with a confidence that surprised the others.

"Really?" asked Koschei. "How?"

"Though some of my memory is still hazy, I am certain I have been here before."

The others exchanged glances.

"Forgive me for doubting you," said the Russian suspiciously, "but that seems a bit convenient. Almost as if you are part of the plot to lure us into the Fiend's trap."

"All I can tell you," said Lola, "is that if I *am* a double agent, I am as much in the dark about it as you are. Now, will you follow me?"

Izanami shrugged. "We all knew this was a bad idea from the beginning. I guess we shouldn't be shocked to find out we were right. I'll follow you. What have I got to lose at this point anyway?"

"What do *you* say, Orpheus?" asked Koschei.

"I have made some bad judgments, some of them quite recently, and this may be another one," he said, "but my instincts tell me she is our best—and perhaps only—hope. I shall follow her."

Lola wished she had as much confidence in herself as Septimus seemed to have. She was still adjusting to her new memories, and they did not yet seem completely real to her. She had to work on trusting them and avoiding the fear that she was merely hallucinating.

"We must all join hands," she said. "We are in Astaroth's Umbra. We must proceed to the Penumbra."

"Should you be speaking his name here?" asked Izanami nervously.

"It does not matter. He knows we are here. From here on his name cannot cede any power he does not already possess."

Koschei looked to Septimus. "Is that right, Orpheus?"

The demon hunter was uncharacteristically chastened. "I have no choice but to bow to her knowledge. I seem to have become the student now."

"What's this about an Umbra?" asked Izanami.

"Astaroth's realm does not conform to anything we know in our world. All our mortal senses can do is try to make whatever sense of it they can, drawing on the natural laws of our own physical world. In those terms, the Netherworld exists in the form of what we would recognize as a shadow. We are now in the umbra of that shadow, where the light is completely blocked. We need to move to the penumbra where reflected light mitigates the darkness. There our senses will be able to perceive the reality of this place in a way that approximates our own reality. Now everybody take someone else's hand. I will lead you where we need to go."

"Am I the only one who is completely gobsmacked by her?" asked Koschei.

"I'd say we all are," said Izanami.

As they joined hands, Lola closed her eyes and concentrated. Her confidence in her knowledge grew steadily. She opened her eyes to see something not unlike a moonrise. A dim light gradually illuminated everything around them. Though they were doing nothing actively to move, they experienced a sensation like travel. A fantastic landscape revealed itself. There was ground beneath their feet, yet it was not ground. It was more like a solid form of vibrating energy. Their current location was flat enough, but they were surrounded by formations in shapes none of them had seen before in nature.

To Lola's mind it was like being immersed in a three-dimensional M.C. Escher drawing. It was alien and unsettling—unlike anything she had seen before. Yet it was hauntingly and disturbingly familiar. She took a deep breath, even though there seemed to be no air and her lungs did not seem to require it.

"My friends," she said, "welcome to the Netherworld."

22
The Netherworld

"IF THIS FELT in any way real and not like some weird dream," said Izanami, "I think I would be nauseous."

"I may have experienced something like this once before," said Koschei, "after a long night of drinking vodka. Better not to remember that. So where do we find this woman we have come to retrieve?"

"I need to establish a psychic link," said Lola. "With luck the amount of time she and I spent together before she was taken will be enough for me to sense her and make contact."

"Let me try," said Septimus. "After all, I have spent much more time with her than you have."

"That would have been a very long time ago and, besides, you're talking about Justine and it is Maria we have come for."

"Aren't they the same person?" asked Izanami. "How can you be sure?"

"Because I just know," said Lola.

"Wait a minute," said Koschei, "I am confused. Have we come to rescue one woman or two?"

"One," said Septimus.

"I don't know," said Lola. "One definitely. Maybe two."

"Well," said the Canadian, "will somebody please make contact with at least one of them? The sooner this is over, the happier I will be."

Lola and Septimus both put their fingers to their temples and closed their eyes. Both went into a trance-like state.

"I think I sense her," said Lola, "but what you are doing is interfering."

"Yes, she is close but something is blocking me."

Lola lost patience with him. "You have to stop what you're doing, Orpheus, and let me."

"Very well, but I shall have my turn afterwards."

Koschei gave a sideways glance in Izanami's direction. "This Sapphire has certainly made things interesting. She and Orpheus bicker like children."

"Orpheus can't accept the idea of not being in charge," said the amused Canadian.

"I know where we need to go," said Lola. "Follow me."

For such a simple command, it was frustratingly difficult to obey. Each step took them in a different direction than they intended. They found the only way to proceed was to trick their feet by intending to go in a different direction than they actually wanted. Only Lola seemed to march forward with a minimum of confusion. Even Septimus found it difficult to get his bearings.

"You can tell she has been here before," said Izanami impressed. "Not easy going for those of us only here for the first time. That includes you, Orpheus, eh?"

"That is correct," grumbled the demon hunter. "This is my first venture into this realm."

The surrounding shapes shifted as they moved but not in any way they would have logically expected. Movement aggravated their disorientation. A true shadow realm, the dimness of its light intensified the feeling of being adrift.

Though their bodies detected nothing that could be called temperature, their minds experienced a numbing coldness. Similarly, their noses had no sensation of smell, yet in their souls they perceived an odor like something burnt to a crisp.

The group was startled when the all-encompassing shade was pierced abruptly by something like a shooting flame. It was an unsettling event that would be repeated, though in no discernible pattern. There was no heat from the flame, yet all could feel its clear potential to sear—if not one's body—then one's soul.

"I don't like this," said Izanami. "There. I said it. I don't like this at all. I have a very bad feeling about this."

"You always have a bad feeling," taunted the Russian. "Besides, what is there not to have a bad feeling about? Are we not in the very place men have feared and spoken about in hushed whispers for millennia and called hell? If you are ever to have a bad feeling, this would be the one place to have it, no?"

Septimus said nothing. He was uncomfortable with the way Lola had taken charge. It made him more apprehensive about being led into a trap. Had the strange young woman from Seattle been sent to be his undoing?

Lola led them down a route that could be best described in earthly topographical terms as a valley. Their path then transformed inexplicably into a climb. As they neared a summit, their senses were assaulted by the brightest and most searing blast of light yet. As the shade returned, they saw before them an imposingly tall figure.

Septimus recognized him immediately. It was the same baleful presence he had encountered all those centuries ago. It was Astaroth. The demon hunter looked toward Lola, curious to see if she was surprised by his sudden appearance. All Septimus could tell for certain was that this was not her first time gazing upon him.

The same malign voice he remembered now echoed once more in his mind. "Ye are brazen beyond words. This is my realm."

"We have come for the one who was called Justine Browne," said Septimus.

"That matter was settled."

"I have come to unsettle it. She went with you willingly the first time. Not so the second time."

Izanami and Koschei shared a glance. Both were thinking the same thing. They had come for a battle to end all battles. Instead they had wandered into something akin to a legal argument.

"I have strict principles of conduct, mortal," bellowed the Fiend in all their heads. "Now that she is back, I am entitled to keep her. She first came willingly, and she then came willingly again. Here she shall remain."

Septimus shouted as loud as he could, "I... say... *no!*"

"You say no?" All felt the Fiend's sheer disbelief echoing in every corner of their minds. "You have no say here. Your lives and souls were forfeit by default once you set foot in my domain."

"You will not profit from my ignorance as you did before. While I acknowledge your power, I assert my rights, which by your own code of behavior you are bound to respect."

"Do not dare to speak to me like this in my own house. Do not come before me and my legions and use impudent words. You are no one here. Do you understand? No one!"

"He's not no one, you evil thing!" shouted Izanami angrily. "He is the one person who can stand up to you. He's the demon hunter Orpheus! He... he's... Sep..."

Septimus and Lola looked at the Canadian in horror. The Fiend roared with laughter. Izanami threw her hands over her mouth, unable to believe what she had nearly done. If Septimus was curious about how she had learned his true name, he did not show it. The look on his face was unwavering and resolute.

"You pick *now* to suddenly join his fan club?" said Lola. "You have never had one good thing to say about him since I met you."

"It's okay," replied the Canadian defensively. "I stopped before I said it, didn't I?"

The Fiend extended a huge arm in Izanami's direction. They all watched with alarm as his gargantuan fingers curled around her body and lifted her close to his face. She panicked to see her diabolusbane fly from her hand, as if of its own accord, and fall at Septimus's feet.

"What were you saying?" the demon's voice echoed in their minds, as he drew her still nearer.

"Nothing. I wasn't saying anything."

"Finish what you began."

"I don't want to."

She struggled for her ordinary blade, as useless as it would have been to her, but his grip on her was too strong.

"I insist."

"Insist all you want," she screamed. "You can't force me to talk if I don't want to."

"But I can," replied the eerily soothing voice. "My rules are quite fair. Once you have begun to speak, I am within my rights to insist you finish—on pain of annihilation if needs must."

"Then annihilate me. I'm not talking!"

"Do not be a fool, Izanami," said Septimus calmly. "Say what he wants to hear."

"But what will happen?" she asked the Fiend. "What terrible thing will occur because I broke that stupid rule? You already know his name, don't you? Why does his name matter anyway? It's just sounds coming out of my mouth. Why are they different from any other sounds coming out of my mouth?"

"They have meaning to you," intoned the disembodied voice. "They therefore have value to me. Now speak."

Desperation etched on her face, she looked down at the demon hunter who had been her mentor. He looked up at her with calm eyes and an expression that nearly resembled a smile.

"I was actually trying to support you for once," she said plaintively. "I was trying to show some gratitude to you for being my teacher, even when I probably didn't deserve it. I got carried away. I guess that will teach me to try to be nice."

Septimus nodded solemnly. With a look that suggested forgiveness, he bowed his head.

Izanami shut her eyes. "No!" she shouted. "I won't say it! Now just finish it!"

"You silly stubborn girl!" cried Septimus angrily. "Release her, Fiend. If she will not say it, then I shall. I shall tell you my name. I shall be the one to speak it."

Time seemed to freeze. A deathly silence descended over everything.

"Is this what you want to hear? I am Orpheus! I am Grandfather! I am Eliot Bridge! I am Feidhlim! I am Tim!"

Lola, Koschei, and Izanami were stunned by the power and rage in his voice.

"I am the demon hunter Septimus Bridge! Do you hear? Septimus Bridge! Are you satisfied now? Release my friend!"

In an instant the colossal hand that had held her vanished, and Izanami fell like a stone. She appeared crippled by the experience.

The Fiend's voice proclaimed, "The utterance of a mortal's true name in my realm now alters the situation. I am released from any obligation of courtesy. If ye value your existence, ye will now be gone. Ye despoil my dominion. One of ye shall remain. The others shall leave or else be extinguished."

His visage vanished as the echoes of his words reverberated in their minds. The landscape around them shifted, or did it? It was as if a full moon cast a gloomy light as it rose on the horizon, but it was not the terrain's shadows that grew shorter. It was the demonic topography itself that straightened and extended. It was now as if they stood on a black plain with a roiling purple sky.

From several directions hordes of demons rushed toward them. As Izanami struggled to stand and recover her diabolusbane, the others raised their weapons. As quickly as she could, the still-shaken Canadian stood with them.

These creatures were similar to the guardian on the hilltop, though not as tall but still a good height. Despite the odds, Izanami and Koschei relished the fight. As stupefying as this world was to their senses, physical battle was at least something that was second nature to them—unlike the strange debate between Orpheus and Astaroth. Izanami, in particular, was determined to throw herself into the fight and not speak again. All were relieved to find that fighting hellions in the Netherworld was not particularly dissimilar to fighting them on earth. The main problem was their sheer numbers. Never before had the demon hunters confronted so many all at once.

As Lola wielded her weapon against one adversary and then another, she pondered the Fiend's words. He seemed to have confirmed that Maria was indeed Justine. As much as it pained her, she would have to accept that Septimus had been right all along.

As these thoughts played themselves out in her mind, the demons Lola fought were taken aback by the ferocity those thoughts woke in her combat. It did not matter to her what history Septimus and Justine had. Even if Maria was her reincarnation, she was a different person now. She had lived an entirely different life. Lola was as determined as ever. Being reunited with the girl from Cork was her driving motivation.

As for Septimus, he fought more vigorously than any of them. He had waited more than three centuries for this moment and he was determined not to fall short. Yet he was troubled by certain things that still did not add up. His understanding of the Fiend and this realm was still incomplete.

The one reassuring thing for all of them was that, despite their supernatural nature, the demons were not invincible. When used with skill, the diabolusbane could incapacitate them if not actually destroy them. Yet for every creature that was vanquished, two more appeared to take its place. There was no end to the battle. Would this be their fate then? Doomed to battle for all eternity?

All their various musings in the heat of battle came to abrupt end when disaster struck.

Koschei dispatched a particularly obstinate demon by lodging his diabolusbane squarely into its breast. As it writhed on the ground, its tail wrapped around the weapon, pulled it free, and whipped it in so many directions that Koschei could not regain it. As he attempted vainly to retrieve it, he spotted two particularly vile creatures overpowering Izanami. She had still not recovered fully from being squeezed in the Fiend's grip, and they took advantage to throw themselves on top of her, competing viciously to be the one to finish her off.

"*Umri, mudak!*" shouted the Russian like a madman, as he grabbed the larger one with his bare hands. "Get off her!"

The two creatures then turned their attention to Koschei. Without his diabolusbane, he was defenseless. Relentlessly, the large one grabbed his arm and then his leg. As he twisted furiously in an attempt to free himself, the second one grabbed his other two limbs.

Seeing her friend's plight, Izanami screamed his name as she scrambled frantically in his direction, but she was not fast enough. One of the monsters had sunk its teeth into the Russian's neck.

"Let him go!" she shouted, still struggling to reach him.

As blood streamed from the gash in his throat, Koschei managed to turn his eyes in his friend's direction. She was surprised to see something nearly like a smile on his lips. He then slowly closed his eyes.

The demon that had bitten him reared its head, blood dripping from its brown, uneven teeth. It contorted its face horribly, as if it might be laughing. The other creature looked at Izanami mockingly, as it slowly and deliberately tightened its grip on Koschei's arm. Without shifting its gaze away from her and with a sudden, rough motion, it separated the limb from the Russian's body.

"No!" she cried. "Koschei! No!"

Lola and Septimus looked on in horror. Indeed, all the combatants had paused. The demon swarm watched with something akin to admiration. The three surviving mortals stared in shock.

Septimus shook his head wildly, his black mane whipping in the smoky dimness. He screamed, "No! This wrong! Everything I do is one bloody mistake after another! It ends now!"

Raising himself up, he clenched his fists and vibrated as if about to explode. A golden glow came over him and intensified in brightness until it seemed to have illuminated the entire Netherworld. Lola and Izanami gaped in awe. Though they had by now often seen him use his powers, they had never before seen anything like this. He pointed his fists in the direction of the Canadian, and a blinding beam of light emanated from them in her direction.

"I send you back! I should never have brought you here. I should have had the courage of my own conviction. I should have brought none of you. I should have come alone."

There was an explosion of light and Izanami was gone.

"Is she...?" stammered Lola.

"She is back where she belongs. She is safe. I shall never ask anyone ever again to risk anything for me. Koschei's death will be on my conscience for all time. As are all those in which I had a part all those years ago during the wars in England and Ireland. No more. No more. It is over. And now, I send you back as well, Sapphire."

"No!" she cried. "I'm staying. I'm seeing this through. I'm not going anywhere until I see Maria again!"

"It is not up to you. Farewell."

As he had before, Septimus clenched his fists and concentrated his energy. He began to glow again. Lola was intent on stopping him, determined to remain, but her body was exhausted. Instead, she focused her mind on staying, on resisting his power.

There was an explosion of light all around her. For a minute or two, all she could see was the whiteness of the light. She had no idea where she was. Gradually, her sight returned. She was relieved to see that she was in exactly the same place. Breathing heavily, Septimus stared at her, perplexed.

"You should be gone. How did you thwart me?"

"I don't know. I just didn't want to go. I told you. I am in this 'til the end."

"Then the battle will go on until you perish here like Koschei. What purpose will that serve?"

"What battle?" asked Lola, looking around.

While they had been talking, the army of demons had melted away. The two of them stood alone.

"Astaroth!" shouted the demon hunter.

There was silence.

"Bring her to me! I am taking her with me. You have no right to keep her!"

Above them the visage of the Fiend appeared, this time larger than before.

"It is over," said its disembodied voice.

Lola looked around and saw a figure stumbling in the distance. For a moment she stared in disbelief and then ran to her as fast as she could. She put her arms around her. She could scarcely believe it was true. She was hugging Maria.

"Are you all right? How awful it must have been for you. Talk to me, blue-haired girl. Is it really you?"

The Irish woman stared at her in disbelief.

"Lola? You came for me. You actually came for me. How did you ever get here? I've been pure mad out of my mind, so I have. I don't understand any of it."

Septimus joined them and found her words curious.

"Has your memory not returned, Justine?"

She looked at the demon hunter as if she were having trouble remembering exactly who he was.

"Oh, Septimus. It's you. I'm sorry, but I don't think I'm your Justine. You had me nearly convinced I was, but I don't think I am. I'm sorry. I know you wanted me to be her."

Septimus's mouth was agape.

"But then…? How…? Where is Justine?"

The voice of the demon again echoed in their minds.

"You and the woman may leave, but the one who belongs to me will stay and remain forevermore. Now go."

"Wait. No," said Lola. "We're not going anywhere without Maria. We're not leaving her here. If she has to stay, then I'm staying too."

"There is no choice in the matter," bellowed the voice.

"Wait…" said Septimus. Though still dazed, his face looked as though a fog had been lifted. "I think I finally understand now. Did I really get it so wrong? Was I really such a complete fool? What a bloody, ridiculous idiot I have been. Three-and-a-half centuries and I have not learned a bloody thing. I am the biggest cretin in the entire universe!"

Lola became more agitated. "Orpheus! Septimus! Do something! We can't leave her here. Find a way to make him let her go. You have to!"

He looked at Lola and laughed. "Do you really not yet see?"

"See what?"

"So much of your memory has come back but not all of it."

"I don't know what you're talking about. You're not making any sense. Please don't go all weak-minded on me now, Tim. We have to save Maria. We have to do it now."

He grabbed her by the arms and stared into her eyes. "You need to concentrate. You need to remember."

"Remember? Remember what? I already told what I remember. I was Tyra Knagenhjelm in my previous life. I fought demons under the name Eurydice. What does any of that have to do with what is happening now?"

"How to say it? No, wait, there is an easier way. You will not like it, but it will be much faster. You will understand completely then."

"You're not making any sense."

"Please forgive me for what I am about to do. I think perhaps you will forgive me afterwards—once the memories have returned. At least that is my hope."

Lola was completely confused. She was certain Septimus had lost his mind. As she stared at him, he stood hesitating. Finally, he did the last thing she expected. He leaned over and kissed her on the lips.

23
Reckoning

LOLA FLEW into a rage.

"How dare you! How... how dare you! You absolutely had no right to do that. Are you insane?"

"But do you remember now?"

"Remember what? Jesus, Mary and Joseph! Whatever are you at, Tim? Whatever in the bloody name of our Lord in Heaven are you at?"

"Keep talking. It is coming back. I can hear it in your voice."

It was true. More forgotten memories flooded into Lola's mind.

"No, this can't be right. How can I remember...?"

"Just accept it. It will get easier. I promise."

"This is impossible. This is absolutely impossible."

Maria watched with growing concern. "Lola, what's wrong? What's happening to you?"

"I... I remember now. It's coming back to me. I remember when I was a child in Menlough Castle. I remember my mother, my stepfather, my brothers, my sisters. I remember the day I was married off to a man twice my age. I remember moving to Baile an Choirrín. I remember..."

She looked at Septimus with wide eyes.

"Oh my God. I found you in the shed, fighting with the stable boy. I... I was actually in love with you. The first and only time I was ever in love with a man."

"Keep talking. Tell me everything that comes back to you."

"They hanged me. They thought I was a witch. All the neighbors who had lived beside me for years. They turned on me. They lost their minds. They... they murdered me. I had done nothing, yet they imprisoned me, put me on trial, killed me. How could civilized people do that? How could they do that to me? I never harmed anyone in my life. It was madness. They all went mad, and I paid the price. I felt the pain of the bones in my neck snapping from the pressure of the rope. Then everything went black. I remember seeing you, Tim, on Cnoc Meadha. Then I was here. I was here for what seemed an eternity. But I did not give up. I had nothing but time. For centuries I had nothing but time. I waited. I observed and learned. I absorbed the power of this place. Eventually, my knowledge grew so much that I could make my escape. I broke free and was gone before the Fiend could stop me. I hid myself from him by being reborn as Tyra, but he sent his demons to track me down. Over time they succeeded. By that time, though, I knew them well. I knew their tactics and their weaknesses. I could evade them, and when I could no longer evade them, I could fight them. I fought them for many years."

"Why did you not come to me? Why did you not seek me out?"

"I couldn't, Tim. The Fiend never abandoned his intention to claim you back. I could not risk leading him to you, of putting you in harm's way. Staying away from you was the only way I knew to protect you."

"That was foolish. I would have done anything for you, risked anything. I suspect there were other reasons you did not seek me out, but that is neither here nor there now. What happened next?"

"Astaroth never gave up hunting me. He pursued me for years. With time the pursuit only became more relentless. In the end there was no escape. The only way to save myself was to die and be reborn yet again, this time as a completely different person with absolutely no memory of my previous lives. And it worked. Yet the Fiend still did not give up. Because I had successfully severed all connection to the Netherworld, he could not touch me directly, but he found a way to lure me back anyway. He found the perfect bait. He found..."

She looked at Maria, who was listening to all this dumbfounded.

"He found you, Maria. My perfect physical double. Oh my God. No wonder I could not stop looking at you. I was looking at a mirror."

Lola gasped as she put all the pieces together in her mind. "Oh my God. I am, like, the universe's ultimate narcissist!"

Septimus watched her, his eyes full of sympathy. "I was such a fool. I should have seen it. I should have sensed that it was you. I allowed myself to be distracted by this girl's uncanny physical resemblance. I did not perceive the spirit within you. I should have recognized that you were my Justine in a modern guise. You had all her qualities. I simply did not see them because I was not looking for them in a young woman from Seattle. How could I have been so blind?"

She took his hand. "Oh, Tim, my poor Tim. I hope I can make you understand."

"I do understand—now."

"No, I mean, you have to understand that I am not the same woman that you knew. I am a completely new and different person now."

"I know."

"Those times in Baile an Choirrín. They were so very long ago. I was literally a different person. The Justine you are looking for no longer exists. She died there on that hilltop overlooking the lake, there next to An Choirib."

"I know."

"And poor Maria," she said, turning to the Irish woman. "You have been put through hell, and it had nothing at all to do with you. I am so sorry this happened to you."

The two women were on the verge of tears.

"Can we go home now?" asked Maria.

"Oh my God," said Lola. "When the Fiend says 'the one who belongs to me,' he means *me*. He tricked *me* into coming back. Now I am trapped here."

"No," said Septimus resolutely. "You shall not be staying."

"I appreciate the sentiment, but there is nothing you can do. Please take Maria back to her life and to her family. She is the innocent one in all of this. Promise me you will look after her."

"No, Justine, you will have to take her back yourself. I shall remain."

He clenched both his fists and shouted as loudly as he could. "Astaroth!"

The Fiend's visage appeared high above them. His voice boomed in their ears. "Insolent! You dare to use my name here? Do not test my patience."

"Do not try to intimidate me, you beast. I know you too well now. I know your tricks, and I know the rules by which you must abide. Most importantly, I know your limitations. I understand now. I have standing. You must hear me out. You must heed my demands which are legitimate by your own laws of conduct."

"You overstep, mortal, but…"

"Not mortal," interrupted the demon hunter. "By your own hand and by your own error, you made me immortal. You cannot treat me as you would a mortal. I am in a different category altogether."

"Continue, but bear in mind that, unlike my power, my patience is not without limit."

"Three-and-a-half centuries ago you tricked me into letting this woman take my place in the Netherworld."

"The fact is that she confounded the two of us. It was your soul I coveted, not hers, but I was bound by the terms of our arrangement."

"I do not believe you. I do not believe that you coveted my soul more than hers, and I do not believe that you were bound. I have had centuries to play that night out over and over in my mind and examine what happened from every possible angle. You feigned being snared by some legal condition, but in reality you willingly seized the opportunity to have her instead of me. Why?"

"I shall not be lectured by the likes of you. What can you possibly know of these things?"

"You could have taken me that night, but you chose not to. You seized the chance to take her instead. Again, why?"

"I am not required to reply."

"You owe me an answer. Tell me why you carried away Justine Browne to your foul domain instead of the man who had deliberately sought you out, who was more than resigned to going with you."

"You answer your own question. You were resigned."

"Explain."

"For one your age, you were world-weary and more than ready to die. She was in her prime and had fought death to the very end. She had so much more vitality for me to feed from. Of course, I preferred her. I have always preferred her. She shall remain here for all time."

"She shall not. You have no right to keep her. We had an agreement, and you reneged."

"You are in no position to enforce the terms of our agreement. You do not hold the power here."

"No, I do not. Unless you consider reason and honor forms of power. I assert my moral right to have our agreement upheld. I know, Astaroth, from the way you have always dealt with me to my face that your own nature values probity and integrity—even when dealing with lesser beings such as myself. I call on your own code of conduct to do what you know is right. I am not asking for your permission. I am telling you what I am about to do. I shall send Justine Browne back to her own world while I remain in this realm, as per the terms of our agreement."

A horrifying roar could be heard as the Fiend's image dissolved into a violent display of flame and smoke. His voice boomed like thunder.

"You do not sit in judgment of me. I am supreme in this domain. You cannot dictate to me in my own house. Never before has there been such insolence."

"You know I have reason on my side," said the demon hunter calmly. "Your display of rage is the proof of it."

The noise died down, and the flames and smoke melted away. Very quickly all had turned still and quiet.

"What… what happened?" stammered a terrified Maria. "Where did he go? What's going to happen now?"

Septimus was exhausted. "He knows I am right. Though he has no possible response, he will never acknowledge I won the argument. The fact that he has gone quiet and slithered away is evidence enough that he has conceded. I shall now send you back to where you both belong."

"Wait," said Lola. "Were you serious about staying? You can't, Tim. You can't."

He smiled faintly. "I can and I shall. It is the only way. There is no possibility whatsoever of you and me both going back, and this is what I truly prefer. Moreover, it is the only thing that is just. Believe me, I stay here more than willingly."

"It's not right," said Lola, a tear streaming down her cheek. "It… it's not fair."

"Fair? I shall tell you what is not fair. A man who has committed all the wrongs I have committed and then been rewarded by a lifespan far outstripping anything that nature intended. Every additional day I tread the earth is the epitome of unfairness. What is fair is that you will now be the one with everlasting life. You will use it for something good, something worthwhile. You will not waste your endless years brooding and regretting as I did. You will live and love, and the world will be a better place for it. I am resolved to spend eternity in this place and repent for everything I did and everything I did not do. This is nothing less than fitting and just. Before you go, just know one thing, Lola Blumquist. Know how much I love Justine Browne and how much I always loved her. The memory of that love will be my only comfort in the endless eons ahead of me."

"Lola," said Maria, "we cannot just leave him here. Can we not do something? Is there not some way…?"

"We can refuse to go," said Lola. "We can stay here until we think of something. Until we can change Astaroth's mind."

"I'm afraid you would then be here for eternity," said Septimus. "No, you have no say in this. I am sending you back. Farewell."

Septimus closed his eyes. His entire body glowed. Energy flowed out of him and enveloped the two women. They felt its warmth all about them as the shadows of the Netherworld melted into a blinding light. Then the shadows returned, and they saw that all was as it had been before.

The demon hunter's shoulders slumped. He was on the verge of tears. "I failed. Once again I have failed. Will I never be allowed to right my many wrongs?"

"It's all right, Tim," said Lola. "We'll all go back together."

"But how?"

"I don't know. We'll figure something out."

"No, we won't, and if you would stop being so stubborn, you would admit it."

"All I know is that I'm not going to leave you here."

"You have to. It's the only way."

"No, it's not. There's always another way."

"Not this time. Don't you understand, Justine? In any case, this is what I want. I want to stay here. It is what I deserve and the only thing that will give my soul any peace. You escaped this place before. Your power is actually now greater than mine. You have the capability to leave. I cannot send you back, but you can take yourself back. I beg you, take your friend and go. Must I get on my knees to beseech you?"

"Tim, I can't."

"You must."

Lola looked at Maria shivering and frightened. She had to admit that Septimus was right, even though it broke her heart.

"You're right, Tim. With you here in my place, there is nothing to stop me from leaving of my own accord and taking Maria with me. Okay, I'll leave, but it's not what I want."

"I do not need you to want it. I just need you to do it."

"So, I guess this is goodbye."

"Farewell, Justine. I shall love you for all time."

Awkwardly at first and then affectionately, Lola hugged Septimus. She gave him a light kiss on the cheek.

"As hard as it is for me to believe now," she whispered, "I did truly love you once upon a time. That can never be erased."

"That was worth waiting three-and-a-half centuries to hear. Now, waste no more time. Take Maria Murphy home."

Lola stepped back and took Maria's hand.

"Come on, Irish girl," she said quietly. "Time to keep the promise I made to you."

Lola closed her eyes and stood motionless. Her entire body shimmered with light. Energy flowed out of her and enveloped the two women. As before, they felt its warmth all about them as the shadows of the Netherworld melted into a blinding light. A disconcerting sense of falling overtook them.

When they could see again, they were lying on grass in the dark. A cold wind blew on them and made them shiver. They could hear the roar of the sea. They were on a hilltop.

"Where are we?" wondered Lola. "Are we back on Cnoc Meadha?"

They stood and got their bearings. Below them they could see a familiar structure. It was Bridge House. They were back on Riesgado Island.

Maria was in shock. "Have I gone mad. Did any of that actually happen? It's so unbelievable."

"I have a lot to catch you up on, Irish girl. So much happened while you were gone. Everything is so different now. Everything I thought I knew was wrong—or at least incomplete. I have to get used to being, well, not a different person exactly, but much more than I thought I was. It's a lot to take in."

"Is it really true? That Justine he was on about, the one he thought was me? It's actually you? The two of you knew each other in Galway all those years ago?"

"Yes, it's true. I can remember it now."

"The two of you were in love?"

"Yes, we were, but it was so long ago. It is like it all happened to some other person. I mean, I was another person. I'm not Justine anymore. I have not been her for a very long time."

"So you must be sad. Now that he's gone, I mean."

"Yes, but I know in my heart this is what he wanted. I can accept that."

The wind howled with increasing intensity.

"Looks like we got here in time for yet another storm," said Maria.

"This feels like a full-blown hurricane," said Lola, as the two of them were blown off their feet.

"Lola," said the Irish woman nervously, "it feels like the ground is moving."

"You're right. This feels like an earthquake. What are the odds we would get a hurricane *and* an earthquake, all at the same time?"

"Lola! Look!"

She saw what alarmed Maria. Bridge House, like the ground beneath it, was shaking violently.

"Jeepers!" cried Maria. "It's going to fall into the sea!"

Lola was seized with panic. "Oh my God! Kyle!"

"Right. Kyle. Where is he anyway?"

"He's in the house! We have to get him out of there before it's too late."

They sprinted toward the building. Between the wind and the ground shaking, it was all they could do not to fall again. They careened down the path to the door of the old stone edifice. Lola pulled open the oaken door. Inside curtains swayed and objects flew off the shelves. Maria followed her friend up the stairs.

"Where is he?" shouted Maria.

"At the very top, I'm afraid."

It felt like forever to reach the attic. It felt as though the house might tumble over the cliff's edge at any moment.

They burst into the room, and Lola was relieved to see Kyle exactly as he had been left, the dim glow still covering him. He lay perfectly still, completely oblivious to all the movement around him.

Maria ran to his side and yelled at him. "Kyle! Wake up! We have to get out of here."

He did not move. She frantically grabbed his feet. "Hurry, Lola! He's not waking up. We have to carry him down."

"He's too heavy, believe me," said Lola, recalling the trouble she and Septimus had getting him up the stairs. "We have to find a way of waking him."

"But how?" said the Irish woman, as she grabbed his shoulders and shook him. "It's like he's in a coma or something."

"Septimus put him under a spell. I'll explain it all later. Right now we have to break the spell."

"But how? Septimus is gone, and he's not coming back. What do we do?"

"Let me think. I actually know a lot of stuff. Maybe even more than Septimus by this point. I just need to remember it. I'm still pretty confused though. It's hard to gather my thoughts. Give me a minute."

"Lola!" said Maria in a panic. "We don't have a minute!"

Lola gestured to her to be quiet and then closed her eyes for several seconds.

"Okay," she said, as she opened her eyes. "This is what we're going to do. Just trust me and go with it."

"Yes?"

"Kiss him."

"What?"

"Just lean over and give him a smooch on the lips."

"You're joking me, right?"

"No."

"This isn't Sleeping feckin' Beauty, now is it? Be serious."

"I am."

"Then you kiss him."

"Me? No way! Go on. You know you've been wanting to ever since you met him."

"Well, maybe, but not like this. Not without his permission."

"Trust me. He's a guy. He won't mind."

"I think he would rather it was you kissing him."

"Well, that's not going to happen. If you're going to do it, do it now because this house is about to go over the edge."

Her eyes closed, Maria leaned over and put her lips awkwardly on Kyle's. She was unnerved by how cold they were and wondered if he was even alive. She pressed her lips harder against his and was pleasantly surprised to find them warming. They had a taste that was both salty and sweet. His skin had a delightful smell like a mixture of warm milk and saltwater. He exhaled into her mouth, and his breath was pleasurably warm.

"You can stop now," said Lola drily. "He's awake."

Maria did not move. Kyle's arm, behaving as if it had a mind of its own, reached up slowly and stroked her hair.

"I hate to break this up," said Lola urgently, "but the house is about to crash into the water. You can get back to this later."

Maria stood up. Kyle lay there in a daze, blinking his eyes. He licked his lips and smiled absent-mindedly.

"Kyle!" shouted Lola. "You have to get up. We have to get out of here. Right now!"

The women helped him to his feet as he tried to gather his wits.

"Where are we? What's going on?"

"There'll be lots of time for catching up after we get out of this deathtrap. Now come on!"

As quickly as they could manage, they helped him negotiate the stairs to the ground floor. Maria pulled him by the arm as they rushed out the front door. The wind whipping at their faces, they lumbered across the grass and did not stop until they were under the shelter of the trees. They stared back at Bridge House as it swayed back and forth.

"I do not think that house is going anywhere," said Maria. "No matter how much the ground moves beneath it, it keeps standing. I think Septimus anchored it to that spot with his magic. As scary as it was, we probably weren't in any real danger."

No sooner had she spoken those words than the edifice teetered to one side, stopped as if frozen in time, then fell to pieces into the roiling waters below.

Lola surveyed the remaining fragments of walls and foundation sadly. "I think Septimus's magic is pretty much all gone now."

24
Ballard

THE WINDS FINALLY began to die down.

Stunned, the three of them could do nothing for several minutes except look at one another.

Kyle mostly looked at the Irish woman, self-consciously licking his lips. "Maria, you're back," he said finally.

"I am indeed. Thanks to Lola... and to Septimus."

"Where is Septimus anyway?"

"He's gone," said Lola. "He won't be coming back."

"What does that mean? Are you saying he's dead?"

"That's hard to say. No, he's just in another place—but he's there forever."

"That sounds like the kind of thing people say when they just don't want to come out and say someone's dead."

"We'll have a long, philosophical talk about it sometime, Kyle."

He turned to the Irish woman. "I wish I could have gone with them, Maria. I wish I could have helped to get you back. I felt pretty useless staying behind and being asleep the whole time. Pretty lame, huh?"

Lola said, "Maria wouldn't be standing here now if not for you, Kyle. You did as much as anyone to get her back. You should be really proud. I admire you so much—especially considering what you gave up."

Lola thought also about Koschei and the sacrifice he had made—for a woman he did not even know. She thought about saying something about him to the others but decided it was not the right time.

"Gave up?" said Maria. "What did you give up?"

"It's not important," said Kyle. "We can talk about that another time. Maybe at the same time Lola and I are having that long, philosophical discussion about death. Right now I have a more important question. If Septimus is gone and he's not coming back, how are we going to get off this island?"

"An excellent question," said Maria. "We're back where we began, aren't we? Stranded with no way of communicating with the outside world."

"I think I can get us home," said Lola. "I'm not one-hundred-percent positive, but I've been remembering a lot of stuff I learned in my previous life."

"Previous life?" said Kyle.

"Yeah, we have a whole lot of catching up to do. Anyway, I've accumulated a lot supernatural energy from the time I spent in the Netherworld. If I can learn to use it, there will be a whole lot of cool stuff I'll be able to do."

Kyle looked at Maria.

"Is she... okay?" he asked quietly.

"I think so. I mean, she was always daft as a brush, but this is something else. After everything I've seen, nothing surprises me anymore."

"I'm going to try teleporting us back to Seattle. We need to all hold hands. Then you need to be patient and let me concentrate because obviously I have never done this before—at least not in this century."

"This is a joke, right?" said Kyle.

"No," said Maria hesitantly, "it's not a joke, but I'd say she's definitely chancing her arm."

"Come on. I know I can do this. You just have to have faith in me."

Reluctantly, the two joined hands with Lola. They held their breath and watched skeptically, as she closed her eyes and focused as keenly as she could. After a couple of minutes, she opened her eyes and looked around.

"Okay, I think I know what I did wrong. It should work this time."

She closed her eyes again. Maria and Kyle's hands were nearly crushed by the strength of her grip. The minutes dragged.

"Do you need to say some magic words?" asked Kyle helpfully.

"Okay, it's definitely going to work this time. Hold on. This time we're headed to Seattle for sure."

"Three's the charm," said Kyle, still wanting to be helpful.

Lola was more determined than ever. Kyle and Maria nearly had their fingers broken by her grip. The Irish woman was about to protest when they were bathed in an intense flash of light.

For one horrific moment Maria feared she was going back to the Netherworld. She opened her mouth to scream, but it filled with water. Her mind flashed back to the moment she nearly drowned after *Transcendence* sank. In terror, she imagined that everything she remembered since the sinking was a mere hallucination, that the boat had only just sunk and she was still drowning in the sea.

As her head cleared, she became aware that she and the others were indeed bobbing in painfully frigid water. She struggled to keep her mouth above the surface. She feared for her life. The others were not nearly as concerned, as they clearly knew how to swim. Lola was annoyed, and Kyle was actually laughing.

"I know where we are," he said. "That's Shilshole. You nearly got us there, Lola. Really close."

"Sorry," gurgled Maria. "Not really much of a swimmer."

"I'll get the hang of this," said Lola. "I'll get it right next time."

"Uh, help?" bubbled the Irish woman.

Kyle used his arm to help buoy her.

"Come on. I'll help you swim to the pier. It's not far."

"Hey," called Lola. "What about me?"

"What about you? You're a great swimmer. I've seen you. You don't need any help."

As the three made their way to the dock at Shilshole, Lola was surprised not to be getting the same attention from Kyle as before. Though she always complained about it, she had actually gotten used to it. Something had definitely changed between him and Maria.

As the three rested and shivered on the pier, Kyle could not stop laughing. "That was the coolest thing that's ever happened to me!

How did you do that, Lola? Was it hard? How does it work? Can you teach me? That was amazing!"

Maria was less impressed. "Would you have a trick up your sleeve for drying us off or warming us up, like?"

"Hey!" said Kyle. "Can you turn back time? That would be cool. What about time travel? Is that real? This is so unbelievably amazing."

"I imagine," said Lola, "the first thing you two will want to do is call your parents and tell them you're all right. They must be beside themselves. I don't even know how long we were gone."

"I don't imagine there is a phone nearby we could use?" said Maria.

"The easiest thing is probably to go to my house," said Lola. "I hope you don't mind walking. I suppose I could try teleporting us."

"That's all right," said Maria quickly. "A walk will do us no harm—even if I *am* freezing."

Lola felt slightly guilty seeing her friends in their drenched clothes. She was still wearing the suit Septimus had conjured for her. It was already bone dry and keeping her warm. She wished she knew how do the same for her friends.

As they plodded down the bike trail in the dark, Lola said, "You know, once we get to my house, things are going to start happening quickly. You'll talk to your parents and you'll find they've been frantic for days. You'll probably find out there were stories about you in the newspapers every single day. Reporters will want to interview you. They'll want to know exactly what happened out there on the water."

"None of them are going to believe it, though," said Kyle. "I mean, *I* don't even believe it."

"I know," said Lola. "That is why you have to decide exactly what story you are going to tell and stick to it. In fact, the two of you should agree right now on your story so that you are both consistent."

"What about you, Lola?" asked Maria. "There were three of us in it, you know. What story do you think we should tell?"

"I'm not going to tell any story. I'm only going to ask one thing from the two of you. Please don't mention me. Don't tell anyone I was on the boat with you."

"What? How can we do that? People will have missed you. They would have been looking for you too. Your name would have been in the papers along with ours."

"I don't think so. I pretty much know what I'm going to hear on my voicemail when I finally get the chance to check it. There will be a call from Sheila at the temp agency saying she is very disappointed I did not turn up for work and that my services are no longer required. There may be a message or two from friends wanting to know if I want to go out for a drink on the weekend. That will be it."

They began to climb the path up the hill.

"I am certain that's not true," said Maria. "I am sure there are people who have been missing you."

"Look, I'm not looking for sympathy. I'm just being realistic. I've been kind of a serious loner for the last while."

"Surely, you have relatives who check in on you?"

"I have aunts, uncles, and cousins all right, but none that live very close or that I talk to on a regular basis."

As they reached the end of the path and the beginning of Northwest 64th Street, Maria said, "Yes, but my friend Sinéad knew that three of us were going on the boat. I'm sure the authorities spoke with her. She would have mentioned you. I'm sure she would have remembered your name. We talked about the song titles and that would have stuck in her head. The police would surely have tried to make contact with you and then realized you were missing as well."

"Yeah," said Kyle. "And as soon as my mom realized I was missing, she would have called you. She would have figured out you were missing too."

"Yes, you're right," conceded Lola, "but what I am saying is that I want you to lie about that part. I want you to say that I decided to leave town for a while at the last minute and I didn't go with you on the boat."

"But why? The three of us all went through this together," said Kyle. "We should stick together the whole way."

"I know what you're saying, Kyle, but the fact is I'm not the same as the two of you. I've changed. No, it's more than that. I was always different, and I know that now. I need to go off by myself and figure things out. I need to learn exactly who I am and what I can do. I need to figure out what my future is, what my purpose is. I won't be able to do that if I'm the focus of press attention for a week. Besides, I don't want my name publicly connected to Riesgado Island. I don't want it to turn up when someone does an information search about it in the future. There may be people—or things—that will come looking for me. I am tied to a different world now. I need to be careful, and I need to be ready."

"So, are you going to be like Septimus?" asked Kyle. "Are you going to be a demon hunter?"

"I don't know. With any luck maybe demons aren't going to be a problem anymore after what Septimus has done. I just don't know, but somehow I have a feeling this is a larger battle that will never be over. And the universe seems to have decided I am going to be part of it."

By this time they had arrived at Lola's house. The three of them stopped and stared at her front door. To Maria in the dark it looked smaller than the previous time she saw it. None of them made a move to go in.

"I guess what I'm saying," said Lola, "is that this is basically goodbye. I mean, we will always be friends and all that, and I hope I see you both often in the future. But I'm being realistic. Things are going to get crazy and your families and your other friends are going to want to spend a lot of time with you for a while. Once you go inside and use the telephone, it's all going to be different. For a long time."

There was still no move to go into the house.

"We could wait until morning," said Kyle hesitantly. "You know, hold off and not call anybody until the sun comes up. We could just take a few hours for ourselves. Just to spend some time together and talk. Maybe make some sense out of what we have been through."

Maria was doubtful. "I know my mam is sick with worry. I don't think I can do that to her. I can't make her and Dad wait any longer to know I'm safe and sound."

"Maria's right, Kyle. We'll have to find time to get together later. You can't put off letting people know. It's not right."

Kyle nodded, and they headed toward the door. Lola remembered she no longer had her keys, but a quick gesture with her hand produced a flash that sprang the lock open. They walked in.

"The phone's over there," said Lola. "Go ahead. I'll get some blankets and clothes. After all you've been through, it would be a bit anticlimactic to end up dying of pneumonia. And I'm definitely going to make some coffee."

"You go first, Maria," said Kyle. "I get the feeling your parents are probably freaking out even more than mine are. Hey, Lola are you going to make the coffee like Septimus? You know, by snapping your fingers?"

"He didn't do it by snapping fingers," she said. "No, I'm going to make it the only way I know how. I refuse to let some things change. At least for now."

After a long and emotional conversation, Maria hung up the phone and handed it to Kyle.

"That was my youngest brother Conor. Mam and Dad and my sister Deirdre are here in Seattle! They flew over as soon as I was reported missing. It seems I am all over the news in Cork. They've already been planning my funeral Mass. He gave me the number of the hotel where they're staying, but he's going to ring them in the meantime. I cannot believe what a fuss everyone is making. Anyway so, once Kyle is off the phone, I'll ring them and arrange to meet up."

"While you're waiting," said Lola, "do you mind if I try something? You know, as kind of an experiment?"

Maria was the tiniest bit apprehensive. "Like what exactly?"

"Do you trust me?"

"No, not really. I mean, it depends."

"Close your eyes."

"Why?"

"Just do it. You'll see."

"I really don't care for these sorts of games."

"It's not a game—exactly. I just want to try something. Please?"

"Well, I suppose you did go to hell and back for me. I suppose I do owe it to you."

Maria closed her eyes and waited nervously. Her head shivered at the sensation of cold, rushing air that quickly turned warm. Her scalp had a tingly sensation. She opened her eyes to see Lola's smiling face.

"Go look in the mirror."

She went into the bathroom and let out a shriek.

"My hair! You made it blue again!"

"Yeah, I wasn't sure it was going to work, but I think it looks okay. I just wanted to see my blue-haired girl one more time."

"The funny thing, Lola, is that I already decided I was going to leave it natural. I had actually reached the expiry date of my blue-hair phase."

"Well, you can always change it back."

Maria looked doubtful, running her fingers uncomfortably through her tresses. "I don't know, Lola. This doesn't feel anything like normal hair. I think you've actually changed the pigmentation of my hair follicles. What about your own hair? Are you going to change it back as well?"

Lola stood beside her in front of the mirror. She nearly had an out-of-body experience seeing both their faces together in the reflection. "I think I'm going to leave it white for now. It's sort of symbolic of the fact that I've changed, that I'm a different person now. Besides, Kyle told me it was really hot."

"Hey, what are you guys doing in here?" asked Kyle, having finished his phone call.

"How did it go?"

"Man, that was intense. My mom was actually crying. She never cries. They're on their way over here now from Laurelhurst. I don't think Dad is even going to make a big fuss about the boat."

The phone rang.

"That will probably be my parents," said Maria. "Conor was going to give them the phone number."

The Irish woman answered the phone and immediately became engaged in another emotional conversation.

Kyle looked at his friend with concern.

"You were right, Lola. It's really hit the fan now. Things are definitely going to be crazy for a while. We're all going to go our separate ways."

"It's only right, Kyle. You and Maria need to spend time with your families, and they need to spend time with you."

He struggled visibly to find the words to say next.

"Are you, you know, going to be okay?"

"Yeah, of course, I am. I'm going to be fine."

"I don't like to think of us going and leaving you here alone."

"I'm used to it. I like being alone."

"You could come stay at my parents' for a few days. They wouldn't mind. They've always liked you."

"That's sweet of you, Kyle, but I think you know as well as I do that your mother and I are never going to be the best of friends. No, I'll be happier in my own house. I have a lot of things to do."

"If you're sure."

"I'm sure."

"Call me if you need anything. Or if you just want to talk."

"Yeah, the same goes for you."

The next half-hour was a blur of activity. Kyle's parents arrived and talked a mile a minute. They had one question after another, but Lola was not sure they were actually paying much attention to the answers. For now, their sheer relief at having their son safe and alive took precedence over curiosity about what exactly had happened during his disappearance. They could not wait to get him home to talk to him privately.

"I told you when we bought that boat," muttered Kyle's father to his wife, as he opened the door of their Lexus, "renaming it was bad luck."

"Oh, Dad," laughed Kyle, "that's just an old superstition."

As dramatic as their visit had been, it was nothing compared to the next one. Maria's parents and sister arrived in a taxi, and her mother Imelda bombarded Lola with a million questions and assaulted her with several forceful hugs. Maria's family—and Maria herself—were impressed when Lola spontaneously spoke a few words of Irish to them. No one was more surprised, though, than Lola herself. The Murphys wore themselves out with expressions of gratitude to the angels who had seen Maria and her friends home safely. After a final exhortation of "Thanks be to God" they too were gone.

Lola sat down exhausted. She heaved a sigh and took a sip of her coffee. It had long since gone cold.

25
Chiharu

FOR SEVERAL WEEKS Lola barely left her house. She spent much of her time sitting around and listening to music. Sometimes, though, she sat in silence. Yet time did not drag for her. In fact, the days flew by all too quickly.

She relived old memories. She reexperienced her childhood in Menlough Castle. She recalled her mother and her stepfather and each and every one of her six brothers and five sisters. She cried to think of them all now dead. Some were full siblings, some half-siblings, some step-siblings, but she had loved them all. She remembered her wedding night with a much-older husband she barely knew, then did her best to put it out of her mind. She recalled how at first she hated living in Baile an Choirrín. How she did her best to nurse Henry Lynch when he fell ill with the plague and suffered for nearly a week. How it was almost a relief when he finally died. How she found a purpose in life running his property afterwards. She remembered her time with Septimus Bridge and tried to put it in perspective.

While Lola's solitary days during this time were reflective, her nights were haunted. She sometimes woke up in terror, having relived her trial and execution as a witch. She laughed grimly at the notion this was indeed what she had now become. Thanks to her time in the Netherworld, did she not now have the powers of a witch? What was she going to do with them? She wished she could have Septimus back for just a single day to talk with. While she knew all too well he was flawed, he had something she felt she lacked—long centuries of experience in the so-called real world. She had so much to learn and to relearn and no one to help her. She recalled, though,

Septimus himself had found his way mostly on his own, and so would she.

One day she had a phone call from Kyle. He wanted to see her, so they arranged to meet at the tavern in the U District.

"Sorry. I meant to call sooner. It's been crazy."

"I know. I saw you on TV. You're practically a celebrity."

"Yeah, I'm getting kind of tired of it. Strangers actually come up to me on the street. And my mom checks up on me ten times a day like I'm still a child. She's paranoid that something's going to happen to me again."

"It's hard to blame her. It had to be pretty scary for her."

"She wants me to come work with her. She never wanted me working in a store anyway. I think it's so she can keep an eye on me."

"A lot of people would give anything for a job in that company."

"Probably, but not me. I'd be bored."

"So what are you going to do?"

"I think I might go traveling for a while."

"Really?"

"Yeah. I have some money saved up, and I know Dad would lend me some more if I asked."

"He's not making you pay him back for the boat?"

Kyle shrugged.

"He didn't make a big deal about it. He said it was insured."

"I wonder if I can guess where you're thinking of traveling."

"Yeah, I think you know. I'm going to Ireland. In fact, I'm leaving tomorrow."

"Going to see anyone in particular?"

"Maria and I have been doing a lot of video chat. I… I really like her."

"Yeah, she's something special."

"I suppose it's kind of crazy, just picking up and going over there, but what the heck. It's not like it can be any crazier than what I've already been through. Should be a lot of *craic*."

Lola smiled at his awkward use of the Irish word. "Yeah, it should be good *craic* all right."

"Is it weird?" he asked.

"What?"

"I mean, you really liked Maria."

"I still do."

"Will it bother you if, you know, we're like... together?"

"You don't need my permission, but since you asked, you and she are two of my favorite people in the world. It would make me very happy to think of the two of you together. You want to know the really weird thing about it, though?"

"What?"

"You used to really like me..."

"I still do."

"Well, as hard as it is to believe, once upon a time I looked exactly like Maria."

"You did? When was that?"

"A very, very long time ago."

"You mean...?"

Lola put a finger to her lips. "Shhh..." She smiled. "Don't worry, you're not the only man to get confused between the two of us."

"Maria says she's tried calling you a bunch of times and you never call back."

"Yeah, I've been kind of bad about that. I'll call her. Yeah, I'll call her. Maybe tomorrow morning when it's still daytime over there."

"I'll send you a link so you can do a video chat."

"Okay, sounds good."

"I should probably go and finish packing."

"Yeah, thanks for this."

"For what?"

"You know... this."

Kyle stood and said, "I really miss you, Lola."

"I think you're supposed to actually go away first before you miss someone."

"You know what I mean."

"Yeah, I miss you too, Kyle."

They hugged, and Lola was surprised to find that she did not want to let him go. "Take care of yourself, Joe Cool."

Without another word, Kyle got up and left.

That night Lola found she could not sleep. She checked the time and decided to use the link Kyle had sent her. Within moments, she saw Maria's face on her laptop screen.

"You still have your blue hair!"

"Jeepers! It's you. I thought you'd fallen off the face of the earth, so I did."

"How have you been?"

"Grand. I've got a job. Got a few bob in my pocket. Thinking of moving into a house with a few of my mates. It's all good."

"I saw Kyle."

"Does he have his bags packed?"

"I think he's getting there. So you finally got him to go to Ireland."

"Okay, so I know what you're thinking."

"You probably don't."

"You're thinking, what does a really sound girl like Maria Murphy see in a big dumb Yank like him?"

"My opinion of Kyle has changed a lot. I have a lot of respect for him now."

"You're just saying that. Well, he's sweet and he's gorgeous and I absolutely love him to bits. I cannot wait until he gets over here."

"Be good to him, Irish girl. He made a big sacrifice for you."

"I know. He saved my life by giving me his life vest. And it was nearly at the cost of his own. I'll never forget that."

"You need to get him to tell you sometime about how he gave up part of his life so you could be saved."

Kyle had obviously not told Maria about his shortened lifespan. What neither Maria nor Kyle could know was that, because of the time Maria had spent in the Netherworld, she would likely have a significantly lengthened life. Lola wondered if she should say something but decided that sometimes people were better off not knowing too much about their destinies.

"Part of his life, you say?" said Maria. "If I have my way, he'll be giving up all of the rest of it for me. Sorry, getting ahead of myself there. C'mere, I have to get you to come visit as well. You need to sort out my hair."

"What's wrong with your hair?"

"Look at it. It's still blue."

"Well, change it if you want a different color."

"Believe me, I've tried. It won't wash out, and when I try to use a different color on it, it just goes back to blue. What the feck did you do to me?"

"Sorry about that."

"No worries, but I'm really past my wanting-blue-hair phase now. Oh well. So what's new with you?"

"Not much. Been doing a lot of thinking. Still trying to figure things out."

"You will. You're too brilliant not to come up with all the answers."

Several days later Lola decided to go to the tavern again. As she sat at the bar, she noticed Kurt heading for the sound equipment to play some recorded music.

"Please don't let it be a Blondie song," she muttered under her breath.

The first track was an unusual selection for the tavern. Apparently in honor of Margarita Night, it was a ballad sung by Los Lobos in Spanish called "Bella María de mi Alma."

Lola sighed, recalling her Spanish class at U-Dub. "Beautiful Maria of my soul. What are the odds?"

She fought back a tear as she surveyed the place. There was no one she knew, and so many of them were younger than her. Well, technically all of them were far younger than her.

"This is ridiculous," she said to herself. "I don't think I'll come here anymore."

She grabbed a Metro bus back to Ballard. Sitting in a seat directly in front of a drunk couple having an argument, she wondered why she still took the bus. After all, with more practice she would soon be able to teleport herself anywhere she wanted with nearly pinpoint accuracy. She knew the answer to her own question. Teleporting left her feeling drained in a way she did not like. More importantly, riding the bus made her feel like a normal person. Still, on this occasion she was relieved when the bus journey ended.

As she put her key in the front door lock, she had a sudden premonition that was borne out when she found the door was unlocked. Cautiously, she stepped into the house. All was dark, quiet, and still.

She did not turn on the light. She stood as still as a statue. As the seconds ticked by, she heard nothing. Her thoughts rambled. For some time she had been nagged by the idea that Astaroth might send someone—or something—after her. Perhaps members of one of his cults. Perhaps a stealthy demon that had penetrated the barrier between worlds. She longed for the self-confidence she could only vaguely recall having in her previous life as Tyra Knagenhjelm.

She continued to wait. She heard a noise. It was soft, barely perceptible. It came from the kitchen. Making no sound, she stepped in that direction. She edged her back along the wall right up to the kitchen entrance, then waited. Had she imagined it or was it simply one of those creepy noises old houses make? Had she let her nerves get the better of her?

Deciding that anything would be better than standing there waiting, she swung around into the kitchen and was met immediately by a blow to her side. It knocked her to the floor. She sprang up instantly and struck back at her attacker, who then fell against the table sending the unwashed breakfast dishes crashing to the floor.

Her opponent reacted as quickly as Lola had, bouncing back to swing around with a powerful leg kick. The force of it threw Lola against the refrigerator. Seized with anger, she leapt at the intruder and forced her to the floor. The adversary reacted instantaneously by rolling over and deftly pinning Lola against the linoleum where she struggled fiercely.

There was something familiar about the body on top of her. Lola's frantic efforts could not overcome the strong arms holding her down, but they did shake her foe's long black hair sufficiently to reveal her face.

"Izanami!"

"So it is you!"

"Of course, it's me. This is my house. This is where I live."

The Canadian made no move to release her arms.

"You can let me go now," said Lola.

"Tell me something only you would know."

"What?"

"You heard me."

"What are you talking about?"

"I need to know it's really you. Prove to me you're really Sapphire."

"I don't know. Ask me a question."

"Tell me where we first met."

"The name of the pub? I don't remember. It was in Gastown, in Vancouver. Is that good enough?"

Izanami relaxed her grip. When she did, Lola immediately seized the opportunity to roll over on top of her.

"Hey! No fair!" protested the Canadian.

"No fair? You want to talk about no fair! You break into my house. You attack me for no reason in my own home in the middle of the night. You want to talk about no fair?"

"I had to be sure it was you. I've heard stories. Hardly anyone has ever come back from the Netherworld, but some say they come back possessed—with demons inside them."

"Well, that didn't happen to me. Did it happen to you? What are you doing here anyway? How did you even find me?"

"I've been hunting demons a long time. If I can hunt one of those things down, it wasn't going to be too hard to track down the likes of you, Sapphire. Or should I say, Lola Blumquist?"

"Hey! You're not supposed to say a demon hunter's real name out loud, remember?"

"That's a stupid rule. It was Orpheus's rule, and Orpheus is gone. That's right, isn't it? Is Orpheus gone?"

"Yeah, Orpheus is gone."

Lola nearly added that he and Koschei were both gone because Izanami did not heed Orpheus's "stupid rule," but she said nothing.

She was not sure how much difference Izanami's slip had really made. Lately she had come to the conclusion that things were always going to turn out the way they did.

"I knew it," Izanami said. "There was always something weird about the way I could sense him, even when he was nowhere around. I just always knew he was out there somewhere. That feeling was gone when he cast me out of the Netherworld. I could just tell he didn't come back. The jerk. You know where he sent me? He landed me on Grouse Mountain. I had to walk all the way back into the city. Are you going to let me go now?"

Lola ignored the question. "So now that you know my real name, tell me yours."

"Maybe I don't want to."

"If you want to stand up, you'll tell me."

"You think you can keep me here like this for very long? You're very mistaken... Lola!"

The Canadian suddenly thrust herself upward, throwing Lola off balance. Izanami was quickly on top, but only until Lola had rolled around again to retake the advantage. They continued wrestling for several minutes, but the fight was no longer serious. They were like children letting off pent-up energy. After several reversals, Lola again found herself on top and was determined not to relinquish her position.

"Tell me. Tell me your name."

The Canadian bit her lip.

"My parents named me Chiharu."

"Hey, that's a really pretty name."

"What a really mean thing to say. You know I hate pretty names."

The game was over. They sat up, resting their backs against the bottom cupboards. For several minutes, they did not talk. The only sound was their loud breathing.

"You know," said Lola, "we really have to stop meeting like this."

Chiharu was not in the mood for joking. "Koschei's dead," she said grimly.

"Yeah, I know. I was there too."

"It was terrible. It was the worst thing I ever saw. I think even worse than Ragnar. I think it's because I actually liked Koschei. He was vain and kind of arrogant, but we got on. He didn't deserve to die."

"No one deserves to die."

"He didn't deserve to die like that. On the other hand, at least he was there by his own choice. He knew the risks going in. That counts for something, I guess, but I still feel bad. I miss him."

"Yeah, I didn't know him that well, but I miss him too. I can't forget that he died rescuing my friend."

"It's my fault."

"You can't think like that. He saved you. That's how he wanted it."

"I need to know what happened. I mean, after Orpheus sent me away."

"Yeah, I imagine you do."

"So did you actually rescue her? Who did she turn out to be anyway? And what happened to Orpheus?"

"Septimus traded places with her, just like he meant to back in the seventeenth century. He's in the Netherworld forever."

"And was she Justine or what's-her-name?"

"She was what's-her-name. You want to hear something funny?"

"What?"

"Turns out I'm Justine."

"What? No. Really?"

"Yeah, I'm the one Astaroth actually wanted. I was the one you and Koschei and Orpheus were saving all along."

Chiharu looked at her in disbelief.

"Say, you just got a lot more interesting."

Impulsively, Lola ran a finger lightly down Chiharu's cheek.

"Hey, do you want to stay here for a while. We could, you know, hang out together or something?"

"We're the last ones, you know. The remaining two. It's just us now."

"Really? Just us? Aren't there any more demon hunters out there somewhere?"

"There probably are, but I wouldn't know where to look for them. All the ones I know personally are dead now except Septimus—and he might as well be dead—and you. As far as I know, it's just the two of us."

"Wow, that's kind of a sobering thought."

"It means that, if any demons show up from now on, it is basically up to us to stop them. Just us."

"Kind of scary, huh?"

"Yeah, scary," said Chiharu. "Do you really want to hang out with me? I'm a lot older than you. I finally worked it out the other day. I'm actually ninety-six years old."

"Give me a break. You look and act like you're about eighteen. Anyway, you're just a child compared to me. The other day I figured it out, counting from the first time I was born, I'm actually 397 years old."

"Like I said, you've definitely gotten more interesting. Do I really look like I'm eighteen?"

"Hey, do you want to stay up all night and watch old horror movies? We could make popcorn."

"Sounds good."

The pair were soon snuggled up in Lola's bed watching a DVD on an old television set.

"This is one of my favorite old movies," said Lola. "Do you know it? It's *The Raven*. It's got both Vincent Price *and* Boris Karloff. It even has Jack Nicholson before anyone knew who he was."

"Will it be really scary?" asked Chiharu. "I don't like movies that are too scary."

"So are you going to show me your scars? When I first met you, you said you would show me your scars if you ever got to know me better."

"I did? Well, that was obviously back when I thought I would never get to know you better. I won't show you now. Maybe later. One horror movie at a time."

"You know, I have a scar on my arm where you wounded me. I don't think it's going to go away."

"Sorry about that. Well, at least you'll have something to remember me by."

"I won't need to remember you if you don't go away."

"You're not getting sentimental on me, are you?"

They lay there happily watching the film until Lola noticed Chiharu had fallen asleep. She rested her head on the Canadian's shoulder.

Suddenly the movie stopped and the television screen flickered wildly.

"Shoot," said Lola, reaching for the remote. "That was my favorite part."

Before she could begin figuring out the problem, a woman's face materialized on the screen. It was a face Lola recognized but had never expected to see again.

"Sapphire, I have a message for you."

Lola blinked several times.

"Judith?"

"Yes, I have an urgent message for you."

"Judith, aren't you dead?"

The old woman was annoyed at being interrupted. "Yes, well, I have not been able to rest. It is taking me some time to cross over, and Grandfather has taken advantage of my restless wandering to do some communicating through me. His voice is so very far away, but I can hear it through the pendant he once gave me."

"Grandfather? You have a message from Septimus?"

"What's going on?" asked Chiharu drowsily. "Who are you talking to?"

"It's Judith. The housekeeper at Bridge House. She has a message from Orpheus."

Chiharu blinked several times. "You were right. She doesn't look like much of a housekeeper."

"As I say, this is urgent," said Judith impatiently. "Please listen carefully."

"Yes, yes, what is it?"

"Grandfather says two particularly nasty hellions have breached the fabric of reality and crossed over to your world. They are quite likely to cause a good deal of bother and that you should do something about it. He suggests you try to locate some person called Izanami."

"Yes, yes, Izanami's here. We're both here. So where are these demons?"

"He says they would have materialized somewhere in the desert near a place called Moab, Utah. I am afraid that is all the time I have. Good luck to you."

Judith's image was swallowed by the screen's flickering. Within moments the movie had resumed.

Lola looked at Chiharu. "This is it," she said breathlessly. "The time has come. We're going to have to fight demons by ourselves."

"I don't suppose we could just ignore it and pretend we never heard any of that."

"I don't think so."

"We're probably going to get killed, you know."

"Don't talk like that. You've been fighting demons for years. I spent a whole former lifetime fighting them, even if I still don't remember it all that well. We'll be fine."

"Stop being so annoyingly positive."

"But I'm a positive person. What's wrong with being positive?"

"Because the one worthwhile thing Orpheus ever taught me was that, if anything gets you killed, it's overconfidence."

"Yeah, he *was* always pretty pessimistic."

"We are definitely going to get killed."

"Yeah, come to think of it, that does seem pretty likely."

"This is going to be a disaster. We're definitely going to die."

"We better get dressed."

They stood in their demon-fighting gear and checked their blades.

"Shieldbreaker is ready to go."

"I can't believe you're still calling it by that stupid name."

"Are you ready?"

"No."

Lola could not resist throwing her arms around the Canadian. She surprised both of them by kissing her squarely on the lips. "You know what, Chiharu?"

"What?"

"I have a feeling you and I are going to be best friends forever."

"Yeah, maybe even literally forever. If we don't get killed in Moab, Utah."

"So are you ready?"

"As ready as I'll ever be."

They held hands, closed their eyes, and then vanished in a sudden brilliant flash of light.

About the Author

A native of California's San Joaquin Valley, Scott R. Larson has also lived in Ohio, France, Chile, and for a good while in and around Seattle, Washington. After many years working for newspapers and graphic design companies as well as in the software industry, he currently finds himself in the West of Ireland, not too far from Cnoc Meadha. He spends his days writing books and blogs, including one of the internet's longest-running film review web sites, *ScottsMovies.com*. He is descended from Anabaptists.